PIERCED

SYDNEY LANDON

"But he that dares not grasp the thorn should never crave the rose."

Anne Brontë

ACKNOWLEDGEMENTS

A special note of thanks to my wonderful PA Amanda Lanclos.

A thank you to Kim Killion with Hot Damn Designs for your wonderful cover. And to my editors: Marion Archer with Making Manuscripts and Jenny Sims with Editing 4 Indies. Love you ladies!

And to my blogger friends, Catherine Crook with A Reader Lives a Thousand Lives, Jennifer Harried with Book Bitches Blog, Christine with Books and Beyond, Jenn with SMI Book Club, Chloe with Smart Mouth Smut, Shelly with Sexy Bibliophiles, Amanda and Heather with Crazy Cajun Book Addicts, Stacia with Three Girls & A Book Obsession, Lisa Salvary and Confessions of a Book Lovin Junkie.

To my beautiful flower girl,

I am not sure you received my first or second letters, so I'm writing again. Things have been crazy since I saw you last, but I need you to know you have been in my heart and in my thoughts.

I miss you. It has been six weeks since I saw you last, and I miss the touch of your soft skin. I miss looking into your beautiful blue eyes. I miss your laughter and the crazy conversations we shared.

Please write back to me. Let's work out a place we can meet.

All my love forever,

C x

CHAPTER ONE

Rose

I was fourteen the first time I tried to kill myself. I swallowed a bottle of my mother's Ativan. Unfortunately, our maid found me soon after and put two and two together when she saw the empty pill bottle on the floor. Our neighbor, Dr. Holland, rushed over and forced me to drink something that looked like charcoal. There were more indignities involved that I won't go into, but needless to say, it fucking sucked.

My father railed at me for hours afterward about the embarrassment I had caused him and how horrifying it would be if any of his friends or colleagues found out. My mother pissed and moaned about how I'd wasted her bottle of anxiety medication and how inconvenient it would be for her to refill the script again.

I promised I wouldn't put them through that kind of trouble again and kept my word until I was seventeen. On that last attempt, I slit my wrists in my parents' bedroom. Somehow, the irony of killing myself in the room of the people who I hated so much seemed symbolic. Plus, they weren't due home for another day from their latest mini-vacation, so I never expected I would be saved.

Again, my father was pissed he had to call Dr. Holland. And my mother went on and on about how I'd ruined the carpet in the bedroom. She used the whole "incident," as they'd taken to calling it, as an excuse to have all the carpeting removed from the house and hardwood floors installed. I could almost imagine the conversation she must have had with my father. *We need to be prepared in case Rose tries to off herself again. Just think of how much faster the cleanup will be next time.*

In a strange way, I can almost admire how easily my parents, Hoyt and Celia Madden, bounced back from life's little surprises. Other than being annoyed at having to deal with me, they were surprisingly unscathed when I "acted out." Yes, that was the other term they used to describe their daughter attempting to take her own life. Something that should have been, at the very least, a cry for help was trivialized as nothing more than me going through *those awkward teenage years.* I'd started having panic attacks a few years before my first attempt, which should have possibly tipped them off that I was in distress, but instead, my mother had rolled her eyes and told me to start carrying a bag around in case it was the housekeeper's day off. It fascinated me that she saw it as the housekeeper's role to provide the bag, rather than her own. It also communicated her indifference and scorn loudly.

After the second attempt, I gave up on ending it all and just looked for ways to cope. I was every cliché in the book. *Poor little rich girl, what does she know about the real world?* A valid question maybe. I had, after all, been raised in a big house with actual staff that took care of all of our needs. I wore designer labels and expensive jewelry. I never wanted for material possessions because they were part of the package my father presented to the world. We were the Maddens. We were old money and prestige. The perfect family—or, at least, that's the image my parents desperately tried to project.

Funnily enough, he may have wanted me to dress and act like a lady, but he had instilled in me a love of guns from an early age. Target practice was the only bonding experience I ever had with my father. I had been thrilled the first time he'd taken me with him until I learned it was just another area of my life where I was expected to be perfect. I was a glorified show dog, after all, and any shortcomings on my part reflected poorly on him. I would hazard a guess that I was probably the only little girl in my third-grade class who was an expert marksman. Instead of a doll for Christmas, I got a new handgun. I could go on, but you get the idea.

At eighteen, quite by accident, I found a way to rebel against my parents' dictates, while still appearing to follow them. I cut my leg while shaving and marveled for days over the small imperfection that no one seemed to notice. As silly as it may sound, I felt I had control over something in my life for the first time ever. Thus began my voyage into cutting, or self-mutilation as the experts called it.

I took perverse pleasure in knowing there was a new cut on my inner thigh that no one knew anything about. I could sit at the dining room table across from my parents looking like June freaking Cleaver, and they had no clue as to the wounds I'd inflicted upon myself. I held the power over this small part of my life, and oh, did I relish it. I longed to tell them that their flawless daughter was in reality damaged both mentally and physically, but I knew if it did, they would take that from me as well.

Yes, I'm quite aware of how insane it sounds to be frightened of losing the ability to cut myself, but it was the only piece of free will that I'd been left with. Until I met Jake Ryan during my second year of college. He was thoughtful, considerate, and gorgeous. He was my first official boyfriend and lover. My parents had been okay with him because his parents were a part of Asheville society, but they made sure to point out that he wasn't future husband material. They had bigger aspirations for me. I was just thrilled to be living what felt like a normal life. I also had a real friend in my new roommate, Lia Adams.

For what seemed like but a moment, but was actually a couple of years, things were good. My parents were still overbearing, but since I didn't live *with* them, I was somewhat removed from their demands. I was no longer cutting either as Jake knew all about it and had pleaded with me to stop.

But I should have known it wouldn't last. My roommate and best friend, who had so recently become involved with Lucian Quinn, a very rich and powerful software magnate, was brutally attacked by her stepfather in the basement of our apartment building. Around the same time, I discovered that Jake had been cheating on me for months. It was over. The beautiful illusion I'd been living shattered, and I returned to the only way I knew to cope.

"Rose! Are you asleep with your eyes open?" I come back to the present with a jolt as my friend, Lia, snaps her fingers in front of my face. "Is everything all right?" she asks, looking at me in concern.

"I'm fine, chick." I give her a reassuring smile, dropping my shield into place automatically. Lia is the closest thing I have to a sister, and I love her dearly. She knows me well enough to sense there are areas of my life I keep locked away, but she doesn't push me. After all, Lia understands secrets far too well. An abusive mother raised her, and her stepfather had terrorized her. The fact that she is sitting before me now looking beautifully relaxed and happy is a testament to her strength and resilience. Of course, being married to Lucian and having a gorgeous baby girl probably helps greatly. Surprisingly enough, I'm not jealous of her perfect life. If I feel anything when I see her and her doting husband together, it's a pang of sadness that I'll never have the same. Instead, I'll likely be stuck in some loveless marriage to please my father. "So how is that hot hunk of a hubby this morning? You have that relaxed, sexed-up look going on."

Lia blushes, which somehow amazes me. After all she's been through in her life, I wonder how she can still maintain some degree of innocence. She tosses a Splenda packet at me while rubbing her face. "He's fine. He got up with Lara during the night and let me sleep."

Wiggling my eyebrows suggestively, I say, "So you gave him a great big reward for being a good boy?"

"He supplied the 'big' part," she zings back before clapping a hand over her mouth. "You're rubbing off on me." She sighs ruefully.

I laugh, easily pushing my own problems aside as I enjoy my girl time. "Worse things have happened, my little virginal friend." When she opens her mouth to dispute my statement, I add, "That's not a literal title. You're just still so easy to shock, which is unbelievable considering who you're married to—sex on a stick." I lick my lips and grin as she narrows her eyes. The kitty does have claws when it involves her man. Those two are so in love with each other that it should be sickening, but instead, it's almost comforting to me. Despite everything they've been through, they found and recognized their soul mate in each other.

Ignoring my description of her husband, Lia takes a sip of her latte before saying, "I saw Max yesterday."

My hand tightens around my cup before I can stop it. I see Lia's gaze take in that telltale sign. "How's he doing?" I ask, careful to keep my voice steady. Max Decker is Lucian's lawyer as well as the man I have lusted after for well over a year. I doled out some jail-yard justice when I found out Jake had been cheating on me. I smashed up his car and shot out his tires. Lucian sent Max to bail me out of jail. Then I proceeded to torture Jake a few more times, just to spend more time with the oh-so-sexy and handsome lawyer. Am I proud of it? Well, yeah, actually I am. What I hadn't expected, though, was that I would develop real feelings for the aloof lawyer. Jake might have been the only guy I'd ever had sex with, but even with my limited experience, I knew Max desired me. He may have tried to deny it, but he couldn't hide his body's responses.

Something always stopped him from giving in, though. Shadows in his beautiful gray eyes seemed to match my own. I hadn't seen him since Lia's daughter, Lara, was born, and God, had I missed him.

"He's Max," she says simply. "You know, he's rather surprised me, though, with how he much he enjoys Lara. He's not in the least bit afraid to pick her up. In fact, he goes straight to her when he visits."

"Really?" I ask in shock. I can't imagine my uptight lawyer going goo-goo over a baby. He doesn't seem the type at all.

"Oh, yeah." Lia shakes her head. "The first time she spit up on his shoulder, I held my breath. I mean I wasn't worried about him freaking out or anything, but I did think he might be upset over staining his expensive suit. But he just shrugged and shifted her to the other shoulder while I wiped it off. Luc said he still had the jacket on that afternoon and hadn't even gone home to change."

"Wow," I murmur, "that's actually kinda sweet." Dammit, I didn't need another reason to be infatuated with Max Decker. Next, she was going to tell me that he loved dogs and carried his elderly neighbor's groceries for her. Thinking of him as cold and distant was the only thing that kept me from embarrassing myself by chasing after him.

"He asked about you," she casually tossed out.

It took a few seconds for her words to register. When they did, I could only gape at her. Shouldn't this have been the first thing she mentioned instead of dead last? My cool seems to desert me as I ask far too eagerly, "What did he say?"

She grins as if to say, "gotcha," before saying, "He wanted to know how you had been. I told him you were doing well. He also asked if you were working anywhere and I um … kind of said that you were coming to work with me soon."

"You did what?" I sputter. Maybe she didn't want to admit I was doing nothing but sitting in my apartment every day because my father doesn't think I need to waste my time on some "menial temporary job."

Lia carefully sets her cup down before giving me her big, hopeful, puppy-dog eyes. *Shit, she's up to something. I'd know that look anywhere.* Lia's father, Lee Jacks, recently purchased a medical staffing company in desperate need of new management and a change of direction. He wanted Lia to take over the daily operations of the company and apply the knowledge that came with her new degree in business analysis. "I want you to come to work with me." When I open my mouth to automatically object, she holds up her hand to stop me. "Please don't say no yet. You and I both have the same degree, and together, along with Lee's help, I know we can do it. You're my best friend and the sister I always wanted. Say you'll do it, Rose," she pleads.

My heart feels as if it will jump out of my chest. She can't possibly have any idea how much I want what she's offering. To work alongside her while we attempt to revive a struggling company would be a dream come true. This is the type of opportunity I should be jumping at. Isn't this why I spent four years in college? Instead, excuses pour from my lips. "I couldn't possibly ... I haven't decided what I'm going to do yet. You should hire someone with more experience. I mean you know what they say about friends working together." I do my best to ignore the voice in my head screaming, "Say yes, Rose. Say yes!"

She stares at me with a raised brow as if waiting for my tirade to die down. "To use one of your favorite sayings, I'm calling bullshit. I saw the look on your face. You want to do this, so why are you trying to talk yourself out of it? Have you already taken another job?"

"What? No," I answer far too quickly. Dammit, I should have said yes. That would have been less awkward. Now, she's staring at me intently, and I find myself shifting uncomfortably.

When her chin wobbles, I know I'm screwed. "Don't you want to work together? I can't think of anyone in the world I'd rather have by my side than you—my best friend in the world. Heck, my only friend for so long."

And there it is—the kill shot. Even though I have no earthly idea how I'll manage it, I can't say no to her. I have a mother and a father, but in my heart, I know she is all I really have. The one person who loves me just as I am. I can't let her down, no matter how much this new job pisses off my father. If I'm actually making my own money, what else does he have to hold over my head? A small flicker of unease moves through me as I think of walking away from my family. They've made me doubt that I can ever stand on my own and be anything other than their trophy daughter. Somehow, I feel as if Lia's offer is so much more than a simple job. She is giving me a chance to prove to myself that my life doesn't have to go as it's been scripted. The prospect is both exciting and terrifying. I know with a certainty, though, if I don't take this opportunity, I've as good as given up. Releasing the breath I hadn't even been aware of holding, I say with much more confidence than I'm feeling, "So when do I start, boss?"

Lia jumps to her feet and squeals loud enough to attract the attention of everyone nearby. "This is awesome. You won't regret it, Rose, I swear. We're going to take that company right back to the top." *And that, right there, is why I love having Lia as my friend. She does believe in me. She does see me as more.*

She throws her arms around my neck, and I inhale the smell of baby powder. I think I find it just as comforting as Lara does. "Thank you," I say quietly as I pull back. I can see it in her eyes that she understands I'm talking about more than the job. She doesn't know my whole story and it's likely she never will. I don't want to appear weak in her eyes, but how could she see me as anything else? She lived a life of hell and remained strong. In comparison, I've been treated like a princess but tried to end my existence twice. I never want her to know that. I want to be the woman who *she* sees me as, and she's giving me that chance.

"You're the one doing me a favor." She smiles. "And I know Lee will be thrilled when he finds out you're coming on board. Oh, and I wanted to tell you that Lara and I are taking one last business trip with Lucian this week. He's flying to New York this evening and we're tagging along. We'll be back on Sunday."

Shaking my head, I give her a smile. "You two can't be without each other, can you?" She doesn't even bother to deny it—which I love. Again, I feel a pang of loneliness but force it aside to enjoy my time with her.

We stay for another hour discussing my salary as well as a basic plan to get started. Lia has already been working part-time to get things in place, and on Monday, I will join her. Lara has been going to the office with her, but they have hired a nanny who will begin on Monday as well. I hope the poor woman is strong because Lucian and Lia will drive her crazy worrying about their daughter.

I feel lighter than I have in years as we part ways. There is a spring in my step that has never been there. I have almost reached my car when the sound of a text chimes from my purse. I pull my cell phone out slowly, almost as if it's a snake that will strike at any moment. I know without looking that it's my father since his text tone is the theme from the movie, *Jaws*. I think the sinister melody fits him perfectly.

Dinner at six sharp.

That's the extent of the message. No greeting, no pleasantries. It's from my father, of course, and it's in no way an invitation—it's an order. *Way to piss on my happy, Dad.* It's as if the man is so in tune with me that he knows when I might be anything other than miserable. And when that happens, he immediately seeks to correct it. With a sigh, I unlock my Prius and get behind the wheel. Truthfully, I had planned to tell him about my new job via email, but maybe a surprise announcement would be best.

I'll drop the bomb as I'm leaving, and then turn off my phone for a few days. Easy, right? Even as I sing along to the radio, trying to pretend I'm not scared, my hand trembles and I curse my weakness. As if reminding me that there is another way to cope, my thigh throbs from a recent cut. And I know that despite my best intentions, there will be another mark before the night is over.

CHAPTER TWO

Max

I loosen my tie and toss my jacket over the back of the sofa within seconds of walking through the door. It's been a long day, and I'm exhausted. I open a drawer in the kitchen and pull out the array of takeout menus. Luckily, I live far enough out of the city of Asheville, North Carolina to enjoy the peace and quiet but close enough to take advantage of a delivery service. Sadly, I make my meal decision based solely on what will go best with the beer I intend to have. Pizza it is. Being a man with no one to think of tonight but myself, I go for the Meat Lover's. The last woman I dated would only eat the veggie patch with a gluten-free crust. What a fucking waste of a good pizza.

As if on autopilot, I go through the almost ritualistic motions: pop the top of a much-needed Heineken; take a quick shower to remove the day's grime and shit; throw on the comfort clothes—basketball shorts and a T-shirt; wander back to sit in front of the impressive flat-screen television. *When did I become like a robot again?* Awaiting a college basketball game, I flip channels restlessly. It's nights like these that I miss my friends.

Lucian is my boss at Quinn Software as well as one of my best friends. We spent a fair amount of time together until he got involved with Lia. Not that I begrudge him his marital bliss. I'm damned happy for them both and their daughter, Lara, is about the cutest thing I've ever seen. I find myself dropping by their place with some excuse just to see her. I'm a kid person apparently—who knew?

And Aidan, as much as he and I liked to bust each other's balls, I miss the hell out of him. He'd left town after saving Lia's life. Unfortunately, the woman who had tried to kill Lia was the woman who Aidan loved. Cassie had been certifiable, but Aidan had always wanted to believe that there was good inside her. In the end, he'd been forced to sacrifice her life to save Lia's. Something I didn't know if he'd ever recover from. None of us had heard from him since he left months ago, and to say there's a huge void in our lives is an understatement. Man, I miss him.

The sound of the doorbell pulls me from my somber mood, and I jog embarrassingly fast to answer it. Has it really come to this? The highlight of my night was the fucking delivery guy? Hell, I even think about inviting him in for dinner and a cold one but manage to refrain. I've never been a party animal, so I'm not sure why I suddenly find it so hard to be alone. It had never really bothered me before Rose. I shake my head in denial as I realize what I've just admitted.

How could I possibly be in some kind of funk over a woman I'd never even had a real relationship with? She's Lia's best friend, and I'd helped her out of a couple of situations she'd gotten herself in. That was it. Well, she hadn't missed any opportunity to touch me when we were together. Her straddling my lap in my car the first time I bailed her out of jail is something I'll likely never forget. Having her grind against my hard cock was sweet torture. I'd pushed her away, though, when I'd wanted nothing more than to rip her panties off, pull out my cock, and fuck her until one or both of us passed out.

My attraction to her had only grown after that. I'd tried to tell myself it was just physical, but there was something about her that reached me on a level I hadn't experienced in so very long. I still wanted to fuck her, but I also wanted to make love to her. Spend hours discovering that beautiful body. And even more unsettling, I wanted to take her out on a real date. To have an actual conversation with her that didn't involve screwing her on the table. Okay—maybe, I'd like to do both ...

She was gorgeous with her red hair and mesmerizing green eyes. She had a body that kept me up at night and a sassy mouth that never ceased to amuse me. God, the things that woman blurted out. Maybe it was the fact that her actions were at such odds with her appearance that so captivated me. She dressed like a wealthy, repressed socialite but shot out tires and discussed guns as if she were some outlaw's daughter. Add that she also had no problem putting her hands and mouth on me anytime we were in the same room together for more than a few moments ...

I'm not in the market for a relationship, though, and haven't been in years. Once upon a time, I tried the whole long-term, white-picket-fence thing, and it blew up in my face. I haven't been in a relationship since, and I don't see that changing. I have sex when I want it, and no one's feelings are involved. I avoid women with ticking biological clocks and expectations of something more.

While helping Lucian and Lia through the situation with Lucian's ex-girlfriend, Cassie, Rose and I became closer than I should have allowed. Tragedy tends to unite you, no matter how hard you try to keep your distance. We had both leaned on each other while supporting our friends. We hadn't slept together, but we had shared a few dinners and spent time in each other's arms, without sex. In the end, though, we'd parted ways after Lara was born, and I hadn't seen her since. I missed her, though—worried about how she was doing. I knew she had problems dealing with her parents, but I didn't know how deep her problems went. And truthfully, I think I'm better off not knowing. I'd be tempted to wade in and save her—which would only hurt us both in the end when I walked away.

I'd had a recent momentarily lapse, though, and had asked Lia about Rose. I'd wanted to take it back the minute I'd uttered her name, but my curiosity wouldn't allow it. I'd continued to bombard her with what I hoped sounded like a friendly conversation. I'd been shocked and uneasy to find that they were planning to work together. That meant we would likely be in close proximity at some point as Lucian had asked me to be the legal counsel for Lia's new business venture as well. I'd already agreed and couldn't very well back out now. I would try to handle everything possible via telephone to avoid running into the woman I was trying so hard to forget.

Life had a way of showing you that sometimes you had only as much control as it allowed. Fate had never been particularly kind to me, and I had a bad feeling that it wasn't even close to finished yet. I only hoped I was strong enough to handle whatever was in store for me next.

Rose

I park in the circular driveway at my parents' stately home and take a deep breath before opening my door. Even with the weather turning cold, the grounds are still vibrant with color. We have always had full-time help both inside and out. My parents would never lower themselves to actually do the yardwork, but they damn sure didn't miss it if one single weed made its way into the immaculate beds that surrounded the house.

I feel a certain kinship to the landscaping. We all have a part to play in Hoyt Madden's world and looking perfect is a requirement. There was hell to pay when that didn't happen. Having an off day just simply wasn't allowed, and I'd learned that the hard way through the years. Now, I just wear the plain cardigan sets that cost hundreds of dollars and try not to think about how much they age me. I'd be freaking thrilled over an outfit from Walmart. At least, it might actually have some personality to it.

I glance down at my watch and curse. Damn, I've stood outside for so long that it's a few minutes past six. I hurry up the stone path and come to an abrupt halt when my father himself stands in the now-open doorway. *Shit!* "Good evening, Daddy," I manage to get out of my rapidly tightening throat. I hate this. I hate that I become a wallflower around this man. *Why do I let it continue?*

"You're late," he snaps. "Now, our dinner will be cold because you can't tell time."

I fight back the urge to point out that it's only five minutes, but I know better than to argue when he's in a mood. Instead, I say meekly, "I'm sorry. I was just admiring the lawn and lost track for a moment."

He steps back and motions me ahead with an impatient gesture. "By all means then, let's go before anything else further distracts you. I swear, Rose, I'm not sure how you manage your day-to-day life."

It's childish, I know, but I stick my tongue out when I know he's safely behind me and can't see my face. Just once, could the man not ask me how I'm doing instead of insulting me? I walk straight to the dining room where my mother is already seated and sipping a glass of wine. Our cook, Letty, gives me a quick wink before walking off toward the kitchen. "Rose, you know it's incredibly rude to keep people waiting," my mother murmurs with an exasperated sigh.

"I've already apologized to Daddy," I say defensively as I take my seat at the table. Letty comes back in with bowls of tomato bisque soup, and everyone is silent while we eat.

I've just started to relax when my father says, "Now that you're finished with school, it's time for you to move back home. I'll terminate the lease on your apartment and have

some movers collect your personal effects. We'll donate
any furniture you've purchased to a thrift shop."

"I ... what?" I gasp out. "Why would I do that? I love
where I live now."

"It's hardly appropriate for a young woman your age to
live alone in the city," my mother interjects. "You'll return
home until you marry."

This was fast getting out of control as the two of them
joined forces to tell me what I was going to do. Before I
was even aware of what I was going to say, I blurt out,
"I've taken a job and my apartment is just a few blocks
from it, so I'll need to stay where I'm at."

Silence. Complete and utter silence. A quick glance
shows my mother appears baffled while my father looks
furious. His face is turning an alarming shade of red, and I
know he's seconds away from losing it. "A job," he booms
out as if the whole concept is somehow dirty. "And just
who gave you permission to do that?"

"I don't understand this at all, Rose," my mother adds,
before taking a large sip of wine.

"It's fairly simple," I say lightly. "You go to work, and
they pay you. In this case, I'll be working with Lia at the
company her father purchased. We'll essentially be running
it, so it's a great opportunity for me. Not many people are
lucky enough to find a position like that straight out of
college."

"I should have known that girl was behind this," my
father sneers. "She's always trying to drag you into her
problems. She's trash, pure and simple."

My mouth falls open in surprise, and then I have to
wonder why. Hasn't my father always been critical of
anyone in my life? "Lia is married to Lucian Quinn—who
could probably buy and sell us many times over. How can
you act as if she is beneath us?" I ask incredulously.

My mother refills her glass but remains silent as my
father shakes his head in seeming disgust. "She's a gold
digger who got lucky. Of course, from what I've heard of

Quinn, he's got some strange habits, and she's no doubt part of that."

"Her father is Lee Jacks," I point out obstinately. "I've been told he owns half of the state of North Carolina. Or doesn't that count either?"

"For heaven's sake, Rose." My mother sniffs while rubbing her temple. "You're giving me a splitting headache with this tantrum. Do what your father says and stop being ridiculous. Why would you possibly want a job?" The confusion in her voice is somehow disturbing to me. She acts as if I've just admitted to wanting a scorching case of herpes. Is she really that far removed from reality?

"What's so wrong with wanting to make it on my own? Do you really want me to be dependent upon you my whole life?" I ask, genuinely curious as to their answer. My father opens his mouth with the obvious intention of blasting me before he shuts it again. He stares in a calculating way that has me squirming in my seat.

"So let me see if I understand you," he begins. "It's your goal to get a job and support yourself financially? To be completely self-sufficient—with no assistance from your mother and me, is that correct?"

I clench my hands together in my lap, feeling a moment of panic at his words. Is that what I want? The smirk on his face tells me clearly he's expecting me to back down. And for a moment, I almost do. Then I find myself saying, "Yes, that's exactly what I want."

My mother opens her mouth to speak, but my father holds up his hand, effectively cutting her off. "You heard your daughter, Celia. She is an adult and wants to make her own decisions. I believe we owe it to her to honor her wishes, don't you?"

"Bu—but, what about bridge tonight?" she stutters out. "We need another person to play."

In this one instance, both my father and I are united as we stare at her. Has she even been listening to anything that has been said? We're having a serious discussion about my future and she's worried about balancing her numbers in a fucking game? "I'm sure Rose will be happy to stay for an evening with the Roberts." He then turns to me with a pleasant, almost indulgent smile and asks, "Could you spare a few more hours for your parents before you leave, honey?"

Holy shit, what's going on? I think to myself as I smile nervously. "Oh, uh, sure. No problem. I don't have any plans." *Dammit! Why did I admit that?* Now, they won't believe me if I make an excuse to leave early. He excuses himself to make a couple of calls before the guests arrive, and I take the opportunity to escape to the bathroom and regroup for a few moments. I splash some water on my face, not caring about my makeup and take a couple of deep breaths. Just a few more hours and I'm free.

What follows is something straight out of the twilight zone. I play the dutiful daughter as my father does such a brilliant job as the doting father that even I'm getting caught up in the whole charade. He drops a kiss on my forehead at one point. I find myself wondering if, in a strange turn of events, he's actually proud of me. Maybe by standing up to him and wanting to be my own person, he's now seeing me in a different light. Was it that simple all along? I can't recall anyone ever arguing with him before, so this is probably a first for him.

When I look across the room, he raises his glass to me in a silent cheer and a warm feeling goes through me. I may be an adult now, but it's not too late to attempt to salvage a relationship with my parents. I feel as if this is a new beginning for us. Lia meets her father for breakfast one morning a week, and I find myself hoping my father would be open to something like that. I know it would take a while for me to be comfortable spending one-on-one time with him anywhere but a shooting range, but I'm willing to try.

I'm actually surprised to find that it's almost midnight when the last couple leaves and I gather my purse and jacket to follow. My father drapes an arm around my shoulder as he steers me toward the door. "I hope you enjoyed yourself tonight, honey." He chuckles.

I smile uncertainly, wondering why he's laughing, but shrug it away. He's probably had too much to drink. "It was a great evening," I assure him as I step through the door he's just opened.

As I turn to tell him goodbye, he gives me a smug look before saying, "I'm sure I'll hear from you soon." With those words, the door closes firmly in my face and I'm left to gape after him, wondering what just happened. With a sinking feeling in my gut, I realize that the whole evening was apparently a performance for the neighbors. He might have agreed with me getting a job, but the whole father-daughter bonding experience has all been in my head. How pathetic that I'd imagined a complete turnaround in one evening. I should be grateful I'd avoided an ugly fight over the job. He would see in time that I'm capable of being more than a trophy wife.

I walk away determined that from this point on, I'll do whatever it takes to prove to him and myself that I can do this. He's so certain I'll come crawling back, but he's wrong. I can handle whatever life throws my way, and I'll prove that to him if it's the last thing I do.

CHAPTER THREE

Rose

My mood remains upbeat as I make the drive from my parents' house to my apartment. I stop just short of singing, "I Am Woman." I park in my assigned space in the garage before walking to the main door and swiping my keycard through the scanner. I try it at least a dozen times and the light continues to flash red. The temperature has really dropped outside and a light mist of rain is now falling. It's only been a few moments, but I'm already half-frozen.

I pound on the door, but obviously, no one is close enough to hear it. I'm just turning to go back to my car when an older woman I recognize from my floor approaches with her key and gives me a curious look. I hold up the piece of plastic in my hand. "Mine's not working. I'm glad you came along."

We ride the elevator together and part ways in the hall. Our keycards are coded for both the main entrance and our apartment doors. Therefore, it's not exactly a surprise when the damn thing doesn't work yet again. "Shit!" I snap, before stalking back into the elevator and getting off on the second floor where the building manager, Shirley, lives. I buzz her doorbell impatiently, just barely keeping my temper in check. My clothes are damp, and my teeth are chattering. I remember the late hour fleetingly but can't bring myself to care. It's not my fault their keys are junk.

The door finally opens and Shirley stands there in a pair of floral pajamas with a serious case of bed head. If I weren't so freaking miserably cold, it would almost be funny. As it is, she gives me an impatient look as she asks, "Surely you could have waited until tomorrow to pick up whatever you've forgotten. It's not like I was going to rent the place out again overnight."

I stare, trying to decipher her words. "What're you talking about? My key's not working, so I need you to fix it," I say, extending the card to her.

She puts her hands on her hips as she looks from it to me. Finally, she huffs out an impatient sigh and says, "You can't just come and go as you please after you've moved out. If you left something, then give me a call during regular business hours tomorrow and I'll go up with you to get it." Before I can reply, she plucks the card from my hand and steps back to close the door.

"Wait!" I throw an arm out to keep from her shutting the door in my face. "I live here. Why would you think I've moved out?"

She shakes her head, and then her expression softens as my confusion finally registers with her. "Your father called me several hours ago and wanted to cancel the lease immediately. He paid the fine for the early termination and a crew of movers was here less than an hour later." She gives me an apologetic look and adds, "The paperwork was in his name, so there was no reason for me to question him. He said you were moving somewhere more affordable since you were er ... supporting yourself now."

"That bastard," I whisper in a daze. "I can't believe he did this to me." I stand there dripping in the hallway, not knowing what to do next. I have nowhere to sleep tonight and nothing but the clothing on my back.

I feel a touch on my arm and jump as Shirley asks, "Do you want to come in and call someone?" At her look of pity, I want to collapse to my knees and give in to the sobs building in my throat. *I'm sure I'll hear from you soon.* My father's parting words now make perfect sense to me. He fully expects that I'll come crawling home tonight. Apparently, he made quite a few calls when he excused himself from dinner.

I gather what's left of my pride and give Shirley a wobbly smile. "I'll be fine." I turn and walk away, knowing if I stay a moment longer, I'll break down. I'm determined to hold it together until I get to Lia's. Thank God I have one friend in the world that will help me make sense out of this evening.

I'm walking through the lobby when it hits me. Lia and Lucian aren't home. She said earlier that they were taking some time away this week before she was immersed in her new job. "It's okay. I'll just get a hotel room for the night. No need to panic," I say to myself as I trudge through the now heavy rain toward where my car is parked. Only— when I reach the space, nothing is there. Where is my Prius? I look around, thinking maybe I've stopped at the wrong space—but I haven't. No, surely, he wouldn't have taken my car. I pull my cell phone from my purse to call my father, only to find a text waiting on the screen from him.

Congratulations, Rose. You're now a fully self-supporting adult. I've taken the liberty of removing the things from your life that were a burden. Your apartment lease has been terminated and the clothing and furniture donated to charity. Your car will be sold and your phone service will be switched off within the hour. I've also closed our joint checking account and canceled your credit cards. If you would like to reconsider your stance, feel free to contact me.

In a daze, I walk out of the garage and onto the street. It's nearly deserted at this time of the night. Then, almost in slow motion, my body seems to keep going, while my feet lock in place. A startled cry flies from my mouth as I fall so suddenly that I'm unable to brace myself for the impact. My hands burn and my knees throb. Even my face feels raw as I lay there, taking a silent inventory of my injuries. I slowly pull myself up until I'm on my knees. I rub a hand over my damp face, wincing as pain shoots through my body.

The rain is coming down in sheets now, and I'm shaking as it seems to penetrate my very bones. I see an awning up ahead and get slowly to my feet. I stagger toward the shelter, almost sagging in relief as I'm shielded from the worst of the downpour now.

I have little doubt I resemble a homeless person as I rest my back against the door behind me before sinking to my ass on the cold cement. I drop my head into my hands and start to cry. What am I going to do? I literally have the clothes on my back and the few dollars in my purse. I hate to bother Lia, but maybe either she or Lucian can wire me some money until they return. I don't know what else to do at this point.

A noise nearby draws my attention and I see a group of guys on the opposite side of the street staring at me. They probably saw my tumble a few moments ago and stayed around to enjoy my humiliation. My breath catches in fear as I take stock of my surroundings. Other than the stray car passing by, there is no one around to help me. I get shakily to my feet, keeping a wary eye on them. *He's going to cut off my phone in less than an hour. Shit.* I scroll my contacts list, intending to hit the button for Lia when I see Max's name a few entries below. My finger hovers uncertainly, just as a clap of thunder shakes the earth. Fuck it; I'd call Satan himself if he'd help me. The call connects just as the guys from across the street begin yelling words I can't quite decipher.

Suddenly, a raspy male voice sounds in my ear. "Rose?"

My hands are shaking and my teeth are chattering as I manage to whisper, "Max—please."

"What's wrong?" he asks, sounding instantly alert and so very Max that I begin to sob again. "Honey, where are you? Are you hurt?"

His voice soothes my hysteria enough for me to croak out, "I'm on the street. I … my father took my car and apartment. And there are some men … looking at me." Sniffing, I add, "I'm scared, Max."

"I'm on my way, sweetheart. Just take a deep breath and release it," he says slowly. I do as he instructs, focusing on nothing but his words. "Now, what's the name of the street you're on?"

My mind draws a blank. I begin to panic again as I admit, "I—God, I can't remember. It's near my apartment." Then in a moment of clarity, it comes to me. "Wait, it's Pine Street," I call out. Then I realize there is nothing but silence in my ear. "Hello … Max, are you there? Hello?" I yell out before pulling the phone from my ear and looking at it. Instead of "Lost Call," the display says, "No Service." *No, dammit, no!* True to his word, my father has disconnected my phone, leaving me on a deserted street in the middle of the night with no way to call for help. What kind of man does that to his daughter? At that moment, I fucking hate him with everything that I am. Would it even bother him to hear that something bad had happened to me? No doubt in his mind, it would all be my fault for daring to challenge his plan for my life. He's never been a doting father, but even I'm shocked that he would do something like this. I wonder almost idly how he would have explained my gun collection to the movers. He probably had one of his personal lackeys take those away.

When I finally look around me again, I'm surprised to see that the guys from across the street are nowhere in sight. Apparently, the weather was too bad for them to stay any longer to taunt me. The sad part is that I feel even more alone with them gone. Will Max be able to find me from what little information I gave him? Did he even hear me say I was near my apartment before my phone line disconnected?

I'm trembling unbearably now, and I'm so tired I can no longer remain upright. I lower myself back to my butt and slump against the storefront once again. I'm hurting so much by this point that the numbing effect of the cold concrete is like a balm for my aches and pains. "Max," I whisper just as my body slips away.

Max

I'm freaking the fuck out as I frantically yell Rose's name into my phone. Shit, she said something about her apartment before the phone went dead. I'd pulled on jeans while I was talking to her; now, I quickly push my bare feet into a pair of athletic shoes and throw on a T-shirt. I'm out the door and breaking every speed limit known to man as I push my Mercedes hard toward downtown Asheville. Something's horribly wrong. My playful, self-assured Rose was completely absent in that call. I recognized her voice almost immediately because, God knows, it's played in my dreams night after night. But there was nothing but fear present tonight. She was crying, and *what the fuck* was that about her father taking her car and apartment?

It's a long fifteen minutes before I park in front of her building and jump out. I run to the nearest intersection and have no idea which way to go. I take a left and jog the length of the street, seeing nothing. Reversing directions, I pass my starting point and keep going. At first, I almost miss the form slumped against the glass door of a store. I back up a few steps and see her red hair in the dim surrounding light. "Rose!"

I drop to my haunches, automatically checking her pulse. Thankfully, it's strong and steady. I then inspect her for any sign of injury. Her arms are wrapped tightly around her knees, and fuck me, there's blood there. Her dark slacks look shredded as if she's taken a fall recently. Her hair is wet and stuck to the side of her neck. Her head is down so she's yet to spot me. I don't want to startle her, so I gently lay a hand on her shoulder, saying her name softly. "Rose ... baby, it's Max."

I begin to worry when there's no response. I open my mouth to say her name again, when she jerks awake, literally throwing herself at me in what I can only assume is an attempt to flee. "Ahhh," she screams, trying to push me away. "Let me go!" I move back a few inches, giving her space until she recognizes me.

"Honey, it's me—Max. Calm down, I've got you, Rose. Shhh, look at me." She stills and instead of drawing away, she now clutches my arms, pulling me near.

"Max? You came? You found me," she chokes out on a sob. Heedless of my clothing, I drop down onto the wet surface in front of her and pull her small form into my arms. I rock her against me as shudders wrack her body. *What the fuck has happened to her?*

"Shhh, baby, I'm here," I coo, trying to calm her. She feels like a block of ice, and I know I need to get her into my car and turn the heat up full blast. "Honey, I'm going to stand now. Just wrap your arms around my neck and hold on, okay?" She nods against my throat before doing as I've instructed. Her grip is surprisingly strong, coming damn close to a stranglehold. It's not easy, but I manage to rise to my feet while holding her steady. I check to make sure we're leaving nothing behind before walking slowly to where I left my car.

"Thank you for coming," she murmurs in my ear as she burrows closer. "I didn't have anyone else to call." Her last statement sends a wave of guilt through me. She's been sitting on a deserted street in the middle of the night, freezing to death, and she's apologizing for bothering me. Have I been such an asshole to this woman that she thinks for one moment I wouldn't be here for her anytime she needs me?

"Rose," I say, before pulling away enough to drop a kiss on her head, "let's get you home."

I balance her weight carefully before opening the passenger door and lowering her onto the leather seat. I wish I'd thought to bring a blanket with me, but luckily, the car is still warm. I gently buckle the belt around her and as I pull back, I notice the dried blood and the scratches on her face for the first time. I want to lose it, but know now isn't the time for questions. She needs heat and dry clothing. Everything else can wait.

When I get into the car, I turn the heat on high before driving home at a much slower speed than my journey here. I keep stealing quick glances at the woman beside me. She appears to be asleep, but I still see her shiver every few minutes. What in the hell happened to her tonight? She shifts slightly, bringing her face more fully into view. There is dried blood at the corner of her mouth and one of her cheeks is scratched. She mentioned some men looking at her before our call had disconnected. Did one of them do that? My hands grip the wheel tighter at the thought. Rage fills me as I imagine some bastard putting his hands on her. I've never been a violent man, but maybe I've never had a reason to be before. Tonight, though, I know without a shadow of a doubt, that I'd rip anyone apart anyone who tried to hurt her.

She looks confused for a moment when we arrive at my house, and I gently shake her awake. I help her from the car and place a hand around her waist to steady her as we walk slowly to the front door. We both blink when we enter the brightly lit foyer, adjusting to the glare after the dark interior of the car. I suck in a breath as I really look at her for the first time. "Christ!" I hiss. Clamping my jaw shut to keep from saying more, I lead her down the hallway and through my bedroom to the bathroom beyond. I pause before deciding that she's in no condition to worry about modesty; not that she ever has with me in the past anyway.

Rose keeps her head down as I tug the top she's wearing over her head and try not to feel like a complete pervert at my body's reaction to her lacy, black bra. *Down boy, now's not the time.* The problem is my cock has never been particularly good at listening to me in situations that involve a scantily clad female. Her eyes follow my hands, and I pray she doesn't notice the slight tremble in them as I move next to her feet. She places a hand on my shoulder without being asked and lifts a leg while I remove one shoe and then we repeat the process until the other is off.

Then I attempt to carefully blank my mind as I reach for the button on her slacks and fumble to release it. When I lower the zipper next, it sounds so loud in the enclosed space I find myself flinching. "Holy shit," I blurt out as she kicks her pants away from her ankles and stands before me in the matching black lace panties. I feel hot and cold all at once. Hell, I'm afraid for a moment I might actually pass out. I'm like a horny boy faced with his first nearly naked female body. Then I see her raw, bleeding knees and I feel like five kinds of bastard. I clear my throat, trying to keep my voice level as I ask, "Do you … um, want me to finish doing you?" Her eyes widen as she stares down at me. I wince as I realize my question may have been misconstrued. I begin to stutter out, "I—shit, not like sexually. I mean, not that I was thinking that, because that would make me an asshole. I'm talking about removing your clothes—getting you naked." I slump forward, shutting my mouth before I can cram yet another foot into it.

"I know what you were trying to say, Max," she says lightly. Then I feel something—hands in the damp strands of my hair, stroking me. I allow my head to rest against her stomach as she continues to soothe me. I wrap my arms loosely around her hips and run a hand up and down her thigh, caressing her smooth skin. I'm not certain how long we remain in that position, both giving and receiving comfort before it hits me. She must still be freezing. I abruptly jerk back, breaking the contact between us.

Getting to my feet, I say, "I'm sorry, honey, let's get you in the shower." I pull the door open and turn the dials. Within seconds, steam fills the bathroom. Going into my detached lawyer mode, I ask, "Do you need anything else?" She stares at me as if she wants to say something, but simply shakes her head. I pull a washcloth and towel from the cabinet and lay them near the sink before walking out and closing the door behind me. She is in the process of lowering her panties when I open the door to add, "I'll be right out here." Holy. Shit. There's a tattoo of a rose with a stem of thorns on her shoulder. I can barely keep myself from reaching out to trace the outline with my fingertips—or better yet, my tongue. My heart is thumping loudly as I close the door and lean against the wall outside. And that ass. What I wouldn't give to squeeze it in my hands. *You're a sick bastard, Decker. She's been through a trauma, and you're ogling her.* Once again, my dick doesn't give a damn that he's being a bad boy. He knows what he likes, and right now, she's standing in my shower with soap most likely running over her firm tits and between the crevice of ... *Fuck! Think of something else—like anything that doesn't have to do with sex or vaginas.*

I've almost talked some sense into the monster in my pants when Rose steps out of the bathroom with a towel wrapped around her body—leaving a long expanse of thigh and the curve of her breasts visible above and below the terry cloth. *No, no, no!* In reality, I know that she asks, "Do you have any Band-Aids?" In my mind, it's more like, "Do you have any condoms?"

"I—er, pardon?" I manage to get out, trying to keep my eyes focused above her head.

I hear the confusion as she repeats her request. "Band-Aids?"

"Oh yeah, sorry," I mumble as I jump to action. "I'll just get me some—I mean you, not me. I'm obviously not getting any—because I don't need it, right?" *Dear God, just shut the fuck up. Dude, you've seen a naked woman before. What's the problem? You're making an ass of yourself. She's going to call a taxi and run as far away as she can from you.*

I walk toward the closet in the hallway where I keep my first-aid kit. She follows behind me, making my skin tingle. "Is everything all right?" she asks hesitantly.

Giving her an embarrassed laugh, I grab the plastic kit in one hand and clasp her fingers in the other, leading her to my kitchen. I pull out a chair from the table and she sinks down onto it. Too late, I realize I should have gotten her a T-shirt or something else to wear. *You've got this. Just imagine she's someone else. Maybe Lia. No, that's not gonna work. You don't need to picture your friend's wife in only a towel. That's all kinds of wrong.*

I grab another chair and sit in front of her. I take an antiseptic wipe from the case and begin carefully going over her scrapes with it. Her hands and knees by far got the worst of it, and she hisses as I touch them. I find myself blowing on the injured flesh, trying to ease the burn. I'm sweating profusely by the time I'm finished, and it has nothing to do with the temperature in the house. Since the first time she touched me, every time Rose Madden was near, I've gone up in flames—and today is no exception. I want her so badly my teeth ache. Something about her soft, fragile look now has me in disarray. Vulnerable is not a word I would ever have used to describe her, but that's exactly what she is tonight. As much as this new side of her entrances me, I can't help but miss the devilish twinkle in her green eyes and the sassy pickup lines she uses so effortlessly. I find myself determined to do whatever it takes to get those things back. She's not the kind of woman who was meant to look so defeated. The way I feel right now, I'll fight whatever battle or war needs to be fought to

save her. "What happened?" I ask softly as I begin
bandaging one of her knees."

She's silent for so long I don't think she's going to
answer me when she finally says, "I'm going to work with
Lia."

I nod my head. "Yeah, she told me that. Sounds like an
amazing opportunity for both of you."

"It is," Rose agrees, but her voice is flat and lifeless. "I
told my parents about it earlier this evening when my father
demanded I move back home now that I'm finished with
school."

"And how did that go?" I prompt when she doesn't
continue.

Glancing up, I see her pull a shaky hand through her hair
before a bitter laugh escapes her. She looks down the
length of her body and then back at me before raising a
brow and saying, "Not too well, I'd say. At first, we
argued, and then my father abruptly backed down. That
should have been my first clue that something was wrong.
But foolish me thought that he actually respected me for
being independent and was proud. That warm, fuzzy
feeling lasted until I got to my apartment and the manager
told me that my father had terminated my lease since it was
in his name. He'd literally moved me out in an hour. Then I
left the building only to find that my car was no longer
where I parked it. I couldn't fathom that it had been taken
so I circled the area, thinking I'd forgotten what space it
was in."

By this point, I've given up all pretense of doing
anything other than staring at her in horror. Surely, there
must be some mistake. What kind of man would do that to
his daughter? "Honey, have you spoken with him?
Maybe—"

She holds up her hand, stopping my flow of words. "He
sent me a text while I was looking for my car and told me
that he'd done it all. Said since I was now self-supporting
that he'd taken the liberty of removing all of the things

from my life that were a burden. He also mentioned that my cell phone would be shut off within the hour and my checking account had been closed. So essentially, he took everything from me in just an evening. The sad thing about it is that I sat under his roof and played fucking bridge with my mother and her friends while he was pulling the strings that would make his daughter homeless." She stops, closes her eyes briefly, and then inhales a deep breath. It's as if the utter cruelty of her father's actions are truly hitting her. She shakes a little and I so desperately want to hold her. Before I can, she continues. "He kissed me on the head like he was proud of me, all the while he was sticking a knife in my back and laughing his ass off."

"Oh baby," I choke out, "I'm so sorry that he did something like that to you." I hear my words and know they're completely inadequate. Hell, I'm in too much shock to formulate flowery speeches at this point. I point at her knee and ask, "How did this happen?"

In a small voice, sounding so very much like a child, she says, "I didn't know where to go. I was going to call Lia but remembered she is out of town with Lucian. I was wet and cold, so I just started walking. The rain was really coming down, and I saw a store with an awning, so I ran for it. I wasn't looking where I was going, though, and tripped on the sidewalk. I went down pretty hard."

I swallow around the huge lump in my throat and quickly finish patching her up. I see a shiver go through her small frame and extend a hand to her. "Let's go find you something to wear and get you into bed. Um—the spare bed," I add quickly, wondering why I can't keep my foot out of my mouth tonight. Her unexpected presence has me so rattled I'm making a fool out of myself.

She takes my hand and stands beside me before giving me a look filled with sadness. "Trust me, I know you don't want me anywhere near *YOUR* bed. You've made that more than clear in the past."

Congratulations, Max, you're an asshole. Even though I hadn't meant my words the way she'd taken them, I still feel like shit. I'd simply been attempting to reassure her that she was safe with me. I hadn't wanted her to think she had to sleep with me. In my rush to tell her exactly that, I'd made a mess once again and only ended up hurting her. "Rose, that's wasn't what I meant—"

"It's fine—really. I appreciate all that you've done, believe me. So if you could show me where to sleep, that would be great. I'm exhausted." She yawns as if to prove her point, although she's careful not to make eye contact.

One thing is becoming clear to me during tonight: She's more upset about what happened—or didn't happen—between us than I'd realized. Other than a few glimpses I'd convinced myself I didn't actually see, she's been very blasé about our encounters. At times, I've thought she might care for me, but I've never been able to get a true lock on where she was in her head. She used our sexual attraction as both a distraction and a way to keep an emotional distance between us. And I'd been more than happy to let her because I was no more ready to commit to a real relationship than she was—or so I'd thought. But where had the hurt in her eyes come from? *This is exactly why you didn't want to get involved.* I'd been devastated by love before and damned if I ever wanted to repeat it. Rose had complicated written all over her, and it fucking scared me to death. She also drew me in like a moth to a flame and that was even more terrifying. I didn't want to be with her—but I couldn't stay away. Where did that leave us? Eventually, you either made a decision or life made it for you as it had tonight. She shakes my hand, and I realize I've been standing here in the spare bedroom staring off into space. *Real smooth, Decker.* "Um ... I was going to—?" My last word comes out as a question because I have no idea if I missed something.

"Get me a shirt?" she says slowly, no doubt thinking I've lost it.

While I zone out, she's still in a wet towel after being up all night. Perfect. "Sorry," I mumble before jogging back to my room and pulling a Carolina Panthers T-shirt from one of my drawers. I give it a quick sniff before taking it back to her. I have no idea why guys always check to make sure their laundry doesn't smell. Probably a leftover habit from my college days when I'd wear clothes several times before taking the time to launder them. The smell test was a necessity back then. "Here you go," I say as I hold it out to her. She mumbles her thanks, and then shifts awkwardly. "I'll, um, just be down the hall. You should have everything that you need in the bathroom. If you don't, just let me know."

"All right." She gives a brief smile. "Thanks."

And with that, I'm out of reasons to stay. If things were different, or maybe if we'd had some type of closure to our flirtation, we possibly wouldn't both appear so uncomfortable right now. After the evening she's had, I wish I were free to sleep with her and offer her the comfort she must surely need. Instead, we're acting as if we're little more than strangers. She's had her hand on my cock and I've had my fingers inside her, with my tongue down her throat. But you'd never know it now. If one of us made the first move, then the other might relax enough to reciprocate. It's clear, though, from her earlier comment that she won't be doing that. She feels rejected by me. She called me to help her, but it's like she still thinks she is a burden. Her eyes, when she told what her father had done, were so defeated. Hurt. Pained. Does she really fear I'd hurt her? That I'd turn her away?

Before I can do something that I might regret, she takes the decision from my hands and walks toward the bathroom, shutting the door softly behind her. I sigh, before leaving to make sure the house is locked up. I'm grateful tomorrow is Saturday and I have nowhere to be. I generally work from my home office for a few hours, but I am free to sleep late. I hope that Rose is able to relax enough to as well.

Surprisingly, I'm out soon after my head touches the pillow. Visions of the broken woman next door to me haunt my dreams, as does the realization that tonight is the start of something that neither of us may be prepared for. We've danced around each other for nearly a year. I've been attracted and drawn to her natural charisma and sassy attitude from the beginning but have been determined not to get involved. Seeing her so despondent tonight hasn't changed my opinion of her. *She's still incredible.* Is tonight the start of something for us? *Should I be running and screaming, "Danger, Will Robinson?"* I'm not sure I'm ready to trust a woman with my heart again. Perhaps after dealing with her father, she can't trust hers either. A perfect storm can't be stopped, though. You can only hold on and try to ride it out—hoping you'll survive the aftermath.

Rose

I feel it building. I panic as I try to control my breathing. *No! Don't let me have an attack in Max's house. What if he hears me?* But as usual, the man upstairs is busy and I'm on my own. I push up from the bed and stagger into the bathroom. I begin opening drawers, trying to find a bag of some sort, but there is nothing. My breathing is becoming more rapid, and I'm seeing spots by the time I make it to the kitchen. In some part of my mind, I'm grateful Max left a light on.

There is no time to be picky. I upend some bread and use the plastic wrap to breathe into. I sway on my feet, afraid I've left it too late this time, but the dizziness finally begins to abate and the dots before my eyes are slowly clearing. *Thank God.* I lean against the counter for another few minutes until I'm feeling more under control.

That's when I see it—a knife sitting in the sink.

It's not that I'm scared. No, it's exactly the opposite. The hand still holding the bag shakes as I focus intently upon the sharp, stainless steel blade. I need it—so fucking badly. More than I ever have before.

Suddenly, it's in my hand. I have no conscious thought of moving, but I must have. The one thing that has chased the worst of the shadows from my life. The sharp relief that it brings will push the bad thoughts away—at least for now. Lia told me several months ago about Lucian's battle with cocaine and how proud she was that he had gotten help for his addiction. She's also mentioned he hadn't wanted Lia to know because he'd felt ashamed that she was dealing with all that had happened in her life without a crutch while he was not. And that was almost exactly the same reason I'd never told her about my cutting. It made me feel weak and embarrassed, and it was so far from the image I've worked hard to present to the world. Rose Madden was a strong, kick-ass woman, not a scared girl who resorted to self-harming to cope.

I am falling apart, though, and fear I will have a complete breakdown unless I can divert my attention. I'd once read that your body can only process one pain source at a time, and over the years, I've found that to be true. If I'm suffering from emotional pain, then I can mask it by cutting. A thin line between my thighs can provide as much relief as Vicodin. Sure, the pain from the incision hurts, but it's a different type of discomfort. Strangely enough, I equate it to a good spring cleaning. It clears the cobwebs and allows me to enjoy the space within and around me once again. Am I rationalizing? Almost certainly, but it works. The network of silvery scars left behind is just collateral damage.

That first nick of the razor had been an accident. My father's criticism had taken its toll, and it had happened while rushing through my shower before dinner. His cruel words about tardiness last night hit me again. *Does he really despise me this much?* Watching that thin line of blood trickle down my thigh had ... settled me. Soothed. By the time I was getting dressed, I'd completely forgotten about my earlier upset. From something so seemingly innocent had been born a dark secret that I had managed to keep from everyone in my life except Jake.

Clutching the knife at my side, I creep silently back down the hallway, careful not to wake Max. I don't know what I would do if he stopped me now. I'm already anticipating the feeling of solace as the blade slices into my flesh. I've committed and justified it. I never change my mind when that happens.

I shut the bedroom door and then walk straight into the bathroom. As a precaution, I tug Max's shirt over my head, not wanting to accidentally ruin it. I've learned that bloodstains are almost impossible to remove. I unroll a length of tissue paper next and then find a spot on the cold, ceramic tile where I can easily spread my legs. It's not lost on me that I approach this routine almost clinically. It's so engrained in me that it's as if I'm on the outside observing someone else.

The knife feels unfamiliar in my hand as I tighten my grip on the handle. I normally use a razor or sometimes a needle. I probe my skin, looking for a location that isn't riddled with scars. Finally, I find a relatively smooth area near the crease of my leg. The skin is thin and more sensitive there but also tends to bleed more. *Perfect.* It's harder to gauge the depth in a fleshy area. I lower the tip of the blade, making a small incision. A thin line of crimson wells up, and I watch it idly, waiting to see if it will trickle down my leg.

After what seems like forever, a small amount of blood breaks free from the cut, making a tiny downward track. I frown. *There should be more blood. I need more blood.* I barely feel the sting from the nick. There isn't enough pain to quiet my racing thoughts. The blade must have been duller than I thought.

So I move it a few inches over and go deeper this time. "Shit," I hiss as it slices through my skin like butter. There is no waiting for the results this time. I see blood before I can even remove the knife. I can only stare, riveted by the vivid red against my pale skin. Then fear hits as I realize that I've cut deeper than ever before. *Fuck!*

The blade clatters to the floor as I grab Max's shirt from the floor and attempt to stop the bleeding. "No, no!" I repeatedly chant as panic seizes me. I'm dizzy, but I can't get up to look for my bag from earlier. "Max," I croak out, barely aware that I'm calling for him. "Max, help me!" I sob one more time, not thinking there is any way he can hear me. But then the sound of the bedroom door slamming open reaches me and there he is.

"Rose! Fuck, what happened?" He drops to his knees and begins running his hands over me, beginning at my neck. I have no idea why he's looking for an injury there since I'm holding a shirt to my leg.

"I cut myself," I wince as my injury throbs. There is nothing but the sounds of our rough breathing in the room. Then he seems to freeze. I look up and see the exact moment he spots the knife I'd tossed to the floor.

"Why?" he murmurs quietly almost as if he's talking to himself. I'm so tired that I'm having a hard time keeping pressure on the cut. I'm crashing the way I sometimes do after the high of cutting begins to ebb. My hand slips, pulling the T-shirt away. *So much blood.* Which seems to jerk him into action. He opens the cabinet behind him and grabs another towel, holding it firmly against me. In a strained voice, he asks, "Did you do this to yourself?" Before I can answer, his attention is drawn to the myriad of scars running up and down my thighs. He swallows visibly. "Oh baby, what've you been doing to yourself?"

Silent tears of shame roll down my face, dripping onto my chest. This is it. The time has come. Someone else knows my secret. Confident, carefree Rose is a fraud. Her mommy and daddy pick on her and she's too weak to handle it. I attempt to cover the evidence with my hands, not wanting him to see any more than he already has. "Don't look," I say huskily. "Please, Max, I'm so ugly."

He raises his other hand and runs it soothingly down my face until he's cupping my wet cheek. "Shhh, you don't need to hide from me. I see nothing but a beautiful woman who is hurting. Let me help you. We'll go to the hospital for stitches and then—"

"No!" I say in near hysteria. "I can't go there. They'll see—"

He seems to understand what I'm trying to say, even though my words are garbled. "Honey, the cut looks pretty deep. It needs to be stitched up." I shake my head frantically, and he stares at me seeming lost in thought. Finally, he takes one of my hands and puts it on the towel. "Keep pressing tight while I get my phone. I have a friend who should be able to help us out." He is back almost immediately. He hands me another T-shirt, and that's when I realize I'm completely naked. Without saying anything, he drops his hand to hold the towel in place, while I pull the shirt over my head. *Of course, he doesn't want to see me naked. Could his rejection be any louder?* Especially now that he knows the truth about me. Rose, the fraud. When I'm finished, he pushes a few buttons on his phone. "Matt, there is a guest at my house with a cut that needs stitching." He nods once, and then says, "Thanks, man. I owe you." He ends the call and tosses his phone down onto the floor. "He'll be here soon."

"But who was that and why would they come at well after midnight without any real explanation from you?"

He looks down at his hands and appears to be carefully choosing his words. "I've known Matt for about ten years. He's a good friend and just happens to be a surgeon."

"And he agreed to help me, just like that?" I ask incredulously.

Looking solemn, he says, "I'm not the type of man who asks for many favors, Rose, so Matt knows this must be important."

I glance around me, seeing the knife still sitting on the floor. "Um, do you think we could move to another room before he gets here?"

He surprises me by leaning forward to drop a kiss on my forehead. "Of course. Hold tight to the towel," he instructs as he gets to his knees before sliding his arms under my knees. I don't even think to protest. Instead, I wrap my free arm around his neck and hang on as he swings me easily into his arms and gets to his feet. "We'll go to the kitchen. The light is probably best there. Do you—need some underwear?"

Is it my imagination or is his neck slightly red? It's hard to believe that anything would embarrass the tough lawyer. I'm happy for the distraction, though, as my leg continues to throb. "Do you have a supply of women's panties?" I ask, trying to sound playful, even though I'm strangely jealous at the thought.

He chuckles, shaking his head. "No. Sorry, honey. I was thinking more along the lines of a pair of my boxer briefs. They'll be too big, but it'll give you some ... covering for now."

Then it hits me. My bare ass is resting on his arm. Holy shit. *I'm freaking out over that when he caught me cutting my leg? Unreal.* My face is hot as I mumble, "Oh, um, that would be great."

He lowers me gently onto a chair, then leaves to find some underwear. He comes back, handing me a pair of blue boxers that are silky soft to the touch. "Wow, these feel better than mine." My gaze automatically drops to his crotch area as I imagine him wearing them. I have no idea how it's even possible for me to have such thoughts after everything that has transpired in the last eight hours, but something about Max makes me forget about how screwed up I am. Maybe that's why I've always been drawn to him.

My father uses his strength to intimidate and control, but instinctively, I know Max is different. He's every bit as strong and determined, but he would bring out the best in the woman by his side, not attempt to crush everything that she is. Have I inherited my weakness from my mother? Or has my father crushed me too?

Max turns his back while I gingerly put my feet in the boxers before standing awkwardly to pull them up. They are big but comfortable. I fold the fabric back to expose my wound before sitting back down. We both jerk when the doorbell rings. "That'll be Matt," Max says before going to escort his friend in. I find myself cringing when Max returns with a man who could pass for Brad Pitt. I attempt to smooth my hair down self-consciously before I realize it will hardly matter. He's going to see the mess I've made of my legs. I doubt seriously he'll give a damn if I'm disheveled. He'll probably think it goes with the disaster that I am inside. Max comes to stand behind me, putting a supporting hand on my shoulder. "Rose, this is Matt Foster." We shake hands briefly as Matt stares at me with eyes that seem to see into my very soul. Something about him says he's seen too much. Energy literally flows off him in waves, but there is also world-weariness in his expression that makes him just as human as the rest of us.

He pulls a pair of glasses from his jacket pocket, and I can't stop the grin that briefly curves my lips. He gives me a wry smile in return. "One of the many downsides of getting old," he says lightly. I would estimate he is no more than forty, but he could easily pass for someone younger. Like Max, the hint of muscle flexing as he moves says that he takes care of his body. I wonder idly if there is a Mrs. Foster and think that if so, she's a lucky woman. He goes to the sink and washes his hands before coming back to where I'm sitting. "Now, let's see the cut that Max spoke of."

Dear God, I don't want to show this stunning man what I've done. My knees clamp together, and Max, as if feeling the tension in my body, steps closer and takes over. His hand grips mine and moves it away from my injury. After Matt moves another chair in front of me, he pulls a pair of gloves from the black bag he brought and puts them on. In a clinically detached way that makes me absurdly grateful, he eases my legs apart to get a better look. Gently he pulls the boxers up and away from the tops of my legs. The cut is still seeping blood as he probes it with his fingers. I see the moment he takes stock of the plethora of silvery scars below it. A glance so quick that I wonder if I've imagined it passes between the two men before Max clears his throat and asks, "What do you need me to do?"

Matt gets back to his feet and throws his gloves in the trash can. He rummages through his bag, bringing a vial and a syringe out first then something that looks like a staple gun, as well as a couple of sealed packets. He puts on another pair of gloves before quickly cleaning the cut and the surrounding area. The sting of pain is strangely welcome, yet it's odd to be experiencing that minor rush with an audience. I swallow audibly as he approaches me again with the now-filled syringe. "I'm not going to lie, Rose, this will hurt. But the area will numb quickly and should stay that way for several hours."

I squeeze Max's hand tightly and nod for him to go ahead. When the needle makes contact with my skin, I hiss. Why is it that I can cut my own skin and only feel relief, but when someone else dares to do something similar, there is only pain? Possibly because I'm not the one in control of what's happening to my body? *Is it as simple as the need to be in charge?* "Ouch," I whimper, as the sharp point seems to go straight through to the bone.

"Just breathe, baby," Max instructs, and that's what I do. Listening to his calm voice, I disconnect from what Matt is doing and focus on the man at my side. I feel pressure on my leg as Matt holds the wound together and the staple gun hovers above it. "Look at me," Max says, and I turn to face him once again. I'm so distracted by the warm tenderness in his eyes that I am almost surprised when I hear the click as Matt begins. True to his word, the shot has done as he promised and the staples don't really hurt.

In a surprisingly short amount of time, I hear Matt say, "There. All done." He's even covered the area with a bandage at some point. I thank him before Max follows him out of the room.

When they're gone, I stare down at the white gauze now covering a section of my thigh. Max's boxers are now stained with my blood. I need to change into another pair, but I'm so sleepy that I can barely remain upright. The secret I've kept for all of these years is out. *I feel so exposed. Physically, I am covered, yet emotionally, I'm exposed.* Two people now know that Rose Madden is a cutter. Maybe tomorrow I'll find enough energy to care, but for now, I want nothing more than the sweet oblivion that sleep can bring. While most people might be afraid of the monsters lurking in the dark, the things that haunt me rarely wait until nighttime.

Max

"Who is she?" Matt asks me tiredly as we step out the front door. Matt is a good friend, but I knew there was no way he would leave without wanting to know more.

"It's complicated," I reply, thinking that about sums it up exactly.

Matt shakes his head. "Don't give me that line, man. This woman is hurting herself. You know that, right? Some of those scars on her are years old. This isn't something she just started experimenting with."

"I know," I admit. "I mean I didn't know until tonight, but I saw the same thing you did. I'd just—shit, I'd never have imagined her doing something like that. She has always seemed so happy and carefree. A little nuts sometimes," I laugh, "but still it shocks the fuck out of me."

Matt puts a hand on my arm and gives me a level stare. "She's in crisis, Max. She needs help. Are you in a relationship with her?"

"No," I say as I try not to panic at his words. "Until tonight, I hadn't seen her in a while. She's best friends with Luc's wife." Lucian and Matt aren't friends, but they do know each other socially. "We've danced around something more than a few times, but it hasn't gone further than that, and I have no intention of allowing anything to happen in the future."

In the glow of the porch light, I see the concern on Matt's face. "You need to be very careful with her. I'll email you some information later on physicians I know who deal with this type of thing. She was just inches away from hitting a major artery tonight, and she may have bled out before you could have stopped it."

My gut clenches as I voice my biggest fear. "Has she been attempting to kill herself?"

"No. Generally it's just a very bad way of dealing with stress, emotional pain, or even trauma." Before I can feel relief, he adds, "But it can escalate over time, and it's possible that she could kill herself by accident."

"Fuck," I whisper, shaken to the core. "I can't believe this. I have no idea what to do, other than to watch her every minute of the day. Somehow, I don't think she'll allow that, though."

"Probably not," Matt agrees. "Understand that it's an attempt to be in control of something and while that may happen while she's doing it, afterward, it generally brings feelings of shame. So not only is she dealing with whatever caused her to start cutting in the first place, but she's also more than likely deeply embarrassed by what she's doing. I would be surprised if anyone else in her life knows about it. If they don't, this could go two ways. She may be relieved that someone has finally found out … or she may be afraid of what you'll think of her now that you know. So be as supportive as you can and try to encourage her to speak with a professional or someone in her life who she trusts."

"Thanks, Matt," I say as I give him a one-armed hug. "I appreciate you coming over."

"I'm here for you," he says sincerely, "and I'm here for Rose. Call me at any time if you have concerns." I walk back into the house and close the door behind me. This whole evening seems like some kind of dream to me. Was it mere hours ago that I received the call from Rose? Everything since has been a blur.

Instead of returning right away to Rose, I make a quick detour to clean the mess from the guest bathroom so she won't be faced with it when she does go back into her room. I've just set the trash bag in the laundry room when I look up to see Rose standing uncertainly in the hallway. "Are you okay?" she asks, and I fight the urge to laugh, even though it's not funny. Shouldn't I be the one checking on her?

I give her a wry smile and walk to where she is standing. "I'm fine, sweetheart. What do you say we call it a night— or a morning? I don't know about you, but I'm beat."

She drops her head, refusing to make eye contact as she says, "Yeah, I'm tired." I automatically place a hand on her lower back and lead her back toward the guest room. She stands in the doorway looking very young and uncertain. "So—um, I guess I'll see you in a bit."

I pull her into a brief hug because she looks as if she needs it as much as I do. "I'm just down the hallway. If you need anything, let me know. I'll leave my door open." She pulls away and I try not to feel like I abandoning her as I continue to my own bed. As exhausted as I am, though, I have to wonder if I'll be able to sleep knowing that Rose is lying next door, possibly even more broken than I am.

CHAPTER FOUR

Rose

I stare at the ceiling and attempt to will my exhausted body to sleep. That Max knows my secret is something I couldn't have imagined happening. In all the months that I teased and flirted with him, I never gave serious thought to what would occur if we ever had sex. Maybe I secretly believed I could hide it all from him in the dark of the night.

He's been incredibly supportive and nonjudgmental since he walked in on me bleeding in his bathroom earlier. I knew he had questions; I could see them in his eyes. But to give him credit, he had yet to make me feel like the freak I obviously am. He has to be thinking in the back of his mind that he really dodged a bullet by not getting involved with someone as messed up as me. No doubt, his doctor friend would have pointed that out to him. Matt Foster had been polite and professional, but there was a weariness to him that was impossible to miss. Like Max, Matt was also a very handsome man. I didn't feel the attraction to him, though, that I do to his friend. Of course, the fact that I was sitting before him looking like a train wreck while he stapled my leg might have had something to do with it. It's a little hard to admire someone knowing they must think you're a complete nut job.

My hands twist in the cotton material of Max's shirt as thoughts of my father fill my head. What am I going to do? I'm homeless. I have no apartment, nor can I afford a hotel. I can't even afford the necessities. If not for Max, I would still be on the street.

I burrow more deeply under the covers as shivers begin wracking my body. Dammit, not again! I know another panic attack is just around the corner, and I have no way of coping with it. Then I remember the bag that I had used earlier to breathe in. I scramble from the bed and flip the lamp on. A soft glow fills the room as I look around. It's not here. Shit, Max must have picked it up. I pace the floor, feeling my chest grow tighter.

Before I am even conscious of moving, I'm walking down the hallway until I reach an open door. I stand just inside until my eyes become accustomed to the inky blackness. I can make out a shape on the bed as I creep toward it. I stand there silently, wringing my hands. I desperately need someone to hold me tonight, but I'm incapable of asking. I turn away, not willing to let him see that I'm falling apart yet again.

I've barely made it a few steps when he rears up in the bed, looking around wildly. I may not have been able to fall asleep, but it appears he didn't suffer from the same problem. I see him jerk as he notices me standing there. His arm reaches toward the lamp but freezes as I say quickly, "Please. Don't! I'll go, just don't turn that on." I have no idea why, but I don't want him to see me right now. Some part of me hopes that his mind will conjure up the image that I normally present—not this pathetic women nearly hyperventilating before him. Then as if things couldn't get any more awkward, I blurt out, "Can I sleep with you?" *Oh my God, why did I say that?* I'm so embarrassed; I don't wait for his reply.

I'm almost back to my room when he grabs my elbow, halting me in my tracks. "Why are you running?" he asks, sounding adorably confused.

"I—shouldn't have put you on the spot. I couldn't sleep and ... I didn't know what else to do."

He is silent for a moment before using the hand he still has on my elbow to propel me back to his bedroom and through the door. Despite my earlier plea, he turns the lamp on before turning the comforter on his bed back and motioning me in. As my pride is already in tatters, I waste no time accepting what he's offering. I crawl across the soft mattress until I reach the other side. When I've stopped moving, he gets in as well and turns the light off.

I begin to think I've made a big mistake as I lie rigidly with only inches separating us. I have the closeness I was craving, but it's still not what I need. I want to feel his arms around me, but there is no way I can ask anything more of him. Truthfully, we're not even friends in the real world, so this is awkward. My skin feels tight. My chest even tighter. *Come on, Rose. Breathe.*

I hear him sigh before he asks, "How can I help you? I can sense your fear from here, sweetheart, and I want nothing more than to hold you until you feel safe enough to sleep." I take a deep breath and wiggle my way back to his side. Why bother to worry about rejection at this point? While it might not be pleasant, it could in no way compare to him finding me in the bathroom with a knife on the floor beside me.

He lifts his arm as I reach him and I duck under it, laying my head on his chest. There is no hair there, and I wonder fleetingly if he shaves or waxes. His muscles flex as he begins rubbing my back, lulling me into an almost trance-like state. Then he shocks me further by humming. I don't recognize the tune, but his husky, masculine voice fills the silence, and I find I'm incapable of thinking of anything else. I want to remain awake, just to hear him, but the pull to sleep is too strong. It's been months since I've

slept beside a man. *Don't think of that douche now, Rose.*
You don't need that additional pain and embarrassment. So
warm. So comfortable in Max's arms. This may be the only
night he allows this. I drift away, secure in the protective
circle of his embrace. Tomorrow, I'll be alone again, but
this is what I'll miss the most.

Max

I wake disoriented as something brushes against me.
Even though it's been a long time, I still remember the
unmistakable feel of a woman in my arms. Sunlight streams
through the partially closed blinds as I take a moment to get
my bearings. The previous night comes flooding back, and
I glance down to see a cascade of red hair sprayed across
my chest. After months of avoidance and denial, Rose
Madden is in my arms—although certainly not in the way
I've fantasized about. Darkness exists inside her that I
never would have guessed.

Possibly, her obsession with firearms and revenge upon
her ex-boyfriend should have clued me in, but both were
presented in such a lighthearted manner that I hadn't a clue.
Matt says that she harms herself by cutting to have some
sense of control over her life, which surprises me. If there
is one woman who I would have said was in command of
the world around her, it's Rose. I'll admit that knowing I've
read her completely wrong is unsettling. As a lawyer, I
literally make a living being able to figure out what makes
someone tick. Now, I find that there is yet another facet to
her I never expected. She's a beautiful, intriguing, and
troubled puzzle I need to solve, if for no other reason than
to help her. Now that I know what she's been doing, I can't
turn my back. I'd never forgive myself if something
happened and I wasn't there. *Does Lia know?* I wonder,
thinking if she'd confided in anyone, it would be her friend.

She shifts again, and I try not to think about the last woman who shared my bed. It's been so long since I've let anyone past the wall I've built around me. I have sex when the need is there, but I don't have relationships. Luc and I were actually a lot alike before he met Lia. I knew he was a goner even before he did. She was the one he couldn't walk away from. I know because I've had that before, and it's damn hard to deal with when it's jerked away. Luc was strong enough to take a leap of faith—but I am not. I will be her friend and help her in any way that I can—but that's all I have to give her.

When a snore loud enough to do a man proud fills the room, I can't hold my laughter back. It's the comic relief I desperately need. She does it again, and I marvel that such a tiny thing can make such a loud noise. Dear God, this woman may need sinus surgery along with everything else.

Apparently, my shaking body is enough to disturb her, and she jerks awake with an adorable snort. I watch her with a grin on my face while her eyes scan the room in confusion and then come to rest on me. "Wh—what?" Before I can fill her in, I see it all coming back to her. Her look of puzzlement gives way to embarrassment as her face turns a deep shade of red. "Crap, I'd really hoped it was just a dream," she mumbles as she drops her head.

"That's not exactly what a man likes to hear when he wakes up in bed with a woman," I tease, trying to put her at ease.

Never one to back down from a joke, she fires right back, "I seriously doubt a man would take a woman he'd found carving herself like a Jack-o-Lantern in his bathroom to bed at the end of the evening unless he was into some strange shit."

I'm strangely relieved she is able to make light of the previous night. I'd been afraid that things between us would be at the very least strained in the light of day. "I'm a lawyer, sweetheart. I've seen a lot and heard even more.

Not much can shock me at this point. Were you working on the eyes or the mouth last night when I walked in?"

A giggle escapes her as she shifts from my chest and falls onto her back. Her hands come up and cover her face as she continues to laugh. "You're sick, Mr. Decker. Has anyone ever told you that? You shouldn't make fun of the fucked up."

I nod my head in agreement. "I've been told that a few times, but my mother never got around to teaching me manners." My stomach growls as I finish my sentence. I turn to study her, thinking she looks more gorgeous than any woman has a right to after an evening of hell. "I'm starving. How about I lock up all of my knives and whip us up something to eat?"

She looks over to see me smirking and raises her delicate finger in the air to flip me off. "Go fix me something to eat before I smother you with this pillow," she threatens as she pats the fluffy mound next to her.

"Your wish is my command." I get to my feet and wink before walking toward the kitchen. I stop off at the bathroom in the hall and take care of business before washing my face and hands. A quick look in the mirror shows the usual morning stubble of hair on my jawline, but I don't usually worry about that on the weekends. My profession calls for me to wear suits more often than not, so I value what little time I can relax and be casual.

As I gather up the ingredients to make eggs and bacon, I marvel at how relaxed I feel. I hadn't expected that this morning. I figured, at best, things would be tense and uncomfortable while we both tried to ignore the elephant in the room. I certainly never imagined I'd be making jokes about sharp objects. I wasn't sure when I began with the teasing if it was the best way to go and part of me was afraid she would either start crying or leave in a pissed-off rage. I was so fucking relieved to hear that giggle. Such beautiful music to my ears. If I'm to help her at all, I think we need to establish that kind of ease between us. I want her to feel as if she can talk to me about anything without things getting too intense for her to handle. As Matt said, if she thinks I'm judging her, then she'll shut me out. And I'm not sure she has anywhere else to turn.

I am plating our meal when she comes into the kitchen. Her hair is a jumble of waves around her shoulders, and she's still wearing my shirt—a fact my cock notices almost immediately. I keep my front turned toward the stove as I try to talk the evil bastard back into a relaxed state. My body has been hyper aware of Rose from the moment we met. The things I've imagined doing to her would either shock or thrill her—possibly both. At this moment, I'm grateful for my loose lounge pants as they give some camouflage to my wayward dick.

I set her food before her, and she gives me a shy smile. "Thanks. This looks great."

"I'm good at everything I do, sweetheart," I joke before thinking better of it. If I plan to keep this just friendship, it would probably be better to stop throwing out the sexual innuendos. That seems impossible around her, though. I blurt them out without thought.

"Prove it," she tosses right back, and despite my resolve, I grin approvingly. As usual, I'm powerless to resist this woman when she turns on the charm. It's hard for me to reconcile the woman of this morning with the one of only hours before. If Matt is correct, and she's been cutting for years, then she has probably become very good at hiding it from the world behind her normal bubbly demeanor.

"I wouldn't want to be the cause of you popping your stitches. Matt would kick both of our asses if that happened," I add lightly as I lift a slice of bacon to my mouth.

We eat in silence for a while before she suddenly asks, "So what's his story—Matt's? How did you first meet?"

I feel a pang of what feels almost like jealousy at her interest in Matt as well as a trickle of unease at the question. Matt and I have a history together and to tell her how we met would be to reveal more than I intend to. Therefore, I keep my answer vague as I say, "We've moved in similar circles." Then I decide to change the subject. "So it looks as if we need to do some shopping today. When I got up, I washed the outfit you were wearing last night, so as soon as it's dry, we can head out. Unless you plan to try to work things out with your father today?"

A shudder runs through her as she shakes her head. "No, I don't want anything to do with him after what he did to me. If I go crawling back now, then he's got me. I'll have to cave to all of his demands, and I might as well be signing my life over at that point because I'll never get back out again." Then she drops her head in her hands and I hear a sniffle. "But I have no idea what I'm going to do. I hardly have any money, no clothing, or other necessities. Lia won't be back 'til tomorrow evening, and I'm not calling and worrying her."

I put a hand on her arm, gently pulling it away from her face. She looks so despondent; it breaks my heart. I should have at least let her finish breakfast before forcing her to talk. "Honey, you don't need to worry about any of that. You'll stay with me until you have everything figured out. For however long you need to. We'll get you some clothing today and whatever else you need." She opens her mouth as if to protest, but I hold a hand up and stop her. "I know that things have been complicated between us for lack of a better word and a big part of that is my fault. At the very least, we are friends, and I hope that you can forgive me for disappearing from your life. We both, it seems, have things going on that we're dealing with, and I deeply regret that I wasn't there when maybe you needed someone."

"Lia doesn't know anything about the cutting," she blurts out unexpectedly. "I'm asking you to please not tell her."

I'm not really surprised at her revelation. Matt had indicated last night that Rose likely hadn't told anyone her secret. "I would never share anything that you didn't want me to. You don't even need to ask. You two are so close, though, so out of curiosity, why haven't you talked to her? Both she and Lucian have had their shares of issues, so you know she's the last person who would judge you."

She shakes my hand off and gets to her feet. I watch as she paces the kitchen for a few moments before looking at me. "I don't want her to know how weak I am. You know what she's been through. My God, she was abused, and then slept in a car after she left home. She found a way to put herself through college and graduate with honors. She's the strongest person I've ever known. I may tease her, but truthfully, I'm in awe of her. Her opinion is so important. I couldn't bear it if she thought less of me. Right now, I'm just not ready to take that risk."

I would like to argue with her, but I don't want to drive a wedge between us. Right now, regardless of how either of us feels about it, I'm all she has in the way of support. I know Lia would do anything for her friend, but it's up to Rose as to how much she wants her to know. "It's your decision," I begin, "and I'll leave it at that. But for today, let's get dressed and beat the crowds to the mall. We should be able to find enough to get you by there, right?"

I'm not sure if it's my imagination, but I think I see her wince before she nods. "That's fine. And I'll pay you back as soon as I get my first paycheck."

I roll my eyes at her. "I'm not worried about that. Let me get your clothes." She's standing in the hallway waiting as I return with her garments from the dryer. "The pants aren't in the best shape, but hopefully, they'll get you by until we can replace them."

She takes them from my hands and buries her face in their warmth, reminding me of a child. There are so many facets to this woman. I wonder if I'll ever see them all. I'm entranced by her, which is not only dangerous, it's damn near irrational. The last thing she needs is a man with issues of his own. She needs stability, and I can only offer her that in the financial form. Emotionally, I'm as fucked up as she is. She turns toward the guest room, then stops and looks at me over her shoulder. "Thanks, Max. I don't know where I'd be today without you rescuing me last night." Without waiting for my reply, she shuts the door softly behind her. I have to fight the urge to follow her. She seems fine, but it will be a while before I forget the sight that greeted me when I stepped into that bathroom and saw the blood. I may have been able to joke about it this morning, but it's something that will haunt me for years to come.

Rose

I deliberately keep my thoughts blank as I shower and then dry my hair. I dress in my clothing from the previous night—and then I see them. There are holes in my slacks. Both knees were damaged when I fell. *I can't go out like this. What if someone sees me? I'm a disgrace—a complete mess.* I'm frozen in place, on the verge of freaking out, when I hear a voice nearby. "Ready to go, sweetheart?" He moves over to stand in my line of vision as if knowing I need him. "You look beautiful and you'll be the envy of every teenage girl at the mall with those ripped up pants. Very retro, Ms. Madden."

I stare at him, slowly coming out of the trace I'd fallen into. I glance down at my clothing, before looking at him once again. He's grinning as if we share some kind of inside joke. At that moment, I understand that he knows. On some level, he gets how hard it is for me to leave the house looking anything less than perfect. It's been drummed into me my whole life. My only purpose as far as my parents were concerned was to look and act the part of a Madden. I'm like some brainwashed cult member who is trying to learn to think for herself. I clear my throat before saying, "Yes, well, haters gonna hate. Bring your wallet,

Mr. Decker. I think I'm going to inflict some serious damage on it."

He gives me a lazy grin that does crazy things to my body. "I have you covered, babe." He waves an arm toward the doorway, adding, "After you, honey." I wonder if he has any idea what the endearments that he uses do to me? Even though I know he means nothing by them, I still feel special; like maybe, in some small way, I do matter. Right now, I need to pretend he feels more than pity for me.

CHAPTER FIVE

Max

The ride to the mall is light and easy. The conversation flows and Rose seems happy and relaxed. I'm not sure what was going through her mind before we left, but I could feel the anxiety coming off her in waves when I walked into the guest room to see if she was ready to leave. She was standing only inches away, but her mind was somewhere else entirely. Sensing she might be overwhelmed by the new wardrobe, I'd done the only thing I could think of. I'd stepped in front of her and diverted her attention. Luckily, it had worked, and she appeared fine now.

When we walk through the double doors of the shopping complex, we both freeze in place. I'm not what you'd call a window shopper. Hell, I can't remember the last time I've been somewhere like this. My suits are custom made, and my casual clothing comes from what I'd classify as a men's store. They sell a little of everything, but you're unlikely to bump elbows with a bunch of teenagers while you're there. The scene before me looks like barely controlled chaos. I have a feeling that if one false move is made, the place will erupt into pandemonium. A glance at Rose tells me she possibly has similar fears. She obviously isn't a chain-store woman either, but we have no choice but to make the best of it. Fuck, I'm a lawyer who handles billion-dollar mergers while sipping coffee; this is nothing. *Don't look like a pussy here. Man up.*

Giving her a bright and what I hope is a relaxed smile, I take her hand in mine, not sure which of us needs it the most. "All right, sweetheart. Let's go get you some clothes. Where should we go first?"

Her head swivels, taking in the area around us. She looks scared out of her mind. Shit. I thought this kind of thing was second nature to a woman, but I'd have to be with the one who is just as clueless as I am. "I—okay, let me think," she stutters as she takes a step forward. Then she throws me under the bus by pushing me forward. "I'm with you so just pick one." *Well, hell.*

I straighten my shoulders as if I'm going to war, and we're off. When I spot a store with women's dresses in the window, I think I've hit the jackpot. "This looks good." I point at a nearby grouping of chairs and say, "How about you check it out while I wait out here?"

She looks horrified at my suggestion. Her eyes widen as she gapes at me. "You want me to go in there alone?" I feel as if I've just suggested she enter the gates of hell.

I have no idea why I feel the need to apologize, but I do it anyway. "I'm sorry, sweetheart. I thought that maybe you'd be more comfortable without me."

Then I see the fire I'm so accustomed to burning in her eyes as she gives me a tug. "Oh no, Decker, you're not getting out of this. I know you're paying, but you're also shopping. I don't have a freaking inkling as to how to do this shit."

"Don't you do this with Lia?" I ask. "Isn't it something you're born knowing how to do?" I know that last line was a mistake when she glares at me.

"I may have a vagina," she snaps, "but that doesn't mean I'm some mall groupie." Then she lowers her voice, sounding achingly vulnerable. "I'm never done this before,

Max. I've had someone else picking out my clothing since the day I was born. My parents didn't trust that I wouldn't embarrass them." She pulls on the tailored shirt that she's wearing as tears glisten in her eyes. "I don't know how to be anything other than this. Yes, I've shopped with Lia before, but that's different. We were buying things for her. Do you know how I dress myself each day?" When I shake my head, she continues. "I have a notebook telling me which pieces to wear together. With every new wardrobe, I get specific instructions so I don't screw it up. It's like fucking designer Garanimals for adults!"

Her face is red, and she looks like a powder keg on the verge of exploding. I think carefully of a reply before I finally settle on, "What in the hell is a Garanimal?"

In an instant, she loses her defensive stance and bursts into laughter. "Oh my God, that's all you got from that whole spiel? Garanimals are children's clothing that come with little tags that make them easy to match up. And before you can ask how I know that, Lia suggested I buy some for Lara instead of the Valentino baby collection that I'd been planning to get."

I wave my hand around me as I say, "So you have been somewhere like this before."

She rolls her eyes. "It's called online shopping, counselor. Something that we should have considered before putting ourselves through this."

It's downright pathetic how little it takes to turn me on. Her calling me "counselor," has me imagining myself bending her over the witness stand while I go balls deep inside her wet heat. My cock is rock hard at the visual, and I attempt to nonchalantly put my hands in the pockets of my jeans, to create some camouflage. "Should we—um, give this a try?" I ask in a voice that sounds unusually high.

Almost as if she has a direct line to my thoughts, her eyes drop to my crotch and her cheeks flush. Any other woman would pretend not to notice, but not my Rose. *She's*

not your anything; get that into both of your heads.
"What's with the wood?"

I look away, feeling like a schoolboy who has just been busted. "You didn't just say that," I groan.

She shrugs her shoulders. "Answer the question, counselor. I mean I know all about the whole waking up with a stiffie, but shouldn't that be over by now? I didn't notice it at the house." She wrinkles her nose and gives me a wary look. "You're not one of those guys who gets turned on by the feeling of women's clothing, are you? It's not going to get you out of shopping with me, but you'll need to carry a shirt or something in front of you to hide that thing. Geez, why did I never know this about you? All this time, I thought you were so straight-laced. We definitely can't buy lingerie if you're getting a boner from looking at a dress through the display window."

By the time she finishes, my mouth is hanging up. I'm in such a rush to assure her I'm not a weirdo that I admit something I'd planned to keep to myself. "I'm hard because I'm with you. It wouldn't matter if we were at a mall or fucking Toys-R-Us. It's just the way my body reacts when you're around."

She looks nonplussed for all of a few seconds before she smirks at me. "I believe I'd keep your sexual references away from a kid's store, counselor, but I like the general theme of your message."

Now, I'm the one with a flushed face. Rather than wait on this train wreck to reach the station, I pull on her hand and stalk into the store we've been standing in front of for far too long. Unfortunately, I know as soon as I look around that there is nothing here for Rose. The place is packed with shirts and jeans that have what I guess are supposed to be fashionable rips and tears in them. If the bored-looking, bubble-gum chewing sales associate is any indication, we've landed in teen hell. Rose's hand flexes within my own as we both stand uncertainly. "I don't think we're in Kansas anymore," she murmurs behind me.

"Let's go somewhere else," I say as I try to pull her back through the door.

When she doesn't budge, I look down to find her staring up at me. She shifts uncomfortably before saying, "I—um, do you think I could look around?"

For a moment, I think she's joking, but a hint of longing in her voice tells me otherwise. Then it hits me. If what she told me earlier is any indication, she was never allowed to be young. She dresses older than her age, and I would bet money that she always has. I doubt she's ever owned a piece of clothing like the ones surrounding us. "Sure, baby, pick out anything that you like," I encourage as she moves timidly forward and begins flipping through the racks.

She spends well over an hour walking every inch of the store as if entranced. At the end of that time, she has only one pair of jeans and a T-shirt over her arm. She comes to where I'm standing a few feet away and says, "I know this will sound stupid, but I would very much like to get this outfit. But I don't want to try it on here."

"Okay," I agree easily. "I'm sure you know what fits you, so it's no big deal, sweetheart." I point at the register. "Let's go pay and move on to the next store." She sets them on the counter, and I notice that her hands are shaking. Then it hits me. She wants the outfit, but this is the first time she's picked something out on her own. Without saying anything, I drop an arm around her shoulders in wordless support and she snuggles into my side. Before I'm even aware of it, I'm dropping a kiss on the top of her head and feeling things that should have me sprinting for the nearest exit. My need to protect her is slamming up against the wall I've spent years carefully building around my heart.

As I sign the receipt for our first purchase, she takes the bag, holding it carefully in her other hand as if it contains a rare treasure. "Thank you, Max," she says sincerely.

"You're welcome, honey. Now, let's see what else we can find." She ends up doing the rest of her shopping in

Nordstrom. A store that has enough of a high-end feel to make her comfortable. This time, she does take a stack into the dressing room. Then I find myself in the uncomfortable position of mentioning the undergarments that she hasn't made any move toward getting. "Er—Rose, if you're afraid that I have some strange panty fetish, you can relax. I know that you need underwear, and if it will make it easier for you, I can walk around the men's section while you pick them out." I pull my wallet from my pocket and take out my American Express card. "Here, take this and buy whatever you need. I'll come back later on to see if you're ready."

She stares down at the card, then back at me before shaking her head. "Oh no, counselor, there will be no running. You've wanted to get in my panties for months, and you're fixing to get your chance." She drops her gaze to see if her words are having the desired effect on me, and dammit, as usual, there's a direct line from her lips to my cock.

I put a hand on the nape of her neck and squeeze lightly. "You have no idea what you're playing with," I whisper in her ear. I'm gratified to feel her shudder.

I think I've taken the upper hand until she pushes back against me, wedging her ass against my groin. "Then show me," she tosses over her shoulder before pulling away from me.

And just like that, she turns the tables, and I'm left wondering if I can remain only friends with the woman who is fast becoming an obsession to me.

Rose

Outside of a few rocky moments when I'd had some twinges of unease—to put it mildly—the mall had been strangely fun. It was obvious shortly after we walked in the door that neither of us was used to shopping with the masses. But it had turned out to be the distraction I desperately needed. I had always loved teasing Max and today had been no exception. Forcing him to help me pick out clothing in Nordstrom had been amusing, but the real fun had been the lingerie shopping.

I would never have guessed that such a confident man would turn into such a bumbling, blushing schoolboy when faced with a pair of cheekinis and a matching bra. When I hold up another set with a matching garter belt, he backs up so fast, he turns over a bin of clearance thongs, bringing the sales associate rushing over. Max drops to his knees to help pick up what looks like hundreds of pairs of skimpy underwear as he apologizes profusely to the motherly employee. She pats him on the arm when they are finished, and then gives me a wink before she walks away.

He surprises me by picking up a handful of boy shorts and pushing them into my arms. "I think these have more … coverage than the others." I smirk as I add them to the small pile I've already amassed. The poor man. Obviously, he's never seen a woman in boy shorts before. I've long been a fan of them, and of all of my underwear, they were the ones that had sent Jake over the edge the fastest. I would have to make sure that Max got a peek at some point. We'd see if he still thought they were a good idea then.

The many problems I had managed to forget during our trip come rushing back when we pull into Max's circular drive and park. He gets out of the car and I follow slowly behind. As he is unloading my bags from the trunk of his car, I stand rooted in place. He gives me a questioning look as he walks up the few steps that lead to his front door. "If you think I'm carrying you in next, sweetheart, you're sadly mistaken. Move that sexy ass now." And with those few words, I am jolted into action. I have no idea how, but Max seems to have the uncanny ability to do and say the right thing. It was as if he knew I was teetering on the edge and tossed out the rope to pull me back in. I trail him into the house and down the hallway as he deposits my new clothing on the floor of my borrowed room. He points toward a set of double doors to the right and says, "There's the closet if you want to hang everything up." Then he gives me a sexy grin before adding, "And feel free to use the dresser to store your new array of panties in."

I laugh at his sudden bravery in discussing my undergarments. "Wow, you've recovered nicely from the near stroke that you had in Nordstrom when I held up a simple piece of silk."

He catches me by surprise when he takes a couple of steps until he's only inches from my face. He lowers his head, and holy mother, he sniffs my neck before running a teasing hand down my side. "Don't mistake me for a fumbling boy, sweetheart, because I'm anything but. I might have been a bit embarrassed at having to walk around a department store while I was hard enough to punch through a wall, but if I decided to take you, those scraps of covering wouldn't stop me."

I moan, ready to hump his leg if it'll bring me some relief from the fire down below. "Mmm … please," I murmur helplessly.

Then the bastard has the audacity to chuckle while I'm panting like a dog in heat. He places a noisy kiss on my cheek before saying, "I don't know about you, but I'm starving. What do you feel like tonight?"

"You," I shoot back promptly, causing his eyes to widen. Before he has time to recover, I stroll past him and toss over my shoulder, "But I'll settle for some kind of pasta with a lot of … meat." It appears that I've rendered him speechless because there is nothing but silence as I make my way to the kitchen and begin opening the cabinets. I have the ingredients for spaghetti laid on the counter when he finally comes in looking a little less cocky and a lot more flushed. I point at the clove of garlic and an onion I've set out. "I bet a macho guy like you can chop those without shedding so much as a single tear."

I don't miss the way his gaze roams hungrily over my body for a split second before he gives me an easy smile. "If I'm in charge of this, then I guess you're handling ... everything else?"

I've never considered food to be sexy, but when I open the hamburger meat and begin kneading it with my hands, we both shift uncomfortably. I have no idea why I'm even touching it considering I normally dump it straight from the package into the pan. This is so much more fun, though. I do fear that Max might chop off a digit with the knife he's wielding since he's so transfixed on what I'm doing. I know it's pure, sick, evil that has me inserting my ring finger into the soft mass almost as if I'm making love to it. *Dear God, I need more therapy than I thought.*

In a strangled voice, Max hisses, "I swear I've never been jealous of ground chuck before, but if you don't stop touching that stuff, I'm going to embarrass myself right here."

I would love nothing better than to extend his torment, but I'm getting kind of grossed out by the smell and the texture of the former cow I've been doing my best to violate. *Poor Bess, she didn't deserve to end up like this.* I dump the lump into the skillet and set it on low heat to brown. I cross to the sink and thoroughly wash my hands three times before leaning against the cabinets to watch Max mince the garlic. I've never really cooked with a man before, and it's surprisingly erotic. Jake's idea of making dinner was to pick up Chinese on the way over. If he were feeling especially frisky, he'd transfer it onto china before we ate. I give Max my best bimbo stance, complete with hair twirling. "Whatcha doing over there, handsome?"

He rolls his eyes, but I can see a grin pulling at the corners of his full lips. "I'm keeping the sharp objects out of your hands, my beauty," he teases easily as he finishes up. I shake my head at his wise-ass comment, but it doesn't offend me. I'm sure that some wouldn't be able to handle him poking fun at something so personal and serious, but in a weird way, I find that it grounds me. I'm not stupid; I realize that he's concerned about me. Instead of making a big deal out of what he discovered last night and watching me every second of the day, he's keeping it light. I truly believe he feels if he handles it in such a way, then maybe I'll feel more comfortable in talking to him about it, and he's possibly right. He's learned my dirty secret, so the shock value is gone. I couldn't reveal much to him at this point that would be worse. He's still treating me like— well, me. Not some pathetically messed-up creature that needs saving. And I love him for it—in the way you would a favorite teacher who made you feel like an adult for the first time. Oh hell, who am I kidding? My feelings for Max are much more complicated than that. I want him to do dirty things to me that I've only ever read about.

"I think you've already taken care of that, baby." He waves the knife in my face before tossing it into the sink. I give him a blank look before it hits me. Shit! I must have said that last thought aloud. I don't need a mirror to know that my face must be the color of my hair. How many times must I blurt out crazy shit before I learn to keep control of my mouth? "I hope you're referring to me doing stuff that doesn't require Band-Aids or stitches."

"You're such an ass!" I snap as I fling a damp dishcloth and do a little victory dance when it nails him right in the chest. "You really need to speak with your friend, Dr. Foster, about some sensitivity classes. I'm sure he wouldn't be happy to know that you're making fun of me in this way."

He nods his head in agreement before adding, "While I'm speaking to him, I'll get his advice on those *dirty* things that you want me to do to you."

Refusing to be outdone, I purse my lips and put my finger to them as if deep in thought. "Maybe I'll talk to him myself. Matt is awfully hot. I mean I can hardly get his big

... medical bag off my mind. What do you suppose he's hiding in that thing? From the size of it, I can only surmise he has some large instruments. And with all of his schooling, he must surely be well versed in using them." Max has gone deadly still, and there is a glint in his eyes that I've never seen before. Heedless of the danger, I move in for the kill. "Since you two are friends, I'll just leave you out of the equation altogether and see if Dr. Foster can take care of all my needs."

He's on me before I even see him move. His hand is at my neck and his mouth is on mine. His tongue plunges into my mouth, stamping unmistakable ownership as he holds me immobile in his grasp. My nipples are hard as glass as I press them wantonly against his broad chest. Resistance is the last thing on my mind as he controls every lick and sip. I wrap my arms around his neck, bringing us into closer contact. He takes advantage of the proximity by grinding his huge bulge into my mound. "Mmm," I moan, feeling myself already on the verge of an orgasm. He trails kisses down my neck, stopping to suck on the soft tissue there. *Holy hotness, is suppressed lawyer Max Decker giving me a hickey?* I'll gladly bear any battle wounds he chooses to give me as long as he doesn't stop what he's doing. I move one hand from his neck and grasp his cock in a bold move that surprises even me. "I want you," I hiss as he pinches my nipple through my top.

"Sweetheart, you have no idea how much I want to lay you out on that granite behind you and fuck that pink pussy," he growls. His hand is on the snap of my pants and it's like Niagara Falls between my thighs when a high-pitched sound has us wrenching apart. "What the—?" Max looks around frantically.

"Oh, no!" Smoke is billowing from the pan where the hamburger meat was once simmering. Max turns the power off under the burner. He then extends an arm to the smoke detector that has my ears ringing and removes the batteries. We both breathe a sigh of relief at the immediate silence. "I guess I'm not going to impress you with my meat handling, after all," I joke as we stare at the charred mess that remains of my attempt at spaghetti sauce.

Max smirks as he runs a hand through his hair, leaving it adorably disheveled. "Well, it was either divine intervention or a strong hint that we're supposed to order a pizza."

I cringe when my giggle of agreement comes out a bit too high-pitched. "I'll clean up in here if you want to order our dinner." I'm still off balance from the recent introduction of Max's tongue to my tonsils. I'd like nothing better than to continue what was so rudely interrupted, but even I know when to accept that a moment is lost. What had happened was spontaneous and so out of character for my straight-laced lawyer. There's no way he's picking up where we left off, at least not right now. I'm disappointed and horny as hell, but I'm also excited in more than a physical way. That bit of insanity showed me that he is far from immune to me. I'd wager that he wants me as badly as I want him, but something has been holding him back. Lia says that even though Lucian and Max have been friends and colleagues for years, Lucian doesn't know much about his past. I sense something is there, though. He has said that he doesn't think it's a good idea for us to get involved because it would be awkward for our mutual friends if it ended on a bad note. I believe he means that to a certain extent. But there's more he's not telling me. He has his demons just as I have mine. Of course, he's recently had a front-row seat to the worst that I have to offer, so I'm more of a fucked-up open book now. Yet he's still attracted to me …

Max waves some takeout menus under my nose, effectively pulling me back to the present. "Just leave everything until it cools off. I don't want you to burn yourself." He points at one of the flyers in his hand and pumps his fist in a show of victory. "This one says delivery in less than an hour, and they have the Italian mega meat feast, which I believe was what you were craving tonight. How does that sound to you, sweetheart?"

I literally choke on my tongue before reaching out to shove him lightly. I lick my lips and suppress the urge to laugh when his eyes follow the movement. "Yum, that sounds amazing. I'm in the mood for something rich and spicy." His lips twitch as he turns away to place the order. I know that our recent kiss and wordplay are getting to him as he discretely adjusts himself before he ends the call. I've always thought that men got the rough end of the deal where horniness was concerned. Women might have to deal with those pesky saluting nipples, but we can blame that on the cold. When a guy is hard, it's like, "Hello, look at me!" Not much of a way to hide it unless they wear loose clothing on a regular basis. Plus, we have better options for masturbation. The only thought we have to put into getting off is with or without batteries. I'm sure they make male-oriented toys, but I have to believe that most opt for the convenience of their hand versus something that isn't even close to a warm vajay. My one and only sexual partner, Jake, made me feel good in bed for the most part. I'm not going to lie. Sometimes, I faked it when I knew my orgasm was particularly elusive that day. Something tells me, though, that Max would never let me get away with that. Jake was a boy—Max Decker is very much a man, with what feels like a monster cock.

Max taps me on the shoulder, giving me a questioning look. "I'm dying to ask you what you're thinking about—but at the same time, I'm afraid to know."

I clear my throat and bat my eyes at him. "Trust me, counselor, you don't even want to go there. It's not fit conversation for mixed company."

His lips twitch. "Yeah, I pretty much figured that. I—um, I'm going to go wash up before the food arrives. Be right back."

He's gone before I can respond. Surely, he wouldn't leave me standing here to go jack off? Even as tell myself it's a bad idea, I'm tiptoeing down the hallway toward his bedroom. I tell myself to stop—that I'm invading the privacy of someone who has opened his home to me. But still, I quietly ease the partially ajar door open farther, seeing no sign of him. I'm on the verge of backing out when I see the light spilling from under his closed bathroom door. *Don't do it! Go back!* My inner voice screams, but I creep forward. I press my ear against the door and hear nothing but silence at first. Oh God, maybe he just had to use the bathroom. I'm beyond sick. I turn and am a few inches away when I hear the first groan. I'm far from an expert, but that doesn't sound like an, "I had bad Mexican food," distress call. Then it comes again and I forget to breathe. He's really doing it. For all I know, he's a serial masturbator who whacks off fifty times a day. But I don't think so. He's in there because of what happened between us in the kitchen.

Maybe it's twisted, but I'm strangely proud that I drove him to this. I'm also completely and utterly excited as I imagine what he's doing while he thinks of me. In a flash, I'm plastered against the door once again, hoping to hear him say my name. Then it happens—the unthinkable. I have no idea how, but the wood surface that had been supporting part of my weight is gone and my arms are flailing at empty space. When the world stops spinning, I am sprawled on the bathroom floor feeling as if I've just wrenched the stitches on my thigh open. But that's not the worst of it. I look up to find Max staring down at me as if I've sprouted two heads. "Rose, what in the hell ..." he begins, sounding bewildered. I believe it's safe to assume he's never had a woman crash his private time before.

"Holy shitballs," I wheeze out as I take in the scene before me. I wonder if he's completely overlooked the fact that his jeans are unzipped and hanging open. That's not what has me so transfixed, though. His amazingly beautiful and very large cock is still in his hand as if he were in mid-pump before I came to be part of the show. I'll never know what would have happened next, because for the second time that evening, a loud noise comes between his dick and me. "Um … Pizza's here!" I squeak as I climb less than gracefully to my feet. I wince as my stitches once again twinge. If I've pulled them all loose, then I'll consider seeing what Max is packing in his boxer briefs a worthy cause. "I think I have enough cash left in my purse to pay for it. You just er—continue on and I'll handle it." Okay, maybe not the best choice of words with that last part, but it just slipped out.

I really have to give him props for maintaining his cool under fire. This would be enough to embarrass anyone, but he's no shrinking violet. A dart of my eyes downward backs that fact up. He remains impressively erect—the one-eyed monster seeming to glare at me for my untimely interruption. I fight the urge to apologize for it, and then almost giggle at that thought. Laughter, when a man is holding his cock, is probably something you can never take back. He closes his eyes briefly as if trying to collect himself, before removing the hand holding his manhood. When it snaps up toward his belly button, I almost sob at the beauty. He puts his impressive package back in his shorts, then gingerly zips his jeans up slowly over the bulge. Even I wince, thinking of how bad that must feel. A stallion that size needs to roam free, not be confined to a stall. He bites off a curse as the doorbell chimes once again. He quickly washes, and then dries his hands before reaching into his back pocket. He removes his wallet and peels off some bills, handing them to me. "Please take care of it." All right, so I automatically assume he's speaking of the big problem that has taken up residence in his jeans. It's something I would take great pleasure in handling for him. He snakes his fingers in front of my face and puts an end to that fantasy. "Rose, the pizza, for God's sake."

It's official, I think glumly as I hurry toward the front door. Max has a pecker the size of my arm, and he's probably never going to let me near it again. And even with everything that is screwed up in my life—that may be the biggest tragedy of them all.

CHAPTER SIX

Max

Just when you think you've experienced everything, life throws you a curveball. In this case, it's more of a nosy redhead crashing in on my jerk-off session. I can't blame her completely. After all, if I had, at least, kept it together until she was asleep, it wouldn't have happened. What kind of host leaves his houseguest in the kitchen while he takes a spank break? The sad thing is that even after the humiliation I've just suffered, I'm still throbbing in my now way-too-snug jeans. The zipper feels as if it's about to cut off circulation to my cock. There's no way I'm going to pick up where I left off, though. Hell, Rose would probably bring the delivery guy in this time to watch.

I can't believe the little minx was listening at the door. Was I that loud? After losing control and touching her in the kitchen, I had been in desperate need of relief. I was so close to the edge that I knew I wouldn't be able to keep my hands off her unless I released some of the pressure that had been building all day. Who am I kidding? It's been building since the last time I touched her all those months ago.

I lean my head against the wall, attempting to bring myself under control. I can't help but laugh as I wonder if this is what it's come to. If not for Rose staring at my dick as if she'd discovered the Holy Grail, I'd feel like some kind of pervert. Who knows what would have happened if not for another timely interruption. I'm beginning to think that my house is a cock-blocker. First, with the smoke alarm, and then with the doorbell. Apparently, it's trying to warn me of imminent danger.

"Um ... is everything okay in there?" I hear called from a distance. "The pizza's getting cold." Then she quickly adds, "But no rush. Take all the time you need. I can totally start without you. I'm used to doing stuff on my own. Shit! That didn't come out right. I really wasn't referring to what I saw when I accidentally walked in on you. I've barely thought about it since. By the way, everyone does it, so don't feel bad. Sometimes two or three times a day. Heck, I've even—"

I literally run from the bathroom before she can finish her last statement. If she's trying to make me feel better, it's not working. Her ramblings are likely to have me dropping my pants yet again if she keeps it up. Already, I can't get the image of her being so horny that she touches herself multiple times. I want to volunteer my assistance with that like a twisted Boy Scout. She gives me an innocent look that I know is anything but as I wave a hand for her to precede me back into the kitchen. When I enter the room, all I can think about is how I had my hands all over her gorgeous body not long ago. "How about we eat in the living room while we watch a movie?" *One that contains absolutely no sex scenes whatsoever.*

We end up watching *Bridesmaids*, which she picks. Of course, the opening scene has a woman being fucked within an inch of her life. Even though Rose claimed to have never seen it before, the smirk on her face says she's a liar. If I've learned nothing in the past few months, I know that she likes to push my buttons. I survive without any further incidents and the rest of the evening is relaxed. I'm in my bed a little past midnight and trying not to dwell on the fact that she's just down the hall from me. I curse Lucian under my breath, blaming him for bringing Rose into my life. I had a perfectly satisfying existence before she came along. Now, I'm restless and edgy. A big part of it can be attributed to sexual frustration, but it's the other part that bothers me. I like her—a lot. She brings out a side of me that has been buried for a long time. *But haven't I been better off since that part was buried?*

I'm still staring at the ceiling when I hear a knock on my closed door before it slowly opens. I reach over to the nightstand and click the light on. Rose is shifting nervously on her feet, showing none of her earlier playfulness. She looks uncertain and shy as her hands clench together. I notice that instead of wearing the gown she'd purchased earlier, she's still wearing my shirt from last night. I open my mouth to ask her what's wrong, and then it hits me. She doesn't want to be alone. Maybe she's afraid of what will happen should the solitude of the night prove too much for her again. I know I should lead her to a less intimate part of the house and offer her some company. Instead, I silently pull back the cover on my bed and move back far enough for her to get in. That's all the encouragement she needs. She hurries over and wraps herself around me before laying her head against my chest.

"I'm sorry," is muffled as she burrows even closer. She shifts slightly, making her next words clearer. "I've never been very good with the dark. I'm almost normal in the light of day when surrounded by people. But sometimes when it's quiet, I lose control."

I tighten my arms around her and drop a kiss on the top of her head. "Shhh, it's okay, baby. Just sleep now. I've got you." I rub her spine, soothing her until she relaxes. Neither of us says anything further. As I drift off to sleep, I know that no matter what the days ahead hold, my life has changed. Since the moment I picked her up off the ground, it's never felt wrong. Her in my home, in my car, shopping together, sharing food, watching a movie, listening to her sassy, quirky wit—it's just felt ... right. Easy. It's as if she's woken me from the stupor I've existed in for so very long, and I fear that I'll no longer be content with my perfectly crafted existence. *But I like sex without emotion, without strings.* Do I? Is that what I still want? I took a chance once and very nearly had it all. Am I strong enough to do that again? I look at Lucian and see how happy he is after finally vanquishing his demons. But not everyone is given a second chance at happiness. What if I try and fail? Would I even survive it this time?

CHAPTER SEVEN

Rose

I barely recognize the person staring back at me from the mirror. It's Monday morning and I'm dressed in one of my new outfits for my first day of work with Lia. Yesterday, I watched movies and surfed the Internet while Max did some work. I did wonder if he was trying to avoid spending time with me, but I couldn't really blame him after my sudden invasion into his life. I know he's a private person, and it must be hard to share his space with me. He went out to pick up some Thai food for our evening meal and came back with a new cell phone for me as well. I'd argued, saying it could wait until I received my first paycheck, but he'd been adamant about me needing it in case of emergencies. After finding myself out of an apartment and a car just days before, I couldn't really argue with that. Instead, I'd thanked him and secretly added it to the amount I already owed him. I wonder briefly how my parents would even reach me, but I also feel relief that my father can't use the phone as a means to control me any longer. If he wants to find me, he'll damn well have to put some effort into it.

Again, last night, I'd gone to him when the darkness proved too much to bear. I didn't tell him I was afraid of hurting myself, but I was certain that he knew. He invited me into his bed in the same manner as the previous night and I'd been weak with gratitude.

Today, I needed to tell Lia what had happened while she was gone. I had decided to swallow my pride and ask her if I could possibly have an advance on my paycheck so I could afford somewhere to live. I knew that she would invite me to stay with her and Lucian, but I won't do that. I have no doubt they would welcome me with open arms, but they're newlyweds with a baby. They deserve their privacy to enjoy this special time in their lives.

My stomach growls as the smell of coffee drifts down the hallway. I study my appearance for another moment and feel my throat tighten. I look nothing like my usual self. I've never worn anything other than traditional, tailored pieces. Conservative and expensive. Today, I'm wearing a form-fitting red pencil skirt with a leopard-print silk blouse along with a black belt and strappy, matching sandals. It's modern and sexy while still being dressy enough for the office. It's the type of outfit I'd often looked at longingly in magazines but had never been free to purchase. My parents would have told me I looked like a whore. Maddens didn't dress in trendy clothing. It was considered trashy and common. I had to admit that it looked better than I could have ever dreamed. I no longer looked like a repressed virgin.

Why then is my skin crawling? Why is my heart threatening to pound from my chest? Sweat gathers on my forehead and begins to trickle down my temples. My hands are trembling and my head is light. *You look cheap. What if someone sees you like this? You'll be an embarrassment.* The voices of disappointment in my head are at an all-time high as I stumble away from the mirror, trying to get away from the ugliness shown there.

On unsteady feet, I make my way to the bathroom and begin looking through the cabinets. Towels and washcloths litter the floor and I toss them aside in search of something to help me dull the noise that threatens to consume me. I am frantic by the time I remember the razor in the shower that I used earlier. For the first time, I don't bother to try to hide what I'm doing by using my thighs. Instead, I pull up a shirtsleeve and push the razor against the sensitive skin of my inner arm. I feel a small bite of pain as it pierces my skin. The protective guard keeps it from cutting deeply, but it's enough to give me what I need.

I lean back against the wall as the familiar peace fills me. As I look down at the bead of blood that wells from the cut, I suddenly feel sick. What is wrong with me? How had I let it come to this? I'd have been better off dying than living this way. I was hurting myself over the style of my fucking clothes.

Then I hear his voice and I know there is no way to hide what I've done. He sounds upset and pained as he says, "Rose, baby. Why didn't you come to me?" *Why didn't you come to me?* Why did he ask that? I've never had anyone to turn to. I couldn't understand why he asked that question. That's it. I drop the razor to the floor and sob into my hands. I hear him leave the room before returning a minute later. He gently pulls my recently injured arm toward him and cleans it before putting a bandage on it. He sighs as if not sure what to do before pulling me into his arms. I melt against him and give in to the tears of desolation that seem to be never-ending. He doesn't say a word, just lets me get it all out. When I'm down to the occasional jerking hiccups, he calmly picks me up and sets me once again on the bathroom counter. He pushes my skirt up to get closer to me. A cool washcloth is pressed against my eyes as he cleans the makeup that is now completely ruined away. I wince as I see smudges of it on his neatly pressed dress shirt. "You're going to need to change," I say huskily as I point at the mascara smears dotting the expensive fabric.

He tosses the washcloth into the nearby hamper and presses closer between my legs. Cupping my face, he murmurs, "It doesn't matter." As he stares into my eyes, he rubs his thumb almost absently across my bottom lip as if trying to discern what's going on in my head. "I can't stand you hurting yourself, sweetheart. What brought it on this morning?"

My first instinct is to say something flippant and pull away. I've never shared this part of me with anyone else, and I feel raw and exposed. I take a deep breath, along with a leap of faith, and tell him the truth. "It's the outfit," I admit, feeling beyond absurd that something so trivial drove me to cut. *Surely other women never feel this way.*

He's quiet for a moment as he ponders my words. He then shifts back slightly to inspect me from top to bottom. "You look beautiful," he says quietly. "But you don't have your shield. You're exposed for the world to see."

"What?" I blink up at him, puzzled by his statement. Is he trying to say that my outfit is too revealing?

He surprises me by leaning down to press a brief kiss on my upturned lips before replying. "You've hidden behind the pearls and the demure sweaters for a long time. Other than Lia and Jake, it's kept people at bay. You're intimidating as hell when you want to be." He laughs. "I've no doubt that you can stop some poor bastard in his tracks with a single look. You're sophisticated beyond your years, and I'm sure that's exactly how your parents wanted it. And after a while, you used it as a way to control those around you. Instead of insecurity, they only saw cockiness and confidence."

I gape at him, not certain if I'm offended or in awe. He has effectively opened me up and pointed out the parts of me that I've worked hard to keep buried. I barely know him, and he's seen through the smokescreens to the insecure woman hiding behind them. "I ... no, that's not it," I deny weakly, but we both know I'm grasping at straws.

One of his hands settles around the nape of my neck, and he pulls me to rest against him. "All right, baby, whatever you say." He's backing down as if sensing my agitation at his all-too accurate assessment. I put my arms around his waist at some point and we remain there for a while longer in silence, each of us lost in our own thoughts. Finally, he says, "Let's go have some breakfast. I'm starving." I nod my head in answer but can't imagine forcing a bite down at this point.

While I'd been getting dressed, Max had fixed us both a garden omelet. Despite the churning of my stomach, I find my mouth watering as he sets the plate before me. I take a hesitant bite and close my eyes in bliss. "Wow, this is yummy," I manage to get out between bites. *Really nice. Distract him from what he saw in the bathroom by inhaling your food like a starving animal.* If the smile on his handsome face is any indication, he's vastly amused that I've eaten half my food, while he's barely had a few bites of his. "Sorry," I mumble, "I guess I was hungrier than I thought."

He waves his fork as if to say, carry on. He opens the newspaper beside him and flips through it while I sip my coffee. "So I was thinking," he begins without glancing up, "there is no use in you moving all of your things to Lia's until you find an apartment. Why don't you continue staying with me? I find your company stimulating—er, enjoyable and—"

"You want to keep an eye on me after my latest razor incident," I insert and know that I'm right when he releases a sigh.

He makes eye contact now and what I see there kills whatever smart comment I'd been about to add. "Honey, I'm worried about you. I realize that I'm probably the last person you wanted to know what was going on in your life—but you're stuck with me. I care about what happens to you, Rose. If you don't want to talk to Lia about what you're going through, then please stay here. You don't have to hide anything from me. If the walls are closing in on you and it's all becoming too much, then tell me.

Believe me, I've been at the end of my rope before, and I know what it feels like to sense the freefall just inches away."

Giving him a disbelieving look, I ask, "Are you trying to say that you've hurt yourself in the past? Because I have a hard time believing you've ever been that weak."

He runs an unsteady hand through his perfectly styled hair, and I swallow hard at the sexy, rumpled look it leaves behind. Damn the man for being so unbelievably gorgeous that I have a hard time concentrating on anything else. "No, I've never cut, Rose. But I have been so overwhelmed to the point that I considered other ... options. It was a long time ago, but I'm not sure I've fully recovered to this day. I was lucky enough to have a friend who stepped up and supported me through the worst of it. I'm not certain of where I'd be today without him."

I stare at him, fascinated by what he has revealed to me. If I had one word to describe the Max who I've come to know, it would be unflappable. The man bailed me out of jail not once but twice after I did insane things to my ex-boyfriend. He might have been exasperated with me, but he nevertheless did his job and didn't flinch when I confessed my latest offenses to him. He might react to the world around him, but he recovers almost immediately. Outside of the surprising hand job I interrupted, he's usually nothing if not predictable. Now, I am forced to reassess everything I thought I knew about him. I've often sensed there was something below the surface that holds him back, and now, he's as good as confirmed it for me. "So you want to what—pay it forward?" I ask, knowing I sound sarcastic, but it's either that or crying all over him yet again.

Instead of being pissed off over my flippant comments, he says gently, "Call it whatever you need to, sweetheart. But I refuse to let anything happen to you."

"That's not your choice," I snap, irritated for no good reason. Other than Lia, I'm not used to anyone in my life giving a shit about what I'm going through. If my parents weren't worried enough after my suicide attempts to lay off the snide comments and pressure to be perfect, then they certainly wouldn't give a shit about me slicing myself. Well, unless I ruined the carpet or forced them to call their doctor friend. Max's concern for me feels intrusive somehow even though I know it's coming from his heart. He's getting too close, and I want to put some distance back between us. "I'm going to ask Lia for an advance on my salary today so I can find somewhere to live. I really appreciate all that you've done for me, and I'll pay you back as soon as I can." I get to my feet, taking my plate to the sink. Max remains at the table, not bothering to argue with me. I feel a sense of relief followed by a strange feeling of disappointment that he's letting it go that easily. Doesn't that prove I don't really matter to him? I've never had a man who was willing to fight for me and he's no exception. No matter how hard I try, I'll never be worth attention.

Then he says something that halts me in my tracks and changes the course of my life forever. "Give me two months, Rose. We'll tell Luc and Lia that we're involved and you're living with me since the issue with your father. That way they won't ask questions you'd rather not answer. We'll be a couple for all intents and purposes as far as the rest of the world is concerned."

I'm completely floored at his suggestion and my voice reflects that. "Why would you do that? What are you hoping to accomplish?"

"I'm going to save you, sweetheart, and you're going to let me." I can only gawk at him, thinking he must be insane. But the tiny part of me that is still capable of hope wants to believe him so badly.

"I'll be fine," I insist, knowing that neither of us really believes it at this point. "I'm not your responsibility. We're basically strangers, and you want to babysit me for sixty days?"

He stands, walking over to me and taking my hands in his. "No bullshit, give me an honest answer. Are you afraid that one day you'll go too far and kill yourself?"

He just voiced the one fear that terrifies me above all others. I've already tried to take my life twice, and I'm petrified I'll eventually succeed. "Yes," I whisper.

He closes his eyes briefly before opening them again. "Stay with me, baby. I'll be your support every step of the way. You have to trust someone eventually—let it be me."

I nod my head and take a huge leap of faith. "Yes." Sixty days. With those words, I realize that I will bind my fate to the man before me for sixty days. *I want that for longer. I want him to become my all—my everything.* But that is not what is on the table here. Sixty days, Rose. Be thankful. It's not forever. *But I now realize, more than ever, that forever is what I wish for.*

Max

I drop Rose at her new office before driving the few miles to Quinn Software. I can hardly fathom what has transpired in just a few hours this morning. I've gone from avoiding relationships and commitments with women to urging someone I barely know to live with me and be my pretend girlfriend if anyone questions it. If that's not putting the cart before the horse, I'm not sure what is.

When I walked in on her this morning and found that she'd cut herself again, I'd damn near freaked out. Of course, I knew she was having a hard time dealing with everything. After all, she'd been sleeping with me every night since she'd been at my house. During the daylight hours, though, she had mostly seemed at ease. Possibly that had lured me into a false sense of security that I couldn't afford to have where she was concerned. She had blindsided me today. The injury hadn't been anywhere near as severe this time, possibly because it had been a razor and not a sharp kitchen knife. That wasn't really the whole issue, though. It was the fact that she'd been upset enough to *need* the pain that bothered me. That was what Matt had helped me understand, anyway. *And she's needed to do that for years if the scars were any indication. How long has she hidden this? How long has she silently suffered? Alone* ...

Since I knew she did not intend to confide in Lia, I just couldn't stand the thought of her leaving me to go pretend to her best friend that she was perfectly okay. And I knew that's exactly what she would do. Hadn't I bought into the show for months now? The woman with not a care in the world. Underneath her public face, it was a different matter. From what I've read, and believe me when I say I have read every article I could get my hands on, most people cut to help them cope with an even deeper emotional pain. It's a form of relief, an escape from building pressure and pain. *How is that possible?* Treating one pain with another. *It's hard to say no to something that feels so good.* She was crying out for help, and no one wanted to hear it. Least of all her self-absorbed parents. They kept heaping the pressure on with no regard to what it was doing to their daughter. I wanted to pay the Maddens a visit and tell them exactly what I thought of their parenting skills. Unfortunately, I knew it would just widen a rift that was already the size of the fucking Grand Canyon. If I ever saw them around, though—all bets were off.

I desperately need to talk to Matt and get some advice and the list of names he's gathering for me. I can only hope Rose will agree to try a session with one of them. I will help her in any way I can, but I'm not naive enough to believe I have the skills to completely cure what ails her. I also don't want to risk doing something to push her closer to the edge. As difficult as that all sounds, the hard part ahead will be convincing our friends that we're suddenly not only acknowledging we have feelings for each other but have decided to live together as well. Holy shit. I am a lawyer and as such, used to dealing with any situation, but this is unfamiliar ground to me. *Will she tell her friends her father kicked her out of her home?*

I park in my reserved space at the office and slowly make my way through the restored old building that houses the corporate offices of Quinn Software. I had originally planned to start my own practice at some point after completing law school. I worked with a big firm in downtown Asheville to get some hands-on experience before taking a job with Lucian. And I've been here ever since. I wasn't just the legal counsel; I was a trusted advisor, confidant, and a friend. That was something you didn't find every day. Lucian, Aidan, and I had become the team that propelled Quinn to the top. We all had very different personalities, but somehow, it worked. Now, with Aidan on indefinite leave, it was up to Lucian and me to ensure that the pending sales, mergers, and contracts that were in the works continued on without a snag. Aidan was a very charismatic man and as such had always been the closer. His absence from our lives, both personally and professionally, had been felt almost immediately. I know it's been especially hard on Luc as he and Aidan have been friends for most of their lives. I'll catch him staring out the window of his office sometimes, and I know he's wondering where Aidan is and if he's okay. True to his word, when Aidan left town, he cut off most forms of communication. He's sent a couple of brief emails letting everyone know he's all right, but that's it. As hard as it must be for him, Luc has respected his wishes and not contacted him.

I go directly to Lucian's office since we have our usual morning meeting to discuss any open issues. His secretary—and second mother—Cindy sits in her usual spot, guarding the keys to the castle or in this case, the doorway of her boss. She's a formidable foe if crossed, but a loyal friend otherwise. She treats us all like wayward sons at times, but we don't mind. Actually, I'm not sure what any of us would do without her—especially Luc.

"Good morning, Cindy." I smile. "You look beautiful today." Yeah, I haven't been on the earth for this long without knowing how to kiss a little ass. Plus, she always looks perfectly put together and deserves the acknowledgment. Although, I'm certain that Sam—Luc's driver and Cindy's boyfriend—has probably beaten me to it.

She studies me for a moment as I stand at her desk before she asks, "What have you been up to this morning?"

Instantly, I feel guilty. I have no idea how she does it. I feel as if I have the word *liar* pasted across my forehead. Which is insane because she couldn't possibly know about the deception that Rose and I are going to undertake? I console myself with the fact that it's necessary to allow Rose time to deal with her demons, but I don't like keeping secrets from those who are close to me. I shrug my shoulder casually before saying, "Just the usual. Is Luc already in?"

I'm relieved when she appears to let her curiosity go and nods. "Yes, go on through. He'll be expecting you. I'll give you a few minutes to get settled, and then bring a tray of coffee in." I'm almost to the door when she tosses out, "You've got lipstick on your collar, in case you missed it."

I resist the urge to slap a hand over my neckline, knowing it will give her too much pleasure to see that reaction. Instead, I step inside Luc's office and shut the door on her soft laughter. In retrospect, it's actually a good thing. It'll lend credibility to my claim of being involved. I still can't help but feel like a kid with his hand caught in the cookie jar. I'm usually a little more discreet than this with my liaisons. Again, I find Luc standing before the wall of windows in his office, looking out onto the street below. I clear my throat before saying, "Good morning."

He takes another moment and then turns to face me with an easy smile. Since I've known him, an internal, restless sort of energy has always seemed to crackle just below the surface. I doubt his mind is ever truly at rest. Now, he has Lia, though, and there's a peace to him I never thought to see. He's blissfully happy with his wife and doesn't care who knows it. The new baby, Lara, they've recently had only amplifies that contentment. At times, I find it hard not to envy him, and it has nothing to do with his monetary wealth. He's living the life that I always saw for myself. The one that was so close then slipped through my fingertips like a fine mist. It's unsettling and no coincidence that I've thought of the past more this weekend than I have in years. Being with Rose has brought it all rushing back, and I'm struggling to deal with the memories that threaten to burst through the walls I've locked them safely behind. "How was your weekend?" he asks as he moves to the chair behind his desk and settles there.

My standard answer of "Good" is on the tip of my tongue when I remember that I need to be a man enchanted by a woman this morning. Hell, I'm not sure at this point if that's even far from the truth. "Surprisingly, very good," I reply easily.

Lucian misses very little, so he immediately notices my unusual answer. He gives me an inquisitive look before asking, "What happened?"

So it begins. I take more time than necessary to settle comfortably as I gather my thoughts. Rose and I had agreed earlier that I could fill Luc in on the issues with her parents. I felt it best that we stick as closely to the truth as possible. "Rose called me around midnight Friday near her apartment, extremely upset. When I got there, she was on the pavement. Cold, wet, and hurt."

All traces of amusement are gone from Lucian's face as he barks out, "What in the hell happened to her?" That's one of many things I admire about my friend. He's fiercely loyal and protective of his inner circle, and Rose entered that by being such a good friend to the woman he loves. I go on to tell him about her disagreement with her father and his retaliation. "She should have called us." He shakes his head looking pissed off. I know it has nothing to do with Rose and everything to do with her parents. "Sam could have let her into our place so she didn't have to worry about somewhere to stay. I assume you found her a hotel?" he asks, and I know it's not really a question. He would never consider for a moment that I would leave any woman helpless, much less a friend.

Showtime. "Yes, of course," I reply. "She's going to be staying with me. If she decides that she wants a place of her own later on, then we'll address that then. For now, we're both happy with our arrangement."

"Your arrangement?" Lucian repeats as if testing the sound. "What're you saying? That she's going to be your roommate or something?"

I adopt what I hope is the look of a man in love or in lust and say, "I believe the correct term is girlfriend. Rose and I have decided we're going to give a relationship between us a go. We probably wouldn't have normally moved in together this soon, but we felt that maybe this was some type of sign for us to take things to the next level." *Fuck. I delivered that whole thing with a straight face—amazing.*

Lucian looks at me as if I've taken leave of my senses. His voice is full of disbelief as he croaks out, "You're involved with Rose? Since when? The last time I saw you two together, you parted ways at the hospital door after Lara was born. Then you've both acted for months as if the other one didn't exist. Now, you're living together. Man, what the holy fuck?"

Sometimes it's a pain in the ass to have people who know so much about you. I hate that he's quizzing me so heavily because it forces me to lie more than I want to. It can't be helped, though, and I'd like to think that Luc would understand if it meant the difference between life and death to Rose. Actually, he'd likely be pissed about both of us for not including him in the full story, but that's not my decision. I promised to be there for Rose, and I'll do whatever I need to do to keep my word to her. She needs the support from someone in her life, and right now, I'm that person. The words flow easily, as the truth usually does. "You know there's always been something between us. No matter how hard I've tried to deny it, she's been under my skin almost from the start."

"No shit," Lucian deadpans. "I'd have to be blind to miss that. Hell, probably not even then. I'm just not sure when you stopped with the denial and let it happen?"

"I've missed her the last few months, even the crazy stuff. I can't see an NRA advertisement without remembering her blowing out Jake's tires. I guess I'm just tired of fighting what seems inevitable." Again, there is a lot more truth than not in my words. It's starting to appear as if pretending to be Rose's boyfriend isn't going to be that much of an act. I feel almost vulnerable, which is strange. Barely one day in and I feel like a train wreck. By the end of the week, I'll probably be sobbing on Lucian's shoulder while asking Cindy to bring me a warm blanket and hot cocoa.

He stares at me as if trying to figure something out. I know he senses there is a lot more that I'm not saying, but he can't put it together—yet. He has little choice but to accept my statement at face value and see where it goes. I know a warning is coming, though, and I'm not disappointed. "Lia would be thrilled to see you two end up together. She'd have been doing some nonstop matchmaking this entire time if I'd gone along with it. And while I think you two could potentially be good for each other, I'm wary about the possibility of it not working out and a rift forming between all of us. Therefore, I'll ask that you be aware of the consequences and treat Rose accordingly. She may scare the ever loving hell out of me at times, but she's a good person and deserves a helluva lot more than that pussy Jake gave her."

"Agreed," I snap as I think of the punk who cheated on Rose. She delivered a lot of her own brand of justice to him in the end, and I have to believe he'd think twice between dipping his dick around town next time. I'd still like to kick his ass, though. How in the world could you have a woman such as her and stray?

After that, we move on to actual work, and I find myself able to relax with the grilling session over. I wonder how Rose is faring with Lia and vow to call her later to check in. I have a feeling we'll both be ready for a drink before the day is through.

Rose

"Yourdoingwhatwithwho?" Lia's words come out garbled as she gapes at me. I'd filled her in on my weekend as we sat sipping a cup of coffee in my new office. We'd been reviewing existing employee files today and are sitting in the small seating area in the corner.

"Um—Max and I have decided to pursue a relationship. You know, a little bam bam," I joke, trying to keep the mood light. Lia doesn't expect serious from me when talking about men, thank God.

"But you've been avoiding each other like a scalding case of herpes," she murmurs, causing me to burst out laughing. That's totally something I can hear myself saying. I think I'm finally rubbing off on her.

"You know I've been hot for the man since the moment I laid eyes on him wearing one of those sexy suits. If I spend more than five minutes in his company, I need a panty change. He's just that gorgeous, and if you could feel the size of what he's packing between those muscular thighs." I make a big production of fanning myself. "Chick, when the chance presented itself, I jumped all over it—and him." *Oh, how I wish that were true.*

Lia's eyes are round as saucers as I continue to tick off Max's many considerable attributes. It's scary how I'm not even pretending. He's everything I'm saying and more. Finally, she holds up her hand and halts me when I circle back to the size of his cock. "Hey, I know," she snaps her fingers to make sure I'm listening, "let's go out to dinner together." She's practically bouncing in her seat now, which is cute for someone who is usually more reserved. God, when did my best friend turn into me?. "Anna has already said that anytime Lucian and I want an evening out alone, she'd be happy to babysit Lara." Grabbing her cell phone, she says, "I'm going to text Luc right now and tell him to arrange it with Max. Her fingers are flying over her phone while she talks. I see her hit the send button and then she freezes. "Oh crap, has Max told Lucian about you two? If not, I just totally betrayed your confidence." She's wringing her hands now and the devil in me wants to let her sweat a little, but I just can't do it. Not after all she's been through in the last year. Torture her with talk of Max's dick size, hell yeah, but I can't accuse her of being a bad friend. I don't have it in me. Not for this girl.

"Cool your jets, sister," I say dryly. "If your hubby doesn't know by now, he will soon. Max was going to tell him this morning, so it's all good." Lia visibly sags in her seat, clearly relieved to be out of loose-lips prison. I give her another moment to relax before I say idly, "So are we talking a swap kind of date or what? I know we can't do it at your place with the whole baby thing happening there, but I'm sure Max would be willing to host. Are you and Luc all caught up on your STD checks?" I smack my lips dramatically while her mouth drops to the floor. "I've wanted a go at Mr. Quinn forever." I throw my arms around her and pull her against me. "You might be the best friend I've ever had!"

Silence … complete and utter silence fills the room as she remains ramrod stiff against me for all of a minute before she dissolves into a fit of laughter. "You ass! You really had me going there for a while. I swear I could almost picture the whole thing playing out. You're such a pervert!"

We both continue to giggle like teenage girls. I'm fanning myself before it's over and hoping that no one is close enough to my new office to overhear our conversation. Just in case, though, I lower my voice for one last zinger before we get to work. "I was kidding, but admit it, you're curious about what my chief counsel is packing under those suits, aren't ya? And trust me, it's—"

She claps a hand over my mouth as her face turns an adorable shade of red. We both let the topic of penises drop while we get to work. We've been at it for a few hours when there is a knock on the door and Lia's father Lee Jacks strolls in. *Holy hot daddy.* I'm not lying when I tell Lia that her father is a stud. As if sensing my thoughts, she turns to me and shakes her head. "Don't go there," she whisper-hisses before turning back to Lee.

I let myself be drawn into their discussion and feel warmth invade me as they both express their pleasure at having me on board. For one of the few times in my life, I feel as if I belong. I'm part of something that my father can't take away from me. I've only felt like this one other time and that was this morning standing within the circle of Max's arms as he vowed to save me. For years, I've felt as if I had nowhere to go in life and nothing to gain. I've existed as would an expensive, well-maintained figurine. Shone to ensure its beauty but voiceless to ensure its silence. Alone. Now, I fear that I have everything to lose, and I pray I'm finally strong enough to stand against those who would take great pleasure in seeing me fail. *How could the man who raised me so easily discard me, throw me literally out onto the streets? How could he? In contrast, Lee Jacks has done everything possible to be included in his daughter's life, to shower her with love despite not knowing of her existence for so many years.* My father probably doesn't understand that the cost of his victory could well be my life. And a part of me has to wonder if he would care either way.

CHAPTER EIGHT

Max

I haven't been on a double date since high school, but it appears I'm doing it tonight. Lia had messaged Lucian during our meeting this morning, and since he rarely says no to his wife, the deed was as good as done. Truthfully, I think the bastard was vastly amused at the prospect of seeing me squirm for an evening. I also believe it's a big possibility that he and Lia want to observe how Rose and I are as a couple. I'm not sure why it was such a surprise to either of them. I might have no intentions of acting on it, but there is no denying the chemistry that crackles when I'm with her. Even Luc had noticed it.

After Rose was so upset over her clothing this morning, I'm wary of what will happen this evening, so I hurry through my own dressing. I slip into a pair of dress pants and a button-up shirt but leave off the tie. We're going to Leo's for dinner. The Italian restaurant is a favorite of mine as well as Luc's.

Rose's door is open when I reach it, and I quickly take in the room, not seeing any sign of her. I note with some relief that the bathroom light appears to be off. Then I spot a glow coming from beneath the walk-in closet door. My gut clenches as I move quickly toward it. I push it slowly open and hiss audibly. She's standing there in a lacy black bra, tiny matching panties, and thigh-high stockings. Her back is to me and I am having a hell of a time tearing my eyes from her tight ass. My hands clench as I fight the urge to touch her. I clear my throat but still my voice is husky as I ask, "Need some help picking an outfit?" Without waiting for her reply, I step around her and peruse the row of clothing hanging there. When I spot a short, black sheath dress, I pull it from the hanger and put it in her hands. A quick glance shows her eyes fixed straight ahead and beads of sweat dotting her forehead. *Oh, baby, where are you?* I think as she seems oblivious to my presence.

I'm not sure what comes over me, but I know at that moment that I need to do something to shock her back to the present and force whatever thoughts are filling her head to flee. I cup her head gently in my hand and lower my lips to hers. I lick the seam of her mouth, coaxing her to let me in. She's still for a moment then suddenly her breath flutters out as her lips part. I waste no time thrusting into the nectar waiting there. When I feel her tongue seek entrance into my mouth, I'm lost. I lower my hands to her ass and pull her snugly against my hard length. "Max," she whimpers as I knead her flesh.

"I'm right here, sweetheart," I groan as I trail kisses down the slender length of her neck. Before I can think better of it, I sink my teeth into the tender skin of her shoulder and feel a shudder wrack her slender frame. "What are you doing to me?" I ask, not really expecting an answer. I lower one side of her bra and feel weak in the knees when her raspberry nipple pops free. Fucking hell, has anything ever looked sweeter? *Just a taste*, I promise myself as I palm a perfect handful before sucking the taut peak into my mouth. Her fingers sink into my hair, pulling me closer as I nip and suck her into a sensual frenzy. My other hand is slipping across the supple skin of her stomach, and well on its way to the apex of her thighs when the music begins playing nearby. The song is so out of place that I pause, trying to decipher what's going on. "What the hell?" I grumble as I look around.

Rose leans her forehead against my chest as she giggles. The sound is so carefree that I'm instantly captivated, regardless of the raging hard-on that is threatening to punch through my slacks. "I ... set an alert earlier," she wheezes out.

I'm late, I'm late, for a very important date. I'm late ...

I stand still, listening, and then I begin to chuckle as well. The song from *Alice in Wonderland*—"I'm Late"—is the tone that she chose. Raising a brow, I say, "Only you would think of that." As I pull back to put some space between us, I can't miss the irony that yet again, I've been cock-blocked in my own home. Either some higher power is trying to save me or serve up death via blue balls. To distract myself from the painful issue in my pants, I hold the dress up that had fallen to the floor during our embrace and help her into it. Having all of her major parts covered right now is crucial to my survival. "You look beautiful," I say truthfully when I've zipped the dress into place.

She gives me a soft smile, before smoothing the fabric across her waist. "Thanks, you look pretty hot yourself, counselor." She eyes me for another moment before adding, "You do realize that we're going to have to be convincing tonight, right? That means making two people who know us very well believe that we're in love, or at least something akin to it." She appears uncertain as she asks, "Will you be able to do that? Pretend you have feelings for me? I know I'm not the type of woman you'd usually date, and they'll be aware of that, as well. Maybe if you imagine I'm someone else, it'll be easier." She looks so damn forlorn now. It breaks my fucking heart to know that I've done this to her with my studied indifference. *After that kiss, how could she still think I'm not attracted to her? I want to strip her out of that dress and fuck her till morning.* She honestly believes I could never love her. Her parents have made sure that her self-confidence never had the opportunity to grow and blossom, and I've unwittingly reinforced those feelings of inadequacy with my fierce need to protect *my* heart.

Even though I know it opens me to a vulnerability I haven't allowed in years, I pull her into my arms and speak with complete honesty. "You may not have moved in here because we were in a relationship, but the fact I don't want you to leave has nothing at all to do with fooling our friends. You terrify me, baby, and it's everything to do with you. When we meet Lucian and Lia for dinner tonight, it will be because you're my date and I want you by my side. You're a gorgeous, intelligent woman who keeps me on my toes with your sassy mouth and incredible body. You're who I want to be with tonight, no one else." *And fuck me if that isn't the absolute, shocking truth.*

An impish light enters her eyes and I'm not at all surprised when she jokes, "You were thinking of me during your one-man show, weren't you?"

Puzzled, I stare at her, trying to figure how what she's talking about. "Pardon?" Then she steps back and lowers her hand to the level of her groin before making an unmistakable hand gesture. I groan, letting my head fall forward. "I thought you were actually going to let that one go."

"Are you kidding?" She smirks. "I've thought of that a million times since then. Do you have any idea how sexy that was?" Wiggling her brows, she adds, "And trust me, you have nothing to be embarrassed about from what I saw. That wasn't a simple choking of the snake; it was more like trying to corral your dragon. Or would you prefer beast? Either is pretty accurate."

I shake my head as I'm hard once again. This woman is going to be the death of me. Still, what man wouldn't want to have their cock referred to as something huge? "Out. Now. Car," I order with a tap on her ass for emphasis. I take her hand and pull her from the closet and out to my car. We're probably going to be late, but knowing how Lucian and Lia are with each other, I doubt very seriously that they'll even notice.

Rose

The hostess leads us to a private table in the corner where our friends are waiting. Lucian has his hand resting possessively on the nape of Lia's neck. Her face is flushed and her eyes are glowing. Either those two have had a quickie in the back or they've been discussing the logistics of it. If ever two people could give me hope for the future, it's them. Lucian Quinn, once the king of "get it and quit it," is now a dedicated husband and a doting father. I'm certain it wouldn't have happened if he hadn't met Lia. He would have continued through life as he was, never suspecting his soulmate was just across town at the local college.

Lucian gets to his feet and kissed my cheek before clasping Max's shoulder. Lia and I hug as if we hadn't just been together a few hours earlier. When we're seated across from them, I'm surprised to feel Max take my hand under the table. I instantly feel warm, not because he's touching me, but because it's not for the benefit of our friends. They have no idea that underneath the tablecloth, his finger is tracing circles in my palm as we laugh at Lia's tale of Lucian's diaper changing disasters.

Lia watches us as if she can hardly believe what she's seeing; Lucian looks faintly amused, but I also see a hint of curiosity in his gaze. Regardless of Max's earlier assurances, I can't help but wonder if his friend is thinking I'm way out of my league. Max is a lawyer, for God's sake, and I'm ... well, I'm the daughter of Hoyt and Celia Madden. That's all I've ever needed to know in order to open doors and blend into society. Now, it seems as if I'm

simply Rose Madden, currently broke and homeless friend
to Lia Quinn. Yeah, on paper I'm not exactly a catch. If
Lucian knew everything that Max does about me, he'd
probably be advising his friend to run for his life.

"So how is the whole living together thing going?" Lia
asks. "I bet it's been a big adjustment." I'm puzzled for a
moment when I see her face redden, and then it hits me.
She's remembering our earlier conversation about Max's
cock size.

I rub my forehead as if in pain and say, "It's been a *huge*
adjustment, but Max has been so patient with me. He's
good at anticipating my needs even before I'm aware of
them."

Lia chokes on her sip of wine, and Lucian pats her on
the back as he looks from his wife to me. The twitch of his
lips lets me know that he's noticed the double entendre in
our conversation. Max's hand flexes against mine under the
table as he says, "Behave," under his breath.

As the evening progresses, I find myself relaxing and
falling a little more under Max's spell. I've mostly only
known the reserved man, but tonight, he's showing me yet
another side. He's charming, considerate, and funny.
Overall, he's the perfect date. I am finding it more and
more difficult to remember that this isn't real. When his
arm settles around my shoulders and he drops a kiss on my
brow, it seems so genuine. I know he desires me; he's
admitted as much. But there's something else in his eyes
tonight when he looks at me. I'm fully in the moment with
him when I feel it. That tingle you get when you're being
watched. I do a quick sweep of the restaurant and see no
one familiar. I'm ready to shrug it off as I gaze beyond
Lucian's shoulder and see my ex-boyfriend Jake staring
daggers at me. And he's not alone. It looks as if he's also
on a double date. He has his arm around a dark-haired girl
who I luckily don't recognize, and there is another couple
sitting in front of them. Freaking wonderful. Out of all of
the restaurants in Asheville, he had to be in this one. I see

their waiter dropping off the check and realize with relief that they're preparing to leave. I lean in to Max and say, "I'm going to the ladies' room. Be right back." Normally, Lia would have accompanied me, but she's just placed a call to their nanny, Anna, to check on Lara, so I wave her off as I leave the table.

I go straight to the last stall and close the door behind me. I've just flushed the toilet when the sound of the outer door opening and women's chatter fills the room. I'm not in the mood for polite conversation with strangers, so I stay where I am, hoping they'll make it quick.

When I hear a snide voice say, "Did you hear Jake saying his psycho ex is here tonight? The woman is a nut job. I can't believe she hasn't been locked up somewhere by now." I freeze, unable to move and am barely breathing. Oh dear God, she's talking about me.

"No!" another voice gasps out. "Why didn't you point her out to me? I knew you two were staring at someone, but I had no idea it was her. Didn't she try to kill him?"

"Hell yes, she did," the girl I assume is his girlfriend says. "She carries a gun and will put a bullet in anyone who gets in her way. A total trashy redneck."

"Girl, you better hope she doesn't want him back." The other girl laughs.

"I'm not worried about her." The girlfriend snickers. "Jake wouldn't have her back if she begged. He said it was bad enough that he had to worry about her waving a gun around all the time. But he said the real mess was what she looked like under her clothes."

"So maybe he should have given her a gym membership." The friend chuckles. "Of course, he was probably afraid to risk pissing her off."

"Oh no, that's not it," the girlfriend interjects. "She's covered in scars from where she cuts herself. He said he'd been forced to hide every sharp object in his apartment for fear of what she'd do if she found them. She's a fucking sicko."

"Damn." The friend whistled. "Poor Jake. They were together for quite a while. Why in the world did he stay with her?"

I can almost see the girlfriend shrug as she says, "He felt sorry for her. Plus, he was afraid of what she'd do to him when he did. That's why we had to sneak around for months until he worked up the nerve to end it with her."

"Didn't she catch you two together?" the friend asks. Their conversation fades away as they leave the bathroom. *Air. I need air.* I slump down on the closed toilet lid and try desperately to get myself together. *Skin prickling all over.* I don't want anyone to know what I just heard. *Heart palpitating.* I'm in shock that Jake would share something so personal with the girl he cheated on me for. *I'm going to be sick. No. Keep it together, Rose. Think of Max. Think of being in his arms.* Think of the words he said earlier tonight, just after he'd nearly brought you to orgasm. *"You're a gorgeous, intelligent woman who keeps me on my toes with your sassy mouth and incredible body. You're who I want to be with tonight, no one else."* Was a single word Jake said to me true? He'd pretended to be so incredibly supportive and understanding, when all the while, he was anything but. To him, I was a joke. Knowing that he'd betray me like that with others is devastating.

"Rose, are you still in here? We were getting worried about you."

I jump as I hear Lia's voice. I have no idea how long I've been gone from the table, but obviously, it's been a while. Getting to my feet, I flush the toilet to give myself an extra moment before opening the door. I plaster my public smile on my face before rubbing my stomach. "Remind me to skip the lasagna the next time," I groan. "That stuff is so rich that it's running right on through."

Lia grimaces, seeming to attribute my strained expression to overindulgence. "The check's already been taken care of if you want to rush Max home before you have to …"

I can't help but laugh as she leaves her sentence hanging. I wash my hands then throw an arm around her shoulders. "It's a bodily function, chick. I know you'd rather talk about Max's enormous cock, but I simply don't have the time tonight. Don't worry, though, I should feel better by tomorrow, and we can discuss it over lunch. Why don't you snap a picture of Lucian's tonight and we can compare them?"

As expected, the combination of bathroom talk combined with Max's asset size has her overlooking everything in her haste to escape from me. She is nearing a sprint back to the table while I follow at a more leisurely pace. Max is on his feet and waiting for me when I arrive. He looks at me in concern as he asks, "Are you okay, sweetheart? I was getting concerned."

"I'm fine," I attempt to reassure him. "Just a little full from dinner." Showing yet another reason she's a great friend, Lia has pulled Lucian from behind the table and they're ready to leave. She probably told him I'm in serious danger of soiling my underwear in his friend's restaurant. God, I love that girl.

We all say our goodbyes. Lucian and Lia live only a few blocks away, so they leave on foot while Max takes my hand and steers me to where his car is parked. Ever the gentleman, he opens my door and waits until I'm belted in before shutting it. He's quiet as he navigates the downtown traffic. When we're in the quieter residential area, he asks, "What happened back there?"

I roll my eyes. I've never been quizzed so thoroughly about a bathroom visit before. "Do you want a verbal or a written report?" I ask dryly.

He ignores my snide remark. "You looked as pale as a ghost when you came back to the table. Something upset you."

"Yeah, about a five pounds of pasta," I snap. "For the love of all things holy, can we please not talk about this? Even I have some limits and giving you an in-depth look into my bathroom habits is one of them."

I see his lips quirk, as his shoulders appear to relax. He's accepting my explanation, and I'm beyond grateful. He's the last person I want to know what Jake said about me.

Plus, if I'm completely honest, a part of me is terrified that he feels the same way.

Does he find me disgusting? Now he's seen my scars, can he ever truly want me? How do you desire someone who's so very far from perfect? Max is the epitome of handsome. Why would he settle for damaged goods? *He won't, Rose. He'll kick you out eventually.*

I feel a sharp pang as it hits me with the force of a lightning bolt. I care about him. Maybe it started out sexual, but he's a good man. One of the best I've ever known. I ache to know what it feels like to be the woman who he finally gives his heart to. But that'll never happen now. He knows how screwed up I am. And like Jake, he feels sorry for me. It seems I'm destined to be a burden to those I care about. How much longer can I continue to do that to them—and to myself? The answer to that question haunts me as the car moves through a darkness that rivals the bleakness of my soul.

CHAPTER NINE

Rose

I would remember this night in the years ahead as a turning point in my life.

I've read that when people decide to kill themselves, there's often no emotion involved. And after Max and I arrive home that evening, I am icy calm. Unlike other times when some stress has driven me to cut myself, this time, I am almost like a robot as I assure Max that I am going to sleep in my own bed due to my continued stomach issues. He's concerned and hesitant to leave me, but I insist.

I will no longer be anyone's burden. *She's a sicko. Jake wouldn't have her back if she begged.* I will no longer be anyone's burden. *I've taken the liberty of removing the things from your life that were a burden.* I will no longer be anyone's burden. *She's covered in scars from where she cuts herself.* I will no longer be anyone's burden. The click of the bathroom door echoes within the pristine white walls. The snap of the plastic razor under my shoe is almost deafening. *Or is that the strong beat of my heart?* By removing the guard, I am creating the perfect blade. There is humming in my ears as I remove my clothing, leaving on only my bra and panties. *Since when do I hum?* There is no plan. I just need the sting of pain. What does it matter if Max wants me to stop? I am little more than a pretty project to him. *I will no longer be anyone's burden.* Tomorrow, I'll pack my bags and find somewhere else to live. But tonight, I need the sweet agony that only the feel of my flesh slicing will give to me. Regardless of wrong or right, I need to bleed.

Max

I'm uneasy. The feeling only gets stronger as the minutes pass. Something happened to Rose tonight when she went to the bathroom, and it had nothing to do with an upset stomach. The woman who'd left the table and the one who'd returned a while later barely resembled each other. She'd been pale, but the most disturbing part had been her eyes. They'd been vacant, eerily so. And that hadn't changed on the drive home. She'd looked exactly the same way when she'd closed the door in my face just moments ago.

I continue to pace the floor, not knowing what to do. I don't want her to feel as if I'm watching her every move, but there is no way I can go to bed without seeing her again. Hell, she's slept in my arms since the first night under my roof, and I hadn't realized how much I've come to crave that in such a short amount of time. I hadn't wanted to admit it, but there had been something so right the first night she'd settled so naturally there.

After a few more circles around my bedroom, I've had enough. She can be pissed off at me all she wants, but I have to know she's okay. In a few long strides, I'm at her door. I knock before trying the knob, only to find it locked. I mutter a curse before pounding on the wood once again. "Rose, open up, sweetheart!" There is nothing but silence. "Baby, if you don't open this door, I'm going to break it down! Fuck," I hiss; I step back, barreling against the thick wood. It takes me a few more tries before the door splinters away from the lock and crashes inward. My eyes go automatically to the bathroom, and I see one of her feet in the doorway. There is no sign of movement as I bolt forward.

"Oh God." I freeze. So much blood. Her eyes are closed and her hair looks like a crimson slash against her white skin. I shut down the part of me that wants to fall apart. Her life depends on me keeping it together—if it's not already too late. I drop to my knees and begin quickly looking for the injury. I have to stop the bleeding immediately. A quick glance at her wrists shows nothing, but possibly more scars. I file that away for another time and focus on her thighs. The blood is definitely heavier there. The once white bandage that covered her stitches is now bright red. I grab a towel from the rack on the wall and wipe the area until I locate a spot just inches above. *Oh, fuck.* Blood is pouring from what looks like a fresh cut, and I fear she's hit an artery this time. I bundle up her discarded clothing and use it to elevate her leg. This type of injury I know can be deadly, and I immediately begin applying pressure to staunch the flow of blood. I use my other hand to check her pulse and am relieved to feel the reassuring thud, although it seems too slow.

Still keeping the steady pressure against her wound, I reach into my pocket and pull my cell phone out. Thank fuck I didn't leave it in my room. I don't bother to call Matt. He'd told me on his last trip here that if I thought it was life threatening, I needed to call 911 instead of him. I give the dispatcher my address along with the situation, and she assures me that they have an ambulance on the way. She offers to remain on the line, but I drop the phone instead of continuing to talk. I need to focus on what I'm doing.

It's on the tip of my tongue to try to rouse her, but if it's an artery, I don't want her waking up to panic. She needs to remain calm so she doesn't speed up the pumping of her heart, which would increase the blood flow from the artery. I hear sirens in the distance and grab the phone from the floor. "The front door is locked," I tell the dispatcher. "I can't leave her so have them break it down." I hear her relay the information, and a few minutes later, the sound of wood splintering once again fills my house.

I'm moved out of the way as the emergency personnel take over. I answer as many of their questions as I can before she's loaded onto a stretcher. They ask that I follow them instead of riding along. I want to argue, but I know I'll just be delaying them by seconds that they may need to save her. I grab the keys to my car and am behind them in seconds. I place a quick call to Matt, letting him know what's happening, and he promises to meet us there. Luckily, the hospital she's been taken to is his, which means he'll be able to get more information than he would have otherwise.

I consider calling Lucian and Lia but decide to wait until I have more information. Rose is against them knowing, but with what's happened tonight, that decision is out of her hands. She needs to be surrounded by the people who love her, and I intend to see she gets that. I also know her parents need to be informed, although I have mixed feelings there. A big part of me feels that they gave up their rights when they tossed their daughter out onto the street because she wouldn't go along with their plan for her life.

The outline of the hospital is visible in the distance, and as I follow the ambulance to the emergency entrance, they stop at the side doors while I screech into the first available space and park. Matt is standing to the side with a grim look on his face as Rose is unloaded from the ambulance. The whole scene sends a flashback racing through my head that threatens to bring me to my knees. I see a look of understanding in his eyes before he reaches out a hand to steady me. "They radioed ahead. They have the bleeding under control. Go around to the waiting area and I'll be out as soon as I've done a preliminary assessment." With those words, he's rushing after the gurney and I'm left on the sidewalk.

The adrenaline rush that I've been functioning on is crashing, and for a moment, I want nothing more than to get back in my car and drive away from it all. *This* hospital is the very place where I once lost the most important thing in my life, and I haven't been back inside since then. The long, sterile hallways inside will haunt me until the day I die. The many prayers I once uttered in a small room here went unanswered, and because of it, I lost my faith in God, love, and myself.

I take a fortifying breath before walking slowly toward the entrance doors. I can't be another person in Rose's life who lets her down. Regardless of my own fears, she needs me. Tomorrow is soon enough to fall apart—today, I'll be strong for the woman who desperately needs someone to believe in her.

CHAPTER TEN

Max

Hours pass as I continue to sit in the cramped family waiting room. Others come and go. Some even attempt conversation with me but quickly give up when I give only clipped replies. I could give a fuck about discussing the weather or how the Panthers are doing in football this year. Rose is all that I can think about—anything else is just a waste of time.

When Matt finally comes in, I feel a moment's panic before I note his relaxed expression. I've been on the receiving end of his bad-news face before, and this isn't it. I feel some of the tension seep from my back as he sinks into a chair and motions for me to do the same. "She's going to be okay," he says without further delay. "She nicked her femoral artery, but thankfully, she didn't completely sever it. We've given her two pints of blood, and I've repaired the artery."

"Thank God," I sigh before scrubbing my hands over my face.

Before I can fully relax, his tone becomes serious. "If you hadn't found her when you did, Max, we would be having a very different conversation right now. For a woman her size, two pints of blood is a lot. People bleed out within minutes with an injury such as hers. This is twice in a few days that she's cut herself. The age of her scarring suggests she's been doing this for some time, but I have to believe it's escalating. Was she upset about anything?"

"I don't know," I admit, "but I think so. We went to dinner with friends, and she excused herself at one point to use the restroom. She was gone a long time, and when she returned, it was obvious something had occurred. She blamed it on an upset stomach, but I didn't believe her. I don't think her parents have her new cell phone number, but she may have called them for some reason."

"She needs help, Max," Matt says bluntly. "I shouldn't be telling you this, but one of my colleagues, Preston Holland, came to speak to me a few minutes ago when he found out that Rose had been brought in. Apparently, he's a neighbor of her parents. He said that they had called him over twice when she attempted to kill herself as a teenager. The first time, she overdosed on her mother's anxiety medication, and the second time, she slit her wrists. He was disturbed by how her parents treated the whole matter and was unnerved by their indifference to something he saw as very serious. He said he tried to talk to her father several times about getting treatment for her, but he always brushed it aside as her being difficult and trying to get attention."

My head is spinning as I remember the scars I'd seen earlier on her wrists. Fuck, she's tried to kill herself before. Did she accidentally cut too deep tonight or was it her intention to do much worse? *Baby, no.* "I don't know what to do," I admit, feeling helpless.

"We don't have to decide anything today," he says, "because I'm going to keep her overnight. But we need to be thinking of a game plan. Going by what you and Preston have told me, I don't know how much help her parents will be. She is an adult, so they don't have any legal bearing on her choices and care, but they are next of kin. I'd recommend treatment in a facility for at least thirty days, but most people are resistant to that step—especially at first. She needs to have the support of people who care about her and will advocate her getting help."

I feel more than a little depressed as I say, "Outside of her parents, to my knowledge, she only has Lia, Lucian, and me."

"Why don't you give them a call and ask them to come by tomorrow afternoon? We can all get together and discuss the best approach. I'm in a bit of a tricky situation here. I can't share anything further with you as her doctor, but as your friend, I'll assist in any way I can. As reluctant as we may be, I need to contact her parents and update them on their daughter's condition. Just try to make sure you're here when and if they visit. I'll keep an eye out as well."

"Can I see her now?" I ask, needing to reassure myself that she's okay. I'd never seen so much blood. The smell. Sticky. Warm. I can't get the image of her surrounded by the pool of blood out of my head. Perhaps, I never will. *What is this girl doing to me? I'm not sure it's good for me to stay ...*

"Sure." He nods as we both get to our feet. "She's probably going to sleep for the next several hours, so don't be alarmed by that. You should go home and get some rest yourself. We'll watch over her here."

I feel my chest tighten as we make our way down familiar halls. *It's not the same. She's fine. Keep it together.*

Matt stops at a door at the end of the hall. "I going to check on a couple of patients since I'm here, then I'm going to catch some sleep. Give me a call if anything comes up. If not, I'll see you here in the afternoon around two."

"I really appreciate it." I shake his hand before he turns to leave. I walk into the darkened room and am almost relieved. Rose looks like an angel as she lies on the crisp, white hospital sheets. She has an IV attached to one hand and still looks pale. Otherwise, she appears unscathed by what happened earlier. I know, though, that looks can be deceiving, and below the surface, she's more damaged than ever.

I pull up a chair next to her bed and sink down heavily onto it. I take her hand and thread my fingers through hers before laying my head back. I'm too exhausted to process the events of the last few hours or to contact Luc and Lia, and at this point, I think that's a godsend. I have no idea what will happen when she wakes, but for now, I can sleep knowing she's alive to face another tomorrow.

Rose

My mouth feels as if it's stuffed with cotton as I attempt to swallow. My eyes are heavy and fight me as I try to open them. Obviously, I didn't sleep well last night or I wouldn't still be this tired. I feel a moment's panic as I think I may be late for work. I struggle through the layers of fog until I'm finally blinking away the vestiges of sleep. Or so I think. I don't recognize my surroundings. *Am I dreaming?*

The sound of a soft snore fills my ears, and I look around to see Max in a chair a few feet away. His head is leaning back at an uncomfortable angle. His dark hair looks rumpled as if he's run his hand through it many times. Then another snore, followed by a louder snort, before he sits up abruptly—looking as disoriented as I feel. "What … Rose?" he asks as if searching for some explanation. I hope he finds one because I have no idea what's going on.

"I think I might be dreaming," I offer. "I guess I brought you in with me. Where do you think we are? Not exactly a five-star hotel kind of fantasy is it?" I laugh hoarsely.

He gets to his feet and stretches. I don't know why, but I sense he's stalling. This is now officially the weirdest dream I've had and that's saying something. Normally, if Max is present, then it at least contains some sexual overtones. But I'm not getting that this time at all. *Shit, did someone die?* He comes to sit next to me, and for the first time, I glance down and see what looks like a hospital bed. There's also a plastic tube taped to the top of my hand. And what in the hell am I wearing? As if sensing my rising agitation, he puts a hand on my arm to brace me. "Sweetheart, what do you remember about last night?"

"Huh? I … um …" I wrack my brain, trying to recall the previous evening. Bits and pieces begin to slowly filter back in, and I am finally able to answer. "We had dinner with Lucian and Lia, right?"

He nods encouragingly. "That's correct. Then you went to the restroom and something happened there to upset you."

Even though it's phrased as a statement, I hear the underlying question. My thought process is still unusually slow as I push myself to remember more. Then it hits me and I'm unable to disguise my quick intake of breath. "I— no, it was just the food. Nothing happened." Whereas I'd been almost languid before; now, it's as if all my senses are in a state of heightened overload. *Flight or fight*, I think hysterically. *He knows what they said. Please, no. Oh my God, what did I do?* I jerk away from his touch, intent only on escaping. I have to get out of here. "Where the hell am I?"

I didn't realize that I'd asked the last question aloud until Max clears his throat and says, "You're in Asheville Downtown Hospital. I called an ambulance for you last night after you nicked your femoral artery." He gives me a look of apology before adding, "Baby, I had no choice. You were close to bleeding out."

All fight leaves my body. I collapse back against the pillows as I stare at the man who undoubtedly saved my life. "I'm sorry," I whisper as I observe the agony on his face. He looks as bad as I feel. "I didn't mean to cut that deep, I was just so upset after—" Too late, I realize I've as much as admitted that something other than the food got to me last night.

He encloses my hand between his, bringing it to his lips. He plants a soft kiss there then lays it directly over his heart. "Tell me what happened, honey. What drove you to hurt yourself last night? No more lies or half-truths between us."

I feel the hot tears spill silently down my cheeks as the last of my walls fall away. I don't have the energy to protect myself from him any longer. Maybe he will think I'm pathetic—but I don't think so. Something about the way he's looking at me leads me to believe he cares— possibly more than I'm able to comprehend. The voice in my head is screaming, *you thought Jake understood, too.* But I push it aside. I have nothing left to lose. If I'm going to survive, I have to trust someone, and right now, that's Max. Taking a deep breath, I begin. "Jake was at Leo's last night with his girlfriend and another couple. I went to the bathroom to regroup, and I heard someone come in. I didn't feel like dealing with them, so I planned to remain in the stall until they left. It turned out to be his girlfriend and her friend, I think. And they were talking about me."

"Fuck," Max snaps before putting his hand protectively over my knee. "Sorry, please continue."

"Anyway, the girlfriend was saying how *Jake's ex-girlfriend was there and how crazy she was.* She mentioned my love of guns and how Jake was terrified of me." Shrugging my shoulders, I say, "You read about stuff like that, you know. Overhearing others talking about you. I could have lived with the crazy part because let's face it, I'm a bit out there at times. But when she moved on to me cutting myself, and the amount of scars that covered my body—I'm not going to lie, it got to me, Max. Until recently, I thought Jake was the only one to know my secret. And regardless of what an asshole he ended up being, I never imagined he would share something so private. Not only that, he belittled me to the girl he cheated on me with." A sob breaks free as I whisper, "How could he do that to someone he supposedly cared about at some point? He knew how terrified I was of anyone else finding out. Yet he told her—of all people. Can you imagine how many others she's taken great pleasure in sharing my secrets with?"

"Oh baby, I'm so sorry," Max says tightly, and then he pulls me into his arms. I can feel the suppressed rage in him at Jake's actions. "I wish you had told me all of this last night. I hate that you had to deal with it alone. I'd like to go find the little fucker and kick his ass. I'll never let him hurt you again."

Out of nowhere, a giggle breaks through the sorrow as I picture Max in his impeccable suit wrestling my ex-boyfriend in the street. I have no doubt whatsoever that Max could snap Jake like a twig if he wanted to. I'm just surprised and more than a little moved by the possessive tone that his voice has taken. He gives me a questioning look, probably thinking I've officially lost it to jump from tears to laughter in the space of seconds. That's what he does for me, though. In the midst of the darkness, he brings the light. "It's nothing. Just enjoying the mental picture of you burying those expensive shoes up my ex-boyfriend's behind. I gotta say, you'll need to stand in line. If I ever see him again, he'll be on the business end of my pistol."

Max pulls back and groans. "It's been at least a month since I bailed you out of jail the last time. By all means, do something that will get you arrested again. The police chief and I are getting to be good friends. We're going golfing next week. And I owe it all to you."

I stick out my tongue at him, unable to resist this playful side. "So when are you breaking me out of here?" I ask, looking around the dismal white room. Immediately, his expression sobers, and he looks away. I lay a hand over his, bringing his attention back to me. "What? Is something wrong?" The irony of that question isn't lost on me. *Of course, there's something wrong. You almost killed yourself.* Have I really gotten to the point that a near death miss doesn't faze me? *Yes, probably more so than I realized.* Was I expecting Max to take me somewhere for a late breakfast while we laughed off my latest lapse in judgment?

He pinches the bridge of his nose, looking as if he's carrying the weight of the world on his shoulders. I've done that to him. I dropped my problems at his door and now he feels responsible for me. Finally, he cups my face in his hands and says, "You can't continue on like this, sweetheart. I know I've said that before, but this is different. I'm very afraid that the next time we end up here, you won't be leaving with me."

"So, is this your way of telling me to find my own ride?" I joke, even though I'm crumbling inside. He's giving me an ultimatum. Either get my shit together, or that's it. He's walking away. And I can't blame him. We're not even in a relationship, and I've turned his whole life upside down.

I jump back when he suddenly yells, "Goddammit, stop with the jokes! What do you find funny about dying? Because I can tell you right now, it's not a laughing matter to me. The thought of losing you is fucking ripping me to pieces." As I stare at him, he lowers his voice to add, "Please, baby, help me. I know it's easier to run from the pain than it is to face it, but that's not working anymore. So many people in life never have the choice, but you do. If you won't do it for yourself, please do it for me."

Then I see a sight that slays me.

He wipes away a tear before it can fall from his eyes. It would be wrong for me to trust him. He's a good man who has good intentions, but he, like Jake, and like my father, must be well and truly ready to wash his hands of me. He seems into me, but who am I to read people well? Only one boyfriend. Only one girl friend too, for that matter. Maybe everyone else in my life has been right to keep their distance. I don't want to be a burden anymore, but I don't know how to escape his care, his pity.

"Max," I murmur. "Tell me what you want me to do. I'll stop cutting. I promise I won't do it anymore." *Liar. You can't stop; it owns you. You're weak.*

As if he can hear my inner torment, he says, "Baby, it's beyond you now. When you're in pain, you're going to hurt yourself to deal with it. But I think the small cuts that you started with are no longer helping you. That's why you're having more close calls. It's no different than a drug addiction. It gets harder and harder to get the feeling you need so you increase the dose, or in your case, you cut deeper."

Before he can say anything else, there's a knock on the door and then it swings open. My mouth drops in shock as I see not only Lucian and Lia walk in, but my parents trailing behind them. I blink a few times, thinking this must surely be some kind of bad dream. "How—?" I ask as I look from them to Max. As if things couldn't possibly get more embarrassing, Matt Foster steps in at the last moment. The silence is deafening, as everyone seems to be waiting for something.

Matt gives Max a look that seems to spur him into action. He clears his throat and gives me an uneasy look. "Rose—sweetheart, I realize that you're probably going to be angry with me, but I asked our friends and your family to come here today to offer you support and also—"

"Oh my God," I say disbelievingly. "This is an intervention, isn't it?" I've never actually been a part of one, but I watch reality television just like everyone else. A part of me wants to sit back and observe the show until I realize I'm the star of this particular one. Then I'm just angry, so fucking enraged. I trusted Max with the worst part of me, and he sold me out. They all know now; I can see it in their eyes—the uneasiness, the damn pity. And the humiliation on my parents' faces. This is their worst nightmare. I've ruined the Madden name. They're probably wishing it had just been alcohol or an oxy addiction. Those are common and somewhat fashionable among the rich. But no, their daughter cuts herself. More proof I can't do anything right. "How dare you?" I hiss as I glare at Max. "You promised you would help me and this is how you do it? By betraying me?"

"Rose." Matt steps forward, holding up a hand as if to stop my tirade. "This wasn't Max's idea. It was mine. We actually spent most of the time that you were asleep arguing about it. But in the end, neither of us could see another way. The people in this room care about you. They're your support system."

"You can't discuss my medical records or treatment without my consent," I snap at him.

He nods his head. "That's correct and I won't be. That's why your friends and family are here. You and I don't know each other very well, but I do care about what happens to you."

Lucian steps forward, and everyone in the room seems shocked when he says in his usual commanding voice, "I'd like to speak to Rose alone if you don't mind." There is some shuffling of feet, but surprisingly, everyone turns to leave. Max looks hesitant, but finally gets to his feet and shuts the door behind him. *Wow, Lucian Quinn really is all powerful. I can't imagine my parents meekly following orders from anyone else. They must surely be dying to tell me what an embarrassment this whole situation has been for them.*

"Is this the tough love portion of the show?" I ask bitterly as I frown at the man I've come to think of as a brother.

He laughs, before lowering himself into the chair at my bedside. He appears completely relaxed as he stretches his long legs before him. "It's love most certainly," he answers, "and yeah, sometimes that's tough." Silence fills the small space as I wait to see what he'll say next. "Don't take this the wrong way, but I always knew there was more going on behind the bullshit blinders you presented to the world."

"If this is supposed to be your version of a pep talk, it sucks," I huff out. How many more indignities will I be forced to endure today?

He has the audacity to wink at me, totally ignoring my blustering. "I know a kindred spirit when I see one, Rose. I spent years addicted to cocaine and only a few people in my life knew it. I was fully functional on it. Hell, in my opinion, it made me a better version of myself most days. Hence, I was never inclined to give it up, even though I knew I was playing with fire. Truthfully, no matter how weak it made me feel that I couldn't stop, I don't know if I ever would have if not for Lia. Loving her meant that my life was no longer just mine to risk. She owned a piece of me and she damn well deserved better that some man who needed to snort a white line in order to deal with day-to-day life. When she caught me using, it was almost a relief. I can't tell you how ashamed I was to have someone who endured what she had discover my secret. I'd never felt like less of a man than I did at that moment."

The fact that Lucian is sharing his darkness with me so candidly is shocking to say the least. I've always liked the man, and can understand why Lia is completely head-over-heels, but we haven't said much to each other, really. *He understands my darkness. He's not judging me. What will he do if I share some of my brokenness and darkness with him, though?* "That's why I didn't want to tell her," I admit softly. "She's been through more than I can even imagine, and she's the strongest person I know. I feel like a coward in comparison. I—I got so tired of never being good enough. No matter what, I was always a disappointment to my family. And every year it seemed to get worse. After a while, I lost sight of who I was and simply became Hoyt and Celia's daughter—the chronic underachiever."

"I understand, Rose, I really do," he says earnestly. "Pain is pain, no matter the root cause. After dealing with the constant negativity that was Cassie, I realize how poisonous words can be. To feel as if you're letting down the people you care about is demoralizing and it chips away at the very fabric of who you are as a person. When Cassie and I were together, there were more times than I even care to admit that I didn't want to go home. The impending verbal backlash from whatever way I'd supposedly let her down that day was a torture that was as depressing as it was predictable. The sad part was that like any repeated pattern, I became almost used to it after a while—but the hurt it caused never lessened. Her arrows found their mark time and time again. Coke gave me a way to escape from all of those memories. I could pretend I was invincible. That I'd never hurt anyone and never been hurt." He dropped his head for a moment, seemingly fascinated with the pattern of the tile on the floor. "I realize now that I was only going through the motions. Nothing touched me until Lia, and even then, I was using it to insulate me from the feelings she stirred within me."

My fingers pluck nervously at the stiff sheet covering me as I admit, "I don't know why I'm like this, Luc. I think something's wrong with me. After what Cassie did to you, I can understand why you'd need a way to deal with trauma. But nothing like that has ever happened to me. I'm almost certain I was actually happy at one time. Then it's as if I couldn't handle life anymore. I started having crazy dreams that made no sense, so I was barely sleeping. Then I ended up taking pills to help me when I got to the point that I was so sleep deprived I couldn't function."

Lucian tilts his head, looking at me in question. "What kind of dreams?"

I shrug my shoulders, but I'm suddenly uncomfortable. "It's nothing horrible or anything. It's just this woman who I don't recognize, yet somehow seems familiar. She keeps telling me that I don't belong—I'm not one of them. Then she begins crying and screaming so loudly that it hurts my ears. Someone pulls me away from her, but I don't see who. I always wake up when she's sobbing, 'I'm so sorry, Poppy, please forgive me.'"

Lucian appears riveted by the dream that has haunted me for so long. The fact that I've had that same dream on and off for over fifteen years is something I've never mentioned to anyone but my parents. They'd brushed it off as they did most things in my life. "Poppy?" Lucian asks. "Do you know anyone by that name?"

Shaking my head, I say, "Nope, sure don't. Points to me for originality in my dreams though, right?"

Giving me a smile I can't help but be dazzled by, he moves in for the kill. "I've been seeing a therapist twice a week who I think you'd like. Her name is Joanna Chase, and she's been a big help to me in gaining insight and control over my addiction." I'm on the verge of blasting him for even suggesting such a thing when he tosses in something that has me rethinking my aversion to a shrink. "I mentioned her to your parents, and they were completely opposed. Let me know in no uncertain terms that you wouldn't be interested in talking to a stranger about your issues."

And there you go, folks. Once again, fucking parents of the year. I know them well enough to guess that this has little to do with me and everything to do with the Madden name. *Rehab, sure. Your daughter in a nuthouse, hell no!* "So I assume you've already made an appointment for me," I say and know I'm right when he gives me a sheepish grin. In that moment, I understand once again why Lia loves this man so much. The fact that he's absurdly hot has little to do with his appeal. It's the man underneath that makes him so attractive. I know without him saying it that he'd do anything in his power to help me. Sharing his personal struggles with cocaine could not have been easy for such a private person, but he did it to show me that I'm not alone. He, better than anyone, understands how crippling the shame and self-loathing is when you can't stop the behavior that is destroying your life.

Lucian gets to his feet and perches in the place Max recently vacated. He pulls me into his arms and hugs me tightly. "Lia and I are here for you. You're family to both of us."

"That's good," I say huskily, "because I might need somewhere to stay. I'm kind of homeless right now, and my parents aren't likely to welcome me back anytime soon after this bit of trashy behavior." I bite my lip as I realize that I've so much as admitted that my romance with Max is a sham. He'd certainly never believe his friend would kick me out on the street or dump me in my time of need. Other than a slight, knowing smile, he doesn't question me on my slip of the tongue.

Lucian winces as he ruffles my hair. "No offense, Rose, but they're kind of assholes. I'm not sure how you turned out so well coming from those two." I roll my eyes, thinking his comment about me turning out well might be a little far-fetched given I'm sitting in a hospital bed after cutting myself. "Anyway, I took the liberty of making you an appointment with Joanna for tomorrow afternoon at four. I'll pick you up around three-thirty."

"Wait … what?" I stutter out. "You're going with me?"

Lucian looks surprised by my question. "Well, of course. I know how hard taking the first step can be. I wasn't kidding when I said we're going to be with you, Rose. And you're more than welcome to stay with us, although I have a feeling Max will be opposed to that idea."

"You know we're not actually involved," I point out. "I don't think you ever believed that we were."

Lucian stands and straightens his clothing before acknowledging my statement. "Maybe not officially, but something has been there since almost the first. I've never known Max to be rattled by anything or anyone until he met you. It may take you both some time to figure it all out, but he's crazy about you and I believe you feel the same." *Lia has certainly worked her magic softening this man.*

I'm still mulling his words when the door opens and a rumpled Max walks in. He looks briefly at Lucian before running his eyes over me as if checking to see if my mental state has deteriorated in his absence.

And it's there, in a hospital room wearing an ill-fitted gown with no makeup on and hair that feels like a rat's nest, that it hits me.

I'm in love with Max Decker.

I've been in lust with him for a while, and I've hoped that someday he would have feelings for me. But a part of me never dared to hope that anything would ever come of it. To become involved with him would mean that he would know my secret and I'm not certain I could have let that happen. Now, I've been laid bare for all to see, and he's still here. Oh God, he hasn't left me. In fact, he's looking at me in a way that gives me hope that Lucian's right. Could he feel the same? Before I can stop myself, I extend a hand, needing to feel his skin against mine. I wonder if he knows that there is nothing simple about the gesture. I've given him the power to bring more pain into my life than I've ever inflicted. For I thought at one time I had loved Jake, but now, I realize that he only ever had a small part of me. I know instinctively that Max would never allow me to hide. A love between us would burn so hot that we'd either be consumed by the flame or welded together so tightly that one simply could not exist without the other. Even as fear fills me at the thought, I thread my fingers through his— anchoring my destiny to the one man I fear I can't survive without.

CHAPTER ELEVEN

Max

I study Rose in relief, thankful she hasn't thrown me out of her room yet. Even though I knew I needed to be the one to initiate the intervention—and to involve Lia, Lucian, and her family—I still feel like I betrayed her. Hell, she'd screamed that very thing at me not even an hour earlier. Now, though, she seems calmer—almost serene. *Fuck, Luc is good.* I'd been surprised when Lucian had insisted on talking with her alone. A part of me had wanted to object even. But it made sense. They're both battling demons, and I was willing to try anything if it helped. Looking at her now, I believe that whatever he said was something she needed to hear.

I wrap my other hand around the nape of her neck and pull her near, dropping a kiss on her forehead then lightly across her lips. "I'm so damn sorry, sweetheart. I don't know if you can ever forgive me, but I didn't feel that I had a choice. You might hate me, but I'd do it again if it meant that you were still here, even if it's not with me."

She uses our connection to pull me closer until my upper body is lying on hers. Our faces are just inches apart as we stare at each other. "I'm not going to lie, counselor. I was beyond hurt and pissed at you—a part of me still is. But after talking to Luc, I also realize that I never needed to hide from my friends." She toys with the hem of my shirt as she continues. "He's made me an appointment already with his therapist, and he's also going with me the first time."

As her eyes mist over, I feel a tug of jealousy that my friend is the one she's leaning on then immediately call myself ten kinds of asshole. I want her to get better, no matter what. Who gives a damn if Lucian is in a better position to understand what she's going through? I should be grateful for his help. It's for damn certain there is nothing romantic involved. Lia owns him, and he'd be the first to admit it. "That's great, baby," I say softly and mean it. "We're all here for anything that you need—even if it's just someone to go target practicing with."

She snorts out a surprised laugh. "You're never going to let me forget shooting Jake's car up, are you?"

"Hell, no," I rasp out as she licks her lips. My cock jumps to attention as it does every time she so much as breathes in my direction. *Down boy—so not a good time for that*, I groan inwardly as I take a deep breath. "Seeing you sitting so demurely in that police station with those pearls on after you'd just taken a gun and a shovel to that bastard's car was about the sexiest thing I'd ever seen," I admit.

Her eyes widen as if riveted by my confession. "Really? I assumed you thought I was crazy. You were so pissed off at having to bail me out."

Unable to resist, I nuzzle the curve of her neck, inhaling her familiar smell, despite the hospital scent now clinging to her. "It's called frustration, sweetheart," I murmur as I drop a kiss on the shell of her ear. "When you climbed on my lap in the car, I wanted nothing more than to spank your ass for teasing me, and then bury myself balls deep in your sweet pussy." *Smooth—talking dirty to a woman lying in a hospital bed while molesting her neck. You'll be lucky if she doesn't call security.* "Sorry, honey, my timing is shit. I shouldn't be saying this stuff right now," I apologize while trying to bring my body back under control.

"Are you kidding?" she groans, "that's the hottest thing anyone's ever said to me. I know it's probably messed up to admit this, but I'm so horny I want to explode."

I gape at her, wondering if I imagined what she just said. "We did not hear that!" My head swivels to the side, and I wince in embarrassment as Lucian and Lia smirk at us. Actually, Luc is doing most of the smirking. Lia's face is red, but her lips are curved in a smile. I realize that I'm covering Rose like a blanket and touch her cheek in apology before putting some space between us. "So," Lia says, "we just wanted to come in and let you know that Dr. Foster is discharging you today as soon as the paperwork is ready. The spare bedroom is all set for you. Luc will pick your stuff up from Max's house, and we can buy anything else you need."

"She's staying with me," I bark out, startling everyone in the room. Fuck, I sound like a psycho. I run a hand through my hair, attempting to compose myself before I scare Rose away with my possessiveness. "Sorry, didn't mean to shout." I put a hand on her leg and rub it reassuringly before continuing. "I don't want you to go, but I can't make you stay. I want to continue holding you in my arms at night when you can't sleep and be there in the morning when you're adjusting to yet another new outfit. I also need someone to burn dinner because that doesn't happen nearly enough for me."

"Don't you need a break?" she asks me uncertainly. "You probably haven't gotten more than a couple of hours of sleep since I've been there."

I drop a kiss on her upturned nose. "I'm fine, sweetheart."

"In that case, I'd love to stay," she says softly. "I'm sure my parents will be thrilled." Looking around, she asks, "Where are they, by the way?" She rolls her eyes, and for a moment, I see understandable insecurity in her expression.

As if not willing to allow herself to grieve, she takes a deep breath and erects what looks like a wall of indifference. "Standing in the hallway with dark glasses on so that no one recognizes them?"

"Er … they left," Lia answers tensely. It's obvious what her opinion of Rose's parents' defection is. After my telephone conversation with Rose's father, then the near argument we'd had in the hallway, I was more than happy to see them go. I could hardly fathom how the man could essentially render his daughter penniless and homeless, then have the nerve to complain about her "antics" embarrassing them yet again. I'd wanted to punch the bastard in the mouth. It may well have come to that had Lia not stepped between us and defused the situation somewhat. There was no way I'm telling Rose what was said, though. She needs support right now, not more disapproval.

"Ah, well, good riddance, right?" Rose says brightly, but I can see the hurt behind the words. No matter what they've done to her recently, she still wants their love and approval. I'm not sure they're capable of the first, and the second seems like a real long shot. After just a few minutes in their company, it had become clear to me why she felt so much pressure to be perfect. They were snobbish pricks that I'd instantly disliked. How in the world Rose turned out to be such a funny and unique person is nothing short of a miracle.

"I'm sure they'll be begging us to join them for dinner soon." I laugh to lighten the mood. Matt comes through the door a short while later with Rose's discharge papers, and Lia offers to help Rose dress in the clothes she brought for her. Lucian motions for me to follow him out into the hallway. "What's up?" I ask, thinking it was something work related.

"Rose said something to me when we were talking that made me a little uneasy. Has she said anything to you about the recurrent dream that she's had for years?"

I shake my head. "No, she hasn't mentioned it. I know she has problems sleeping at night, but I assumed it was a form of insomnia brought on by the issues with her parents. Did she go into detail about it?" Lucian fills me in, and like him, I'm also unnerved. It's not the type of dream I can imagine spanning years. "You think it might be a memory, don't you?"

He rubs a hand over his jaw before shrugging. "In my experience, only memories stay with you for that long. She may have been too young to remember the actual event, but her subconscious could be trying to tell her something. As you know, I've already had a background check run on her. I'm not having anyone that close to my family without it," he adds without apology. For a man with Lucian's money and power, it never hurts to be cautious. I would almost bet that Lee Jacks has also looked into Rose's background. He would be wary of those in his daughter's life. "There was nothing there that we don't already know, so I think we should dig a little deeper. Have the investigator that we've used before go all the way back to her birth and look carefully through those early years." Lucian glances at Rose's door before looking back at me. "I have a gut feeling that something's not right. I realize that her parents have verbally abused her for years, which in itself would be enough to damage her, but maybe there's more that Rose herself isn't consciously aware of."

I slump back against the wall as my mind reels from the possibilities. What in the hell has happened to her in the past? Could both Lucian and I be making something out of nothing? "I've heard of people experiencing traumatic events only to block them out completely for years. Then something happens to open that door and all hell breaks loose."

"It could be what was behind the attempts to take her own life and then the cutting. Even she admitted to me that she didn't understand why she felt the way that she did. She couldn't pinpoint a single event out of the ordinary that led her to it."

"Just a couple of assholes for parents who tore her down at every opportunity. I'm guessing that was a normal day for her and she wouldn't see that as unusual," I retort.

Lucian gives me an appraising look that begins to make me uncomfortable. Finally, he asks, "What made you decide to let her in? You've been in denial for months, but now, you're practically ordering her to stay with you. Don't get me wrong. I've thought you two belonged together for a while, and I've had to almost sit on Lia to keep her from meddling. But what changed? If anything, I would be afraid that all of this would make you run."

I want to ignore his question. Lucian and I aren't exactly the type of men to discuss our feelings, and it seems as if we've done nothing but that since Lia walked into his life. In a way, it's brought our friendship closer than it's ever been. We're more open with each other now. Before, he and Aidan were like brothers and I was more of a cousin. Now, the bond between us has tightened, and I'm grateful. Therefore, instead of walking away, I answer him honestly. "I could have lost her—that's what changed. Nothing that I did could save the last woman I loved. No amount of money, modern medicine, or religion could stop her from fading just a little more each day. But with Rose, I have a chance. I can save her—I *will* save her," I add fiercely as my hands clench into fists.

Lucian looks at me in surprise, and I wonder how he could not know about Melly. There's no way he hired me without the same background check that he ran on Rose. Could that part have possibly been left out? I've never discussed her with him before, but I don't think he's acting right now. He clears his throat before saying, "I won't ask you to tell me any more while we're here, but one day, I hope you'll be comfortable enough to talk to me about her." He gives me a side hug, before patting me on the shoulder. "Lia and I are going to head home. If you need time off or would rather work from home for a while, then just let me know. Rose is our priority and everything else can be worked around. Oh, and I had someone swing by to take care of the door at your house. They've installed a temporary one and will order an exact replacement of the one that you had." I'd mentioned the emergency responders having to break-in to reach us in the bathroom, and Luc, as always, never missed a detail.

"Thanks, Luc," I say around the sudden lump in my throat. One of the best decisions of my life had been taking a job with Quinn Software. I never expected the family that came along with it, but I'm beyond grateful for them. Especially since I so rarely see my own parents; they are usually more than content with the occasional communication via email.

Lia stops to hug me on the way out, and Lucian jokes about his wife spending too much time hugging other men. I grin because I know a part of him isn't joking. If he had his way, she'd never be in the same room with another man again. He's a possessive bastard, and I fully understand. I'm coming to feel the same way about the auburn beauty smiling sleepily at me now. I make a silent promise that nothing will take her from me. I've been given a second chance, and no matter what it takes, this time, I'll hold on with everything I have. God wouldn't be cruel enough to let me find love again, only to rip it away.

CHAPTER TWELVE

Rose

"Holy hell, I'm free! The warden finally let me out of prison for good behavior today." I pump my fist in the air before forming a V for victory with my fingers. "I didn't think I'd ever be plotting ways to escape from a hot piece of man candy like Max, but crap, he found some crazy reason every day for two whole weeks as to why he needed to work at home *every* day. This, of course, was code for, 'Rose, you're staying home with me.' I tried to tell him that you were going to fire me if I didn't get back to work, but he wouldn't listen." I frown at Lia, who simply smiles in return. "Couldn't you have been a little more of a hard-ass? Maybe demanded that I return immediately, instead of saying, 'Take all the time you need, your job will be waiting for you.' What employer says shit like that? McDonald's would have given me the boot after the first day."

When I finally run out of steam, I drop into the chair in front of her desk and she pushes a cup of coffee in front of me. "Are you finished now?" She smirks.

I pretend to sulk for a moment. "Oh, I guess so."

Changing the subject, she asks, "How was your last session with Joanna? Lucian said that you really liked her."

"She's great," I say and mean it. I've been seeing Lucian's therapist twice a week, and so far, it's been nothing like what I'd feared. Her office is more like a well-worn living room, complete with comfortable, overstuffed sofas and a fireplace. Joanna dresses like a new age hippie, and more often than not, she isn't wearing shoes when she opens the door. That one small thing always relaxes me. She's not intrusive and doesn't try to put words in my mouth. Best of all, I've never felt that she's judging me. There's just something about her that makes me want to open up and I have. She warned me on my first visit that she couldn't wave a magic wand and make the urge to cut go away. Her desire is to help me identify my triggers and figure out ways to recognize and deal with them in ways that don't involve cutting. Essentially, I need to retrain my brain. "My parents are completely opposed to it, but luckily, they haven't canceled my health insurance— probably just because they haven't thought about it."

"We can get you covered here," Lia offers. "I'm so happy that you like Joanna. Lucian was really resistant to seeing her, but after his first appointment, he admitted he felt hopeful for the first time that he could beat his addiction for good." Trying to act nonchalant, she asks, "How are things going with Max? Any new developments between you two?"

I glance behind me to ensure that the door is indeed closed before I continue. Fanning myself, I say, "I swear, I've never been so horny in my life. I'm pretty sure both Max and I are masturbating so much our fingers are going crooked. If he doesn't give up the goods soon, I'm going to buy a new vibrator." Wrinkling my nose, I add, "I have no idea what the movers that Daddy hired to clear out my apartment did with my last one."

"Oh my God." Lia holds her sides as she laughs. "I can just picture some guy with a carpenter's crack holding that up and scratching his head."

Wiggling my eyebrows, I say, "He probably took it home to the wife. That thing was a top-of-the-line rabbit. It not only went up and down, but it also did the side-to-side motion. And the rabbit ears—"

"I really don't need that many details about your little plastic friend." Lia smirks.

I lean back in my chair, crossing my legs while I look at my nails. "Oh honey, there was nothing little about it. That baby was the mega bunny model, and as large as it was, I'm certain that Max is bigger." My head rolls to the back of the chair as I huff in frustration. "Do you have any idea how miserable it is to have that whopper nestled between the crack of my ass every night and not be able to do anything about it?" Lowering my voice, I add, "You know I never did the anal thing with Jake even though he wanted to. But I'd take anything I could get at this point from Max. If he wants to explore what's behind door number two, then I'll open the gates and wave him on in."

Lia drops her head on her desk and then makes a gagging sound as if she's choking. "Please, stop telling me stuff about Max! Lucian thinks I've got some kind of secret crush on him already since I blush every time I'm in the same room with him. I told him it was just because you talk about the size of his pecker constantly. And as you can imagine, he wasn't really any happier with that bit of information. Then he wanted to know if we also discuss the size of his package."

"Well, it's certainly not for lack of trying on my part." I pout. "When your best friend is married to a guy like Lucian Quinn, there should be a lot more sex talk. I have to drag everything out of you. Couldn't you at least photograph his pecker while he's asleep or something? I bet the sucker is the size of my leg. I've seen you limping around some days like you've thrown your vagina out of joint."

She giggles before tossing a pen in my direction. "You're such a pervert. Do you ever think of anything other than sex?"

"If I thought of it more, then I wouldn't be going all Edward Scissorhands all over myself, would I?" While Jake and I had been together, my cutting had been at all-time low until I began to suspect he was cheating on me. I'd used sex as a form of escape when I was stressed. The high that an orgasm gave me temporarily distracted me from the urge to harm myself. If Jake suspected that, at times, it had little to do with my desire for him and everything to do with diversion, he never mentioned it. Hell, he was a college guy. I doubt he looked too deeply at why we sometimes fucked three times a day. I have to wonder now if he hadn't known at some point, especially as he learned more about me and how screwed up I was.

Lia's face falls, and I mentally kick myself. I've gotten used to discussing my issues in a humorous way with Max. "I shouldn't have said that," she adds quickly. "Of course, you have other things on your mind. I didn't mean to—"

"Stop, chick. Please don't do that. We've never watched our words around each other and it would kill me if we started now. My twisted sense of humor is the only thing that gets me through the day sometimes, and I need you to be okay with it. Heck, we joked about your mother and your crazy-ass stepfather more times than I can count and you didn't freak out on me. You, better than anyone, understand that laughter takes some of the power from the pain. Yes, I've been cutting myself and it's a serious matter, but it's easier for me to cope this way."

I see the look of understanding on her face as she nods. "You're absolutely right. Normal just isn't you. Thank God, I'm not sure how much longer I could keep up the nice act. I'll ask Lee if he can install a metal detector so we'll know when you're packing any sharp objects." She winces when she delivers her last line and asks hesitantly, "Too much?"

I chuckle; one of the things I love about her is how she cares about others. It's hard for her to even pretend to be mean. I wink at her before saying, "I thought it was good. Why don't we skip the detector, though, and have your hot daddy frisk me?"

"Ugh!" She gags. "Must you lust after my father? If it's something you have to do, then keep it to yourself. It's bad enough that you want to discuss my husband's … size, but I draw the line at Lee." Pointing out the obvious, she adds, "You really need to get some action, don't you?"

"Duh, haven't I been saying that? I don't know how much longer I can sleep with Max and not attack him. I'm ready to throw all my pride away and do something drastic like hump his leg."

She looks puzzled as she studies me. "What are you waiting for then? Do you want him to seduce you or something along those lines?"

With a sigh, I admit, "I know he wants me. I'm not exaggerating when I say that sparks fly when we're together." Looking down at my hands, I add, "He's afraid of breaking me more. He hasn't come right out and said that, but I can read between the lines."

She motions wildly with her hands as she gives me an order. "Go home tonight and have sex. Make him give it to you."

My mouth drops open in shock. She's still glaring at me, which is amusing but a little unsettling as well. Poor Lucian. She must scare the hell out of him when she goes into this bossy mode. "Cool your jets, sister. I get what you're saying, and I agree. It's time to turn up the heat and really let Mr. Decker sweat."

She gives me enthusiastic thumbs up, and then we put the personal talk aside and focus on our work. A part of me never dared to dream I would be here, and regardless of what comes, I'm doing it—living life on my own terms. And I refuse to let anyone take that away from me. Not surprisingly, I haven't heard a word from my parents. In some respects, after so many years of ruling my life, I wonder if they've missed the sick thrill of commanding their subservient daughter.

Max

I've been a nervous wreck all day. I've texted Rose no less than ten times. At one point, Lucian even ordered me to go home, but I knew it would be worse there with nothing to occupy my mind. She sent me a message earlier to let me know that Lia was dropping her at the house around five, and I'd grabbed my briefcase and made my way embarrassingly fast through the lobby of Quinn Software to my car.

Traffic in downtown Asheville is a nightmare, as usual, and I find myself tapping my fingers on the steering wheel impatiently as I move at a snail's pace. When I finally spot my home in the distance, I let out a sigh of relief. I pull into the garage and am at the door leading into the kitchen in seconds. As I step inside, all of my senses are on high alert. I've missed her today. Despite living in each other's pockets for the last two weeks, it wasn't difficult. It's not a concern that has my senses alert, but the need to see her. Touch her. Be with her. The air is fragrant with something that smells amazing. Italian, if I had to guess. Rose is standing at the stove stirring a pot. She turns to give me a cheeky smile as she says, "Welcome home, honey. How was your day?"

I know she is teasing me, but those words sound so damn good that I can't stop myself. In a few strides, I am against her back with my face buried in her hair. My hands go to her hips as I pull her even closer. "Hey, baby," I growl as she pushes her ass back against me.

"Mmm," she moans. "You feel good." My lips are trailing kisses down her neck and my cock is begging for relief when she swats us both down by stepping to the side. She clears her throat loudly. "Um … I can't believe I'm saying this, but I refuse to burn the pasta again. So go set the table while I finishing cooling … er, cooking."

I know if I touch her, she'll cave, and I'm seriously considering it when she trails a hand over the bulge in my pants. "Hold that thought. I plan to thoroughly handle the situation for you this evening." She points the wooden spoon at me. "Don't even think about refusing. I'm done waiting."

Fuck yes. Apparently, we're on the same page tonight. I've been the good guy about as long as I can. I've jacked off so much since she moved in that I am in serious danger of developing carpal tunnel. I could only imagine explaining the cause of that particular injury to my doctor. I even resorted to taking a picture of Rose one morning while she was still sleeping in my bed. The first light of the day had been filtering into the room through the blinds and she'd looked so fucking sexy wearing one of the skimpy nightgowns she'd taken to wearing—no doubt to torture me. The sheet had fallen away at some point exposing the curve of her delectable ass where the gown had ridden up. She'd looked like the perfect mixture of innocent and siren. I'm not proud of it, but that photograph had become regular inspiration in my spank sessions. I always felt a bit like a creeper for doing it, but I couldn't seem to stop myself. She snaps her fingers in front of my face, effectively jolting me back to the present. Obviously, she'd been waiting for a response from me. I surprise myself by slapping her on the ass before growling, "This meal better be fast. Otherwise, I'll be fucking you on the kitchen table and we'll be calling Domino's afterward." Her mouth is hanging open as I leave the kitchen, chuckling under my breath. *That's right, baby, tonight you're all mine.*

I'm rock hard as I gingerly pull the zipper of my jeans past my erection. I've spent the months since meeting Rose fighting my attraction for her. Through it all, though, I feel that it was inevitable we'd end up here. If I'm being truthful, I'm still terrified of letting myself care for another woman, but sometimes in life the choice is taken from you. I can no longer hide from the fact that I'm falling for the beautiful, vivacious, and troubled woman in my kitchen. She's different from anyone I've ever known. My first impression of her was spoiled, repressed, rich girl. That didn't stop me from being attracted to her, but I never would have guessed the number of layers I'd have to peel back to find the true Rose underneath the false bravado.

I've watched her struggling the past few weeks since her hospitalization. I've done my best to keep the mood light so she would be unaware of how worried I've been about her. The last thing I want is for her to feel as if she's under constant scrutiny. But at the same time, I don't want a repeat of what I found the night she almost bled to death on my bathroom floor. I know some of her triggers now, and I try to distract her if I sense she's getting lost in her head. I know that ultimately only she can be responsible for her actions. I can't manage her stress level, nor her need for pain to center herself. But that doesn't mean that I won't try everything in my power to prevent her from hurting herself again.

We've spent every night in each other's arms. She no longer bothers with the pretense of going to the guest room before bed. Her nightgowns are in the drawers I cleaned out for her in my dresser. We stand side by side most evenings as we brush our teeth. I believe she finds comfort in our routine and the ease with which we co-exist. That's not to say you couldn't cut the sexual tension between us with a knife, but even that has become a familiar part of our lives. I've been afraid of initiating sex for fear it would change that dynamic.

Thus far, I haven't learned anything of note from the background check on Rose. A few nights after she came home from the hospital, she became restless in her sleep. She was crying when she awoke. I rocked her gently in my arms as she told me hesitantly about the same dream she'd mentioned to Lucian. I was more convinced than ever that she's blocked out something that happened to her years ago. Either that or she was too young to understand it properly. I am meeting with a new investigator tomorrow who comes highly recommended by Lee Jacks. Lucian had reached out to his father-in-law when we'd been unable to find any further information on our own. I'm going to find out what's haunting my woman's dreams. But tonight, I plan to give her something new to fill her sleeping hours.

"Bad news," I hear from behind me. Turning, I see Rose standing in the doorway, leaning against the frame with a rueful smile tugging at her full lips.

"What's that, sweetheart?" I ask, thinking it can't be too bad if she looks this relaxed.

She moves into the room, never breaking eye contact as her fingers go to the first button on her blouse. She has my attention now that's for damn sure. I'm struggling to keep my eyes from dropping to her chest as another inch of creamy skin is revealed. Fuck it, I'm just a man. There's no way I can take the high road when tits are involved. She shrugs her slim shoulders causing her breasts to jiggle. I growl like an animal, barely hearing her when she says, "It appears I've ruined our meal yet again. I can change clothing if you want to go out to eat. Or we could call—"

"I'm not hungry … for food," I hiss as I bridge the distance between us. I lower my hands to her hips, but let her continue to leisurely tackle the remaining buttons. I note with satisfaction that her hands aren't quite as steady now as she fumbles with the last one. "Need some help, baby?" She shakes her head and bites her lip as she concentrates on the task at hand.

"All right," she squeals as the thin material falls aside and her breasts—in a lacy pushup bra that barely contains them—are revealed. She seems to have forgotten for a moment in her excitement that she's partially naked. I remedy that when my hands come up to pull her bra down and expose her strawberry-tipped nipples. The cold air has the peaks instantly puckering and begging for my attention. "Max ..." she groans as I lower my head to lick and suck one tip into my mouth.

I'm not certain who makes the first move, but we're suddenly a tangle of limbs on my bed. Instead of the hours of leisurely lovemaking I'd imagined, we're both grabbing wildly at each other's clothing. Within moments, we're naked and her hand is on my cock. I'm mere moments away from blowing my load, and that's not how I want our first time to go. I need to slow the momentum or we'll be sitting in the kitchen having dinner within the next ten minutes and Rose will inform Lia tomorrow that I'm the sixty-second man. Hell no, that's not happening. There's plenty of time for quickies later. Tonight, I'll taste the exquisite pussy that I've fantasized about for months. I put my hand over hers, grinding my hips against it for a second before pulling away.

"Lay back and spread your legs, sweetheart." When she remains on her knees staring at my cock as if she's going to weep if she doesn't have it, I straighten my back. This may not have been the best idea since it causes my hard length to bob around like a circus act. "Now, Rose!" I snap, finally jarring her into action.

The sight of her pink pussy glistening with her arousal has me closing my eyes and singing "Ninety-Nine Bottles of Beer" in my head. "Fuck me, Max," she begs huskily, and I fear I'm going to have a stroke. This is like being in a porn movie: Beautiful girl with an amazing body, begging me to fuck her. *Ninety bottles of beer on the wall* ... I gingerly settle onto my stomach, feeling my cock trying to drill a hole into the mattress. I toss her legs over my shoulders. She stiffens under me and tries to bring her thighs together. "No. Please not that," she begs, sounding so different from the passionate woman of moments before.

Then it hits me. She doesn't want me to see her scars. Her hands are attempting to cover the soft skin there as she pulls against my hold on her. "Stop, baby," I whisper. I could release her now and move on to another area of her body, but something tells me that isn't what she really needs. That will only confirm *her* fears that I find her imperfections ugly and that's far from the truth. It pains me to see the evidence of how long and hard she's been crying out for help, with no one listening. The marks are a part of who she is and every one of them tells the story of Rose Madden. Do I hope that another angry red line never mars her body? Absolutely. But I'm in no way repulsed by the ones that do. It's how she has coped with a world that prized perfection above all else. She's begging to be accepted for the person beneath the public face. And I see her. The beautifully imperfect woman who's spent her life feeling as if she was never good enough for the people who were supposed to love her unconditionally.

I nudge her hands aside and begin dropping kisses onto the puckered flesh. A sob catches in her throat as her movements still. "Max," she breathes as my lips attempt to soothe away the hurt she's endured both inside and out. Her hands fall away from her legs and sink into my hair. I seek out and worship each blemish until I reach the one from just a few weeks ago that could have taken her away from me. The area is still a pink pucker, but it's healing quickly.

"You're so beautiful, sweetheart," I murmur against the sensitive flesh there as I tenderly attempt to stroke away the anguish she was feeling the night she hurt herself. The ugly words spoken in that bathroom crushed her so much that she wanted nothing but to flee from it all. "Never think for one single second that I don't adore every inch of this body." I feel her shaking and know that her emotions are close to the surface, so I decide that now is the time to show her exactly what I've been longing for night after night as she slept in my bed.

My head shifts and I've overcome by her scent. A mixture of fucking candy and exotic spices. Unable to help myself, my tongue slips into her folds and I lick her slick cunt. Her hips bow up, and I put my arm over them, bringing her back down onto the bed. "Oh my—sweet, shit!" she yells, and I can't help but grin at her choice of words. *Sweet shit? Yeah, that's a first, but I'll take it.* I suck her swollen clit into my mouth and give it a hard pull as I insert a finger into her wet heat. Her walls are quaking as I alternate fucking her with my mouth and hand. Even though I'm hard enough to cut stone, I'm still almost disappointed when she comes two times in quick succession. *How have I deprived myself of this for so fucking long? Her passion. Her sexual appetite. Her taste.* Her pussy is addictive, and I could eat it all day. Her hands that had been pushing me into her slit are now pulling me almost painfully away. "I want you inside," she gasps out. "Your tongue is killing me."

I laugh as I move up onto my knees before lowering my body down over hers and kissing her softly. I rub my cock against her opening as I grin down at her. "And what exactly do you think my dick is, sweetheart? A walk in the park on Sunday? I'm going to spank this pretty little pussy with it then fuck you until you scream."

As I reach over to grab a condom from the bedside drawer, the little devil bites me on the chin. "You're a lot dirtier in bed than I thought you would be, counselor. Your mouth is downright filthy, and I'm kinda digging it," she purrs.

I smirk in answer as I roll the condom on and decide on a surprise attack. I'm a big boy and I know it. It's probably an asshole move, but I know she's wet enough to take me with possibly only a bite of pain. So I sink into her, bottoming out against her cervix. Her scream fills the room, which might concern me if it weren't followed almost immediately by a moan of pleasure. Her legs come up around my hips, pushing me even deeper. *Eighty bottles of beer on the wall—fuck ... or is it seventy?* I've never been with a woman who seems to love my cock as much as she does. She meets me thrust for thrust, almost chasing my dick down and impaling herself onto it. I'm fast seeing stars and close to severing my tongue as I attempt to hold back. "Come for me, baby. Milk me dry," I beg as we race to the finish. I circle my hips, dragging my root across her clit and feel her detonate under me. My balls tighten and my spine tingles as I pulse a few more times before being taken away by an orgasm that goes on and on. My toes are curling and my ears are roaring as I pull Rose with me and roll to the side—careful to keep our bodies joined. So long. It's been so long, and she's so tight and warm. I do not want to leave her body. My heart is beating overtime, and I'm still seeing stars. Fuck. Me. I knew she was sensual, but holy shit. Finally having her …. At this point, I'd normally be ready to put some distance between my bed partner and me. Say a few nice words then cleanup and move on. But the urge isn't there tonight. I'm in the mood to fucking cuddle, which should be scaring the hell out of me. I haven't done the post-coital snuggle in years—not since Melly died.

Rose melts another piece of ice from my heart as she drops a soft kiss on my chest. "That was …" she begins, and then appears at a loss for words.

"Some sweet shit?" I offer helpfully, and then grunt as she pokes one of her surprisingly bony fingers into my side.

"You're not supposed to judge the words someone says during sex. Your brain can only go in so many directions," she huffs out adorably. "I knew the minute that left my mouth, you were probably laughing your ass off. I don't even know where it came from."

I pull her closer to me; I know we'll have to separate soon, but I want to stay in the moment for as long as possible. A new day is only hours away, but for now, I want to relish feeling like the man I used to be. Before life took away my ability to love. I never thought I'd get that back, but is that where I am headed with Rose? It's only been since her that I've felt this … sense of hope, despite how messed up that must seem. It's her. Love? I think I want that. If only the days ahead could be as peaceful as this moment. But I know with a sense of foreboding that our struggles have just begun.

CHAPTER THIRTEEN

Rose

"You look different today," Dr. Chase—or Joanna, as she prefers to be called—says as she twirls a pen in her hand. The woman is entirely too perceptive. I could utter just a few words, and she is able to put a picture together that is too close for comfort at times. I can see why Lucian likes her, though. Her casual form of therapy is surprisingly relaxing. Sure, we've had some tough conversations, but I always feel better afterward. I've come to think of her as the type of mother figure I always wanted. I'd never confided in either of my parents. They didn't want to hear about school, boys, or arguments with friends. To them, I left home to get an education and anything else was a silly waste of time. Unless it was an affiliation beneficial to furthering their social connections.

I try but am unable to completely keep a smile from my face. I suspect I'm blushing as well but hope she won't notice in the dim lamplight that she favors. "I'm enjoying being back at work," I reply evasively and know there's no way she'll let it go at that. The woman is a human bloodhound.

She props her legs farther under her, displaying wacky knee socks that make me like her even more. She could give a rat's ass about fashion. "That's wonderful. Congratulations." She looks pleased with my news, and I think she's actually been derailed until she says, "Have you and Max been intimate since our last session?" My mouth drops open, and she gives me a slight grin as if to say *gotcha!*

"I—er ... well, hell yes," I grumble. "I fall for that every time." Rolling my eyes, I add, "You lure me and take me down."

Not offended in the least, she laughs and props her head in her hand. "It's my superpower." She fixes me with one of her intent stares. "So how was it?" When I lift a brow, she clarifies, "I mean, were you comfortable with the aftermath? Sex can bring forth some intense emotions, especially when you have feelings for the other person."

I know that Joanna has been wary of Max and I having relations for fear that any problems between us might cause me to cut again. After all, it's only been a few weeks since my last time, and I'd be lying if I said I haven't had the urge. Overall, I'm coping, but I also realize I haven't been truly tested yet. Other than a few stilted emails, my parents have avoided me since I got home from the hospital, and Max has been there every step of the way to keep me from dwelling on anything for very long. I know I can't remain in this bubble forever, though, and that eventually, a stressor may come along and shake my strength. "It was amazing," I say truthfully. "I feel closer to him now, and he seems to feel the same. He's been more affectionate, even before we had sex. This morning we—you know, did it again and it was slower—almost loving."

"You seem surprised by that," she astutely muses. "You've indicated before that he's protective of you, but he appears to have something holding him back. Do you still feel that way?"

"To a degree," I admit. "But it's better than it was. As I said, he's opening up more. We're comfortable around each other and he kept touching me as we were getting ready and having breakfast together this morning."

"So why don't you ask him about his past?" she asks, sounding curious. "Are you afraid he won't talk to you about it or is it something else?"

I run a hand through my hair, trying to gather my thoughts. I'm not sure why this question is hard, but then it hits me and I feel a moment's panic. "I'm scared it will change things between us. What if he can never love me? Right now, I have hope that it will work out, but what if it's taken away from me?"

"That's everyone's fear in a relationship, Rose," she says gently. "To open yourself up to love is also to expose yourself to the possibility of loss. Unfortunately, you're only living half a life without the risk."

"But isn't the reward worth it when it works out?" I ask, hesitantly. A woman my age shouldn't be so damn uncertain of a man, but I can't help it. I've never felt for anyone the way I do for Max. "Damn, you're right. We probably shouldn't have slept together."

"Then why did you?" she asks, looking at me intently.

I blurt it out, knowing she can handle the truth. "Because I was horny and I'm also in love with him. The first was a very pressing need, and the second just made it that much better." I'm surprised at how easily I've revealed the depth of my feelings for Max to Joanna. But there is just something about talking to someone who isn't a part of our group. It's almost as if I want to see her reaction before I tell the rest of the world.

Never one to be rattled by my off-color comments, she points her pen at me and says, "And there you have it, my friend. The two things that will make us go out onto a limb every time—love and lust. No one is immune to the power they hold, and it's probably one of the best parts of that new relationship glow." Then she reaches over and clasps one of my hands. "Enjoy this time, Rose, and take each moment as it comes. Continue to communicate with Max and be open about what you're feeling. If you get overwhelmed or uncertain, then tell him. He's your partner, not someone you need to protect. From what you've told me about him, he wants to be there for you, and as daunting as it may sound, you need to accept that and let him. Love and lust are wonderful, but trust is what will move you forward and give you the building blocks for a lasting foundation." We spend the rest of the hour discussing my parents and also the dream I'd had off and on since childhood. As usual, when I leave, I'm exhausted while also feeling lighter. It's not easy to reveal so many personal things, and at times, I want to resist. But at least I feel as if I'm beginning to face my problems instead of hiding from them. There's a sense of the elusive control I've struggled to have for so many years. Could it have been as simple as letting someone in?

I take a cab back to the office. Lucian has insisted on loaning me a company car from Quinn Software until I'm able to afford something of my own. Someone is supposed to drop it by this afternoon. Strangely enough, Max hadn't been too happy over it. He'd grumbled under his breath that he'd been planning to get me one. But I'd rather borrow one than let Max spend any more money on me. I'm not used to being the charity case in the group and it's unsettling. I refused to accept Lia's offer to pay me for the time I'd been off work. That was more of a handout than I could handle. At this rate, it's already going to be months before I can pay Max back. And I know that's going to be a fight. He's made it clear that he does not intend to take my money. I don't think he understands how important it is to me to feel as if I'm standing on my own two feet. Even if it takes me a while to do that without stumbling.

I pull my phone from my purse to check in with Max. He's always concerned after one of my therapy sessions, and I want to send him a quick text to let him know that I survived. I go warm and mushy when I see a message already waiting from him.

Hey baby, thinking of you and hoping you had a good meeting with Joanna. Miss you.

I startle the cab driver when I throw my head back and begin laughing. Max Decker, normally reserved counselor extraordinaire, used a heart emoticon at the end of his text … and it's about the sweetest thing ever. I hit the reply button and quickly type a response.

Everything went great. Miss you too. Can't wait to be home.

I then add an emoticon of a kitten blowing kisses. It's hard to believe that I'm doing something so normal with him. If he brings out the best in me, then I hope I do the same for him.

As giddy as I am, the fear is still there. I've opened myself to Max in a way that I never did with Jake. I'm terrified that, at some point, I'll disappoint him, and he'll realize that underneath it all, I'm just too big of a mess to deal with. I shake off the negative thoughts as soon as they come. I refuse to do that—to keep buying in to the shit my parents shoveled at me for years. At this point, they're barely even a part of my life anymore. It's all on me. I'm in charge now. There may be setbacks, and some days aren't going to be rainbows and kittens, but dammit, the alternative is unacceptable. Failure could well end up in my death, and that's no longer a risk I'm willing to overlook.

I step out of the car in front of my office and throw my shoulders back. "One day at a time," I say under my breath, as I take another leap into the life I want to live.

At that point, I had no idea that my new resolve would be tested so soon.

Max

Lucian and I take a seat at the conference room table at Quinn Software. Before we say more than a few words,

Cindy escorts in Don Ellis, the investigator Lee Jacks had recommended. I've had several conversations with him on the telephone, but today is our first face-to-face. To date, he's been terse yet professional, and as Lucian and I rise to our feet and introductions are made, I feel a little in awe. I wouldn't want to be on the wrong side of this man.

Don pulls an iPad from his briefcase, and I have to smile at how things have changed. It seems as if handwritten notes are no longer the norm. I rather miss it sometimes. Although considering my vast collection of electronics, I don't think I'd be willing to go back again. He scrolls through the screen before setting it down on the table and clearing his throat. "I found nothing unusual on Ms. Madden's background check." I feel a sense of something like disappointment. "But then I enhanced the search to include her family and things got a little interesting."

When he pauses as if to gauge our reaction, Lucian waves a demanding hand and asks impatiently, "Are you going to continue, or are we supposed to guess?"

Instead of being offended at Lucian's bluntness, Don smirks, which should have told me something big was coming. "There's no record of Celia Madden having given birth—ever."

I process his words before rubbing my neck to ease the tension building there. "So you're saying that Rose was adopted?"

Don leans back in his chair and crosses his legs before shaking his head. "No. See, that's the interesting part. I can't find any record of that either, and believe me, I've been through every database there is—twice."

"But isn't that type of information sealed?" Lucian asks.

Don raises a brow as if to say, *Come on.* "I have ways around that. There is nothing sealed or otherwise to show that Rose Madden was adopted. Essentially, she has a birth certificate with nothing at all to back it up. That in itself is more common than you would think, but generally, there's something criminal involved. Everyone has an origin, and if it's being hidden, there's a reason."

I'm grasping at straws, but I toss it out there anyway. "That's probably not something that most people ever have checked. Maybe it's a clerical error somewhere." I vaguely recall a case that we studied while I was in school at Stanford Law. It's been a while since I've delved into family law, but I do recall very strict punishment.

"It's not," Don says flatly. "Her birth certificate is worth the paper it's written on and that's it. It looks completely normal until you research it and find that there are no actual records to support her birth."

Lucian tosses the pen he's been holding onto the table in frustration. "I knew there was something there. Maybe it's time we confronted her parents. They're a bunch of pretentious assholes, but I didn't actually think they were criminals."

Don holds a hand out hastily. "Don't do that yet. If you tip them off, they'll muddy the trail as much as they can. Right now, it's been years since Rose's birth, and I would imagine they've relaxed their guard. It'll be easier to dig without them being suspicious."

"Do you have any clues as to what we're looking for?" I ask, still reeling from his news.

"I've been running checks into their household staff, going all the way back to when Celia would have supposedly been pregnant. I wanted to see if I could find anyone who might be willing to talk to me. In doing so, I've come across Carl and Patricia Wheeten, a husband and wife who worked for the Maddens for ten years. They both left right after Rose's birth. They had a daughter who would have been fifteen at the time, Daisy Wheeten."

Lucian shrugs his shoulder. "Okay. Do they still live locally?"

"Carl passed away a few years ago, and Patricia lives with her sister in Alabama. But Daisy's the person I'd really like to speak with." If he doesn't provide more information, and soon, then I will snap. Having known Lucian for many years, I can sense his tension too. "She had a baby two days before Rose was born. And I haven't found any record of *that* child from the time Daisy and her *daughter* left the hospital."

"Fuck," Lucian spits out.

The lawyer in me doesn't believe in coincidences. "Did she name the baby Poppy?" I ask, and then hold my breath awaiting his reply.

He gives me a rueful smile. "That I don't know. The birth certificate says Baby Wheeten. And it was never updated. There is also no father listed. Before you ask, I've checked the death records as well. If the baby died, it wasn't recorded through official channels."

"So my girlfriend's a ghost," I murmur uneasily. In a way, I'm relieved that she doesn't appear to be the biological daughter of such assholes as the Maddens. But the question remains … who is she? Could there be a link to the Wheetens?

"She's certainly a mystery," Don agrees before getting to his feet. "I have a few leads to follow up on. I'll be in touch as soon as I know more."

Lucian walks him out, then returns to flop down in his chair. "We certainly don't pick boring women to love, do we?"

"No, we don't," I agree wryly. "Which way are you leaning with all of this?"

He looks thoughtful for a moment. "I'd assume she was adopted if not for the fact that there's nothing to support that. And I know my father-in-law well enough to guarantee that Don knows what he's talking about. If he says he looked in all places, then he did. You and I both never believed that her recurring dream was random, and after what he said, I'm positive there's more."

"Are the Wheetens the key?" I ask, curious as to his take.

"I'll be shocked as hell if they aren't," he replies instantly. "I'd just like to know where they've been for the last twenty-three years. I think we can rule out Rose being abducted because the Maddens are too high profile and have made no attempt to limit her exposure to the public. Exactly the opposite. They've lived in the same house since Rose was born. The Wheetens would know exactly where to find them. The daughter was fifteen when Rose was born, so certainly old enough to know where her baby went."

I knock my fist against the table in frustration. "Then what in the hell are we missing?"

"I don't know." Lucian sighs. "But I'd love to rattle the cage of her pompous ass of a father and see what shakes out." When I open my mouth to remind him of what Don said, he adds, "I know, and I won't do anything—yet. But when and if we get the information that we need, all bets are off."

"I'll drive," I deadpan, thinking I'd love nothing better than to have a few words with Hoyt Madden about the way he's treated his daughter. He doesn't deserve to have a woman like her in his life. Wherever this road leads, I'll be there for her. She's getting stronger every day. After years of having it shredded, I can see her self-confidence slowly building. I pray she's strong enough for what lies ahead because I'm afraid her strength is going to be tested sooner than I would have liked. I'll do everything in my power to ensure that she's ready, but ultimately this is her life and she'll be the one to suffer for the sins of her parents. But this time, she won't suffer alone.

Rose

Lia is waiting for me in my office when I return. She looks nervous, and I'm instantly concerned. "What's wrong?" I ask as I drop my purse onto my desk. "Is everything okay with Lucian and Lara?"

"Yeah, of course." She waves away my question. Then she squeezes her eyes closed for a moment before opening them again. "Please don't be mad at me. It just happened. I was getting a sandwich for lunch, and he was right there when I turned around. Then he asked about you, and, shit, I lost it, Rose. I went off on him, and now, you're going to be pissed off." She twists her hands together in agitation. "I didn't mean to tell him anything. And now, he's here wanting to see you. I tried to get him to leave. But it's not working and—"

"Whoa." She's rambling as she always does when she's upset, and I know this can go all day if I don't stop her. Besides, I'm completely lost here. "What in the world are you talking about, chick? Let's start with who you saw at lunch?"

She hesitates for a few seconds before saying, "Jake."

I don't know why, but I wasn't expecting it to be him. Since that night at Leo's, whenever he's crossed my mind, I've instantly tried to redirect my thoughts. He does not deserve any more of my energy, thought, or time. "What happened?" I ask quietly, motioning Lia over to the small seating area in the corner. I close the door before sitting on the sofa next to her.

She takes my hand, although I think the support is more for her than me at this point. "I picked up my food and was turning to leave Greta's and there he was. He asked how you were and where you were living now. He said he's been by your apartment but found out you'd moved." She cringes before adding, "I have no idea what came over me, but I was in his face before I could stop myself. Crap, Rose, I told him about what happened with his girlfriend and how much it upset you."

"Lia!" I groan in horror. "Please say you didn't tell him about my hospital trip after that?" The last thing I needed was Jake having more information to give to bitch Barbie and her friend. I was a laughing stock with them already.

"No, I didn't tell him about that," she hurriedly assures me. I let out the breath I'd been holding. "But I think he knew anyway, or maybe he was worried that something could have happened," she adds, and my sense of relief flies right out the window.

Air. I need air. Space. I stand and begin pacing the distance of the small room. I can feel the sweat gathering at my temple. My hands are beginning to shake. *No, Rose. You don't have to submit to this attack.* Listen to Joanna's voice here, not your own. *If you panic but* stay in the situation *until you calm down, your panic response will learn that it's not the situation causing the panic.* Okay, I can do this. Jake cannot hurt me. He will not cause a panicked response. Breathe in and breathe out. *Yes, Rose, you can do this.* I stop the pacing, ready to know more. I can't imagine why Jake would care. It sounded from Barbie that he was happy to have me off his hands. "Why would he think that? Are you sure you didn't accidentally let it slip?"

"Of course, not," she snaps. "I believe I'd remember that." Then, as if catching herself, she lowers her voice once again and gives me an apologetic smile. "You guys were together for a long time, Rose, and you said he knows about your—cutting. So wouldn't it be reasonable to assume that he might be concerned?" When I don't answer, she rushes on. "Anyway, I walked off and left him standing there after I gave him a piece of my mind. The next thing I know, the receptionist is ringing to let me know that he's here. During my rant, I told him that you were doing great and we were working together. So he followed me here in hopes of seeing you. He insists that he only wants to apologize."

I drop my head in my hands and moan, "Oh God. Why me? The man cheats on me, then makes fun of me to his girlfriend, and now, he wants what, forgiveness?" I laugh hysterically for a moment, prompting Lia to begin biting her nails. The poor thing, I've been back for two days and she's on the edge of a nervous breakdown. I wonder if our relationship was like this in the past? Has my behavior caused Lia stress or have I hidden it so well that Lia had always seen me as the strong one? Flawless?

She stands and straightens her spine. I bite back a smile as I literally see her put on her game face. "I'll get rid of him. If I have to, I'll call the police and have them drag him out kicking and screaming."

A giggle escapes as that mental picture presents itself. It would almost be worth it. But maybe I need to put the big-girl panties on and fight my own battles. Joanna and I haven't tackled the AWARE technique yet, but she has explained it to me, and I can recall the first letter. A – *Accept the anxiety. Don't try to fight it.* Avoiding Jake is just another way of running from my problems. He should be the one hiding, not me. I've done nothing wrong. "You know what? I will talk to him. I have a few things to say, and since he's here, I'll take advantage of it and unload."

"Are you sure?" Lia asks looking uneasy. "Do you want me to stay with you?"

I have no idea why, but I hitch my pants up, then wince because now, I've got a wedgie. Shit, that always looks so much cooler in the movies. I discreetly pull them back down again and breathe a sigh of relief when things return to their rightful place. I throw my arm around her shoulders and give her a side hug. "I've got this, sweetie. And please don't worry about any of it. I love you for wanting to kick his ass for me. You're the best friend that anyone could have, and I've gotta say, I can see why Lucian can't keep his hands off you. I was kind of turned on myself when you started all that raging about Jake."

Lia blinks rapidly and then falls against the wall as laughter shakes her small frame. "You're such a weirdo," she gasps out. "For a minute there, you had me."

I wiggle my brows as I push her aside and open the door. "Who says I was kidding?" I do my best to keep a straight face as I walk toward the reception area. She is so easy to shock. How could she still be so innocent after growing up in such an ugly environment? I'm grateful she has Lucian. He'll forever keep the wolves at bay and no evil will darken her door again.

Any amusement I feel dies as I see my ex-boyfriend and the man I once thought I'd spend my life with perched on the edge of a leather chair in the waiting area. His foot is drumming nervously on the floor as he stares off into space. As if sensing my presence, he suddenly looks right at me, and I see his eyes widen before he gets to his feet. He stops a few inches away and puts his hands in his pockets. His voice is husky and deep as he says, "Rose, It's ... um, good to see you again." Then he waves a hand to indicate my clothing. "You look different—beautiful—but not like yourself. Shit, that didn't come out right. You always look good. It's just, you've changed." His usual confident manner is nowhere to be seen as he shifts on his feet before glancing over at the receptionist who's watching us with rapt attention.

Not wanting to air my dirty laundry in public, I point down the hall. "Would you like to use one of the conference rooms?" My office would have been more private, but it's also smaller and more intimate, and I'm not comfortable with that. Even though I realize it's impossible, I still want to keep things as impersonal as I can. Plus, I don't want him in my space. He doesn't belong there.

"Yeah, that'd be great." He sighs, sounding relieved.

I flip the lights on in one of the empty rooms and motion him in ahead of me. I take a seat at the head of the table, thinking that maybe it will give me a sense of being in charge. Silly to need that, but I'm happy to take any advantage I can. He settles in the chair next to mine and clasps his hands together on top of the table. "So what can I do for you, Jake?" I ask, focusing on some point beyond his shoulder. I may not love him anymore, but it's still hard to look into the eyes of someone who hurt me so badly. A man I trusted with my secrets. A man I trusted to keep his damn dick in his pants. *Shit, now I'm pissed again, and it feels good—no, great.*

He clears his throat loudly, and I wait for him to ask for water, but he doesn't. He gets right to the point. "Lia told me what happened with Mercedes, and I wanted to say that I'm—"

"Mercedes? That's your girlfriend's name?" I begin laughing and can't seem to stop. I fall against the back of the chair, fanning myself as I attempt to get it together. "Was Volkswagen already taken? How about Volvo? Too tame? Not classy enough for a girl like her?" Instead of being angry, Jake seems to be slinking lower into his seat as if embarrassed. *Amazing*; he cheated on me with a girl named after a fucking car. He doesn't say a word as I have my slightly manic moment before wiping away the tears of amusement that had fallen down my cheeks. "Okay, um, sorry about that." I flex my aching jaw and say, "Go ahead with what you were saying."

"I'm sorry." He says this quickly, probably afraid I'll interrupt him again before he can get it out. "It wasn't like I could hide the fact that you trashed my car," he adds almost defensively, and then he seems to crumble. He actually looks as if he may cry. *This* is not the Jake Ryan I knew. A contrite man he was not. "I should never have told her about the—other thing." He puts a hand over mine, squeezing it tightly. "I promise you, Rose. I never made fun of you to her. Regardless of what happened between us, I'd never do that. I loved you too much—hell, I still love you. I just couldn't be what you needed."

"What's that?" I mock him. "Faithful? Yeah, that was evident with the whole screwing around thing. Us woman are so unrealistic in our expectations, aren't we?" *All right, that may have been a tad bitchy, even for me. But what does he expect? A pat on the head and a fucking cookie?*

"Dammit, Rose, can you just stop for a minute and let me talk?" he bites out. "I know you think I'm a dickhead and you're not wrong. But I'm trying here, okay?"

I want to slap him and stomp out of the room. My hand is itching to connect with his smoothly shaven cheek, but the pleading look in his eyes stops me. Jake's always been an open book. That's how I knew he was cheating on me. I see nothing but sincerity and regret as he stares at me. Maybe I need this as much as he does. We have a lot of history between us, and it's always bothered me that he threw our relationship away and hurt me so badly. Rubbing the bridge of my nose, I say quietly, "I'm listening."

"This is hard for me to admit," he says while studying the table. "But I couldn't handle the pressure of you cutting yourself. I was scared shitless that my actions would drive you to it. Then I moved on to being paranoid that you'd kill yourself over something I did or didn't do. I didn't know how to be what you needed." He looks shamefaced. "When Mercedes pursued me, I was flattered but not interested. I wasn't lying when I said that I love you. I always have, almost to the point of obsession. But it was so complicated—and she wasn't. I didn't have to worry about what I said or did around her because her balls are probably bigger than mine," he jokes weakly.

The urge to feel sorry for him is there again. Then I remember how it felt when his girlfriend made fun of me in the bathroom, and the anger is back, surging through me until I'm ready to explode. "You had options, Jake," I hiss. "Why not just be a man and break up with me? And you certainly could have made the choice *NOT* to tell Mercedes about my scars." I sneer at him. "How could you do that? You damn well knew that I'd never told anyone about that. But you and your girlfriend laughed at me like I was some kind of hideous joke." My voice echoes through the room, and probably down the hallway as well, but I'm too far gone to care.

"I never laughed at you!" He pounds a fist on the table. "I was literally crying in my fucking beer over you one night and I said more than I should have. She was acting the part of the concerned friend, and I told her how much I missed you. Then she asked why I slept with her if I still wanted you ... and it just came out. Swear to God, though, we never joked about it. Actually, it wasn't brought up again. She was lying about that." He sounds almost hopeful when he says, "I'm breaking up with her today. I can't be with someone like that. She isn't who I thought she was—she's not you."

I need to defuse this situation now. Unless I'm wrong, Jake wants more than to apologize. I get to my feet and he does the same. I step back to keep distance between us. I don't need his proclamation of love now. I needed it a long time ago. But not now. I need nothing from him now. "Thank you for coming to talk to me. I know it couldn't have been easy." I can give him that much. I don't think I'll ever be able to forgive him for everything that's happened, but I do feel better knowing that he wasn't tearing me down to others. That hurt me as bad or worse than the infidelity. I try not to think about how many people Mercedes has likely told about my situation. I'm slowly trying to accept that I can't be responsible for the actions of others—only my own.

He bridges the distance and puts a hand on my arm. "Could I take you to dinner—to let you know how sorry I am? If you'll let me know where you're staying now, I can pick you up tonight. Did you move back in with your parents? I called there but kept getting their machine."

"Jake, that's not happening. I appreciate you taking the time to see me today, but I'm involved with someone else. Actually, I'm living with him." As I'm not looking directly at Jake when I tell him, I can't see his expression. But by the quick intake of air and lowering of the head, followed by his telltale stroke of the back of his neck, I can sense he wasn't expecting that answer.

Taking me by surprise, he says, "You always deserved better than me. I hope you've found it now." I'm still speechless as he drops a kiss on my cheek and leaves the room.

I feel as if a weight has been lifted from my shoulders. My past is slowly making way for my future, and the fear I've lived with for so long is losing its grip on me. I'm still in control. *Accept the anxiety. Don't try to fight it.* I'm still in control. Joanna will be proud. Bring on the next bombshell. I've got this.

How I'll regret even thinking that in the days to come because fate took it a little too literally.

CHAPTER FOURTEEN

Rose

I'm shaking my ass and doing a terrible job singing along to Flo Rida's "Going Down for Real" as I wash the breakfast dishes from this morning. Max and I had been running late—for a very good reason—and we'd piled them in the sink before we left. He has what is no doubt an expensive dishwasher, but this little piece of domesticity feels good. *Maybe I'll wash his underwear next; that might bring me back down to earth.*

No sooner has that thought occurred, I hear the doorbell ringing. I swear to God, if it's the Girl Scouts selling those evil Lemonades again, I won't be responsible for my actions. *All right, maybe I'll buy another damn box and eat them all in one sitting. Shit, I need to throw that last empty box away before Max finds it.*

I look through the peephole and feel my heart plummet—what is my father doing here? Yeah, I've been brought back down with a screeching halt. My father is an expert at that. I ponder not opening the door, but then I'll just have to worry about him showing up at my office tomorrow. After Jake, I think I've had enough unexpected visitors there for the week. I take a deep breath and skip the part about pulling my pants up. I learned my lesson on that one earlier. Holy crap, he's literally laying on the doorbell now. *Ask not for whom the bell tolls...*

I wrench the door open just as his finger hovers over the small circle, ready to push it again. "Go ahead, I don't think the neighbors heard you the first ten times," I say sarcastically.

His eyebrows shoot up into his hairline as if he's amazed I would speak to him that way. I have to remember that he has no sense of humor whatsoever, whereas Max or even Lucian would laugh over that line. He straightens the jacket of his suit and grumbles, "What took you so long? I've got better things to do with my time that stand here all day."

I roll my eyes and bite my tongue. I'd love nothing better than to remind him that no one invited him, but I don't. He pushes by me and walks into the foyer. I wave my hand out, saying, "Do come in." He completely misses the slight jab, simply waiting for me to close the door and join him.

For years I was trained to be the perfect hostess, so I find myself reluctantly asking, "Would you like to sit down? The living room is just around the corner."

"Hardly," he huffs out. "What I'd like is for you to go pack your things. It's time for this silly little tantrum of yours to end. You've had your fun and managed to humiliate your mother and me in the process." He looks down at his watch before barking out, "Now, hurry along. We're having the Beardens over for cocktails tonight, and it is rude to keep them waiting."

I'm standing in the bedroom before it hits me: I'm following his orders like a trained dog. I feel sick to my stomach realizing how easily I just bowed to his command. *What am I doing?* There is no way I'm going home. I'm not even sure that I can call it that. *Home.* A penal facility would be more accurate, and the man in the entryway waiting impatiently for me to obey is my warden. I slowly retrace my steps, and he looks confused that I have nothing in my hands. "First of all," I begin quietly, "you saw to it that I had nothing but the clothes on my back when you cleaned out my apartment."

He looks me up and down before saying contemptuously, "Well, if what you're wearing is any indication, you don't need to bother bringing anything with you. You're dressed like a cheap harlot."

I inhale sharply, literally choking on air as I stare at him aghast. He just called me a whore. This is a new low, even for him. The urge to run and change into something he'll find presentable is so strong; it's suffocating me with its intensity.

"You ... need to leave," I manage to get out. My hands shake at my sides.

He has his phone in his hand, typing on it as if I don't deserve a moment of his undivided attention. "And we shall. Hurry. Up." He walks toward the door, and then glances back when he realizes I'm not following him.

Squaring my shoulders, I say evenly, "I said you need to leave. I won't be going with you. This is my home—at least for now."

He's baffled at first as he darts a glance at his watch before raising his eyebrows in irritation. Then, at last, my meaning becomes clear, and he's pissed. I can see the vein throbbing on his forehead as his face takes on a molten-red color. "You've lost your mind! You're playing house with someone you hardly know and making a fool of yourself in the process. What opinion could he have of a girl who gives herself over so freely? You're an embarrassment to the Madden name. Your mother and I have been forced to cover for you, but that can't continue." Pointing to my clothing once again, he shouts, "Sooner or later one of them will see you looking like *that* and it'll be over. We'll be the laughing stock of the club."

"Get out," I whisper as he continues to rant. "Get out. Get out," I chant before bellowing at the top of my lungs, "GET OUT!"

He jerks as if a bullet entered his body. Right now, he'd better be glad I don't have a gun in my well-trained hand.

"Now, listen—"

"Get the hell out of my house and don't come back," I say in a voice so deadly calm that it makes him look uneasy. I've now moved around him and thrown open the door.

The glare he gives as he stalks past is something I've never seen before. It looks like disdain. Not indifference. There's ... contempt. The door slams so hard behind him that a nearby picture crashes to the ground. I stare at it as if not comprehending how it got there. *Broken. Broken glass.*

I'm broken. Broken glass.

The only thing on my mind is escape, and I know how to do it.

God help me because I'm not sure I can stop myself this time.

Max

It's almost seven by the time I make it home. I had a late meeting to review a potential acquisition for Quinn Software that I'd been putting off for a few weeks since it wasn't a pressing matter. But both Rose and I had to return to our normal schedules sometime, and this week has seen me catching up on mine. When I pull into the garage, I smile when I see on one side the company car that Lucian loaned Rose. It feels better than I imagined coming home to someone again.

Going through the motions of retrieving the mail is even more interesting. *Weird, Decker.* I'm whistling under my breath and thumbing through circulars as I open the door and walk into the kitchen. I toss the pile onto the table and am almost in the hallway when something makes me turn and do a quick check of the surrounding area.

Then I see her. "Shit," I hiss under my breath.

Wedged in the corner beside the stove. Even from a distance, I can see her body shaking and her teeth chattering. But it's the glint of the light reflected off the object in her hands that has my heart stuttering. *Be calm; don't startle her,* I think, as I slowly make my way over to her. I've seen this expression on her face before. She's staring straight ahead as if in some kind of trace. I visually inspect her, looking for any signs of blood, but see nothing. *Thank fuck.* Her hand tightens and loosens upon the handle of the blade she's holding, and I fight the urge to wrestle it away from her. I can't risk her hurting herself in the process. I need to be very careful here.

I crouch, bringing myself down to her level. I see no reaction from her to indicate that she's aware of my presence yet. "Hey baby, I'm home. I see you've been in the silverware drawer again." I wince, thinking this might not be one of those times to make light of things. Her expression is still blank, so I settle onto the floor next to her, trying to fit my large frame into the small space. "So what do you feel like for dinner? How about some Chinese?" Giving a forced chuckle, I add, "I'd say pasta, but somehow, you manage to burn it every time." As if my words are getting through to her, the hand that was clenching the knife pauses. Her eyes are still unfocused, so I continue rambling. "Guess what, sweetheart? Cindy and Sam made it official today. Can you believe that? I mean, it's not as if we didn't already know that they were an item, but they have still insisted on keeping it secret at the office. Of course, I guess it has to come out since they're engaged now." I put a hand on her knee, squeezing it lightly. "She came in wearing the ring this morning, and she'd probably shown it to half the building in the first hour alone. Luc looked a little green when I teased Sam about the honeymoon." I laugh. "He said it's too much like discussing his parents having sex."

"Max?" I freeze when she says my name, then feel like I can take the first proper breath since finding her, as some of the fear begins to unwind within me.

I struggle to keep my voice level as I reply. "Yeah, it's me, baby."

She looks confused as if she has no idea why we're both sitting on the floor. Then I see the moment her eyes fall on the knife in her hand. Her face goes deathly pale as she looks down at her lap, obviously searching for signs of injury just as I had. "I didn't do it, Max," she wheezes out. "I wanted to so badly that I was afraid I wouldn't be able to hold out."

I take the blade from her trembling hand and set it to the side. The sound of the metal hitting the tiled floor seems unusually loud. I get to my feet, then lean back down and pull her into my arms. She wraps her arms around my neck and her legs encircle my waist. I walk slowly to the bedroom and manage to maneuver us both onto to bed. I prop my back against the headboard and she releases her legs from my waist to lie on top of me. My arms go around her. One hand strokes her hair while the other caresses her back. "Well done, baby. You didn't cut. What happened, sweetheart?" I ask as I kiss the top of her head. She has been doing so well lately, that I'm thrown by what has happened. This could have been so much worse.

"Jake came to see me today at work," she begins softly. I feel myself stiffen under her as jealousy rips through me. As if she feels the change in me, she rubs my side reassuringly. "That's not what upset me tonight, but I wanted to tell you about it. Lia ran into him while she was getting lunch and told him about what his girlfriend said at Leo's that night."

I sigh, tightening my grip on her. "Shit."

"I wasn't too happy at first," she admits. "I didn't want him to have the satisfaction of knowing he'd hurt me again. But in the end, it was a good thing. We managed to clear the air of some things I'd wondered about. I'm not saying we'll ever be friends again, but at least I don't think he's quite the bastard I thought he was. In the end, he wasn't strong enough to deal with what I'm battling, and I'd be a bitch not to understand that." With a helpless laugh, she adds, "I'm not doing too well handling it either, am I?"

I ignore her question for now and ask instead, "What happened to upset you?"

Her breath quickens against my chest, and it's on the tip of my tongue to tell her to forget it for now. "My father came over. It was ugly, Max, and when he left, I wanted nothing more than to find an outlet for all the pain. I needed the release that cutting gives me. I ran into the kitchen and grabbed a knife from the drawer." She lifts her head and looks at me, her eyes searching for something, and then appearing satisfied when she sees it. "Then I thought of you. These past two weeks here have been the happiest of my life. And I didn't want to lose them. I was at war with myself. I wanted that sharp tip to penetrate my skin more than I wanted my next breath. But at the same time, I couldn't stomach how it would make you feel to find me like that again. And what if I went too far?" A tear drips from her face and onto me as she confesses, "I love you, Max, and that's the one thing that makes me want to fight. I never had a reason before because no one cared whether I lived or died. You may not love me, but I know that you feel something. It's evident every time we're together. I matter to you, don't I?"

She looks so uncertain yet hopeful that it shatters my heart. "Oh baby," I murmur brokenly. I take her face in my hands and wipe the tears with my thumbs. "I love you, too, beautiful girl. I can't fight it anymore. I never thought I'd feel this way again. Hell, I never wanted to, but you own me, Rose Madden, heart and soul."

Our lips lock in a kiss so tender, it shakes my very foundation. There is nothing sexual about it. Quite simply, it's the non-verbal expression of our love for each other.

"Who was she? The woman you loved before me?" I tense. I don't detect any note of jealousy or insecurity in her voice. There is curiosity there and something that sounds like compassion, as if she knows that my first love ended in tragedy.

I've never opened up about Melly before, and it's incredibly difficult. But Rose deserves to know about the person who shaped so much of who I am. I reach to the side and pull the blanket over us as I get my thoughts in order. She seems content to let me go at my own pace. Finally, I clear my throat and begin. "I met Melanie on the first day of college. Actually, we were both running late for class and plowed into each other. I was drenched in her coffee and cursing up a storm. She began laughing hysterically as if seeing me dripping wet with the hot liquid was the funniest thing ever. I should have been pissed, but that was the thing about Melly. It was impossible to be angry around her. She found humor in even the worst situations."

"And you were the serious one," Rose says softly.

I draw lazy circles on her hip as I nod my head. "I was indeed. When you meet my parents, you'll understand where I get that. My father is a lawyer and my mother is a tenured professor. There wasn't much in the way of laughing or being silly in the Decker household growing up. I know they loved me, but they're two people who take everything in life seriously, so I was pretty much the same way. I was facing four years of college and then more years of law school so a girlfriend wasn't anywhere in the cards for me. After that morning, we seemed to run into each other everywhere. We became friends and almost without me noticing, it was more."

Rose traces a finger down my cheek, seeming to understand how hard this story is for me. "You can finish another time if you need to," she offers.

I turn my head to her hand and place a kiss in the palm. "I'm fine, sweetheart. I want you to know everything." I blow out a small breath and continue. "Melly and I were together for all four years of college. When I was accepted into Stanford Law School, I asked her to move to California with me and she agreed. She'd gotten her degree in elementary education and easily found a position as a student teacher at a school there. Everything was arranged and the night before we were to leave, I took her out for a nice dinner and proposed to her—and she said yes." I pause, looking down at Rose to gauge her reaction to my revelation.

"Please don't worry about me. This is a part of your life, and it helped shape you into who you are. Let me shoulder some of your pain as you've done for me."

I hug her to me tightly for a moment before relaxing my grip. "On our way back to the apartment we'd shared for the last year, we were hit while sitting at a traffic light by a group of teenagers who'd been to a party. The driver's blood alcohol level was more than three times the legal amount allowed. There were four of them in the car and two of us. Out of the six of us, only Melly was hurt badly. I had no idea at the time, but later, they discovered she hadn't been wearing a seat belt. I'd never known her not to be buckled up so that in itself was strange. She was thrown through the windshield and onto the hood of the car. I was disoriented after the impact and must have lost consciousness for a while. By the time I was able to get free of my airbag, emergency vehicles were arriving. Melly's airbag had deployed as well, but not in time to keep her from being ejected from the car. Rose, seeing her laying there in that blood, with shards of glass surrounding her, terrified me. When I got to her and found a pulse ..." I pause, trying to shake that horrific scene from my mind. "After that, things were a blur for a while. We were all taken to the hospital where police were waiting to question us. Melly went into surgery immediately because she had so many injuries along with probable internal bleeding."

"That's how you met Matt, isn't it?" she guesses astutely.

Inclining my head, I say, "Yes, he was the attending physician that night. He went beyond the call of duty for us and it forged a friendship that I treasure. He did everything in his power to save Melly. She lived for almost four weeks after the accident. Each time we thought she'd turned a corner, something else happened. I don't think she would have had that extra time to say goodbye to everyone without Matt. She was in a coma for the first few weeks, but then she came out of it and we thought that was a good sign. But her internal injuries were so severe that her organs just started shutting down and they couldn't stop it. She was on a ventilator for the last week, and her parents had to make the decision to remove it when her brain activity ceased."

Rose is openly crying against me and I realize with a start that I am as well. "I was so broken after Melanie's death that I never really grieved her. I locked my heart away and jumped into law school, where I pushed myself to the point of exhaustion. I'd been grateful that my school was so far away from home because it gave me the perfect excuse to leave everyone behind. I didn't have to face Melly's parents, who were devastated by her passing, and I didn't have to pretend that my own parents weren't staring at me as if waiting for me to crack. There was a certain kind of comfort in being completely anonymous and I embraced it. I never once came home the entire time I was at Stanford. After the first two years, my parents stopped asking me and accepted that I needed the distance."

"Thank you for taking a chance and loving me," Rose surprises me by saying. "Just risking your heart again under normal circumstances must have been hard. But then having to deal with my ... problems ... has to be so terrifying for you." She pulls away and moves to sit next to me. "I love you, Max, but please don't let me put you through more hell than you can handle. How can you not be worried that despite my best efforts, you won't lose someone else you care about?"

Her words hit me hard, as they are the same ones I've thought dozens of times since I picked her up on the street that night. I'm scared out of my fucking mind that history will repeat itself in some horrifying way, but that doesn't stop me from loving her. I get to my knees and put my hands on her hips. Looking into her beautiful eyes, I say honestly, "Not loving you isn't an option, baby. You're going to get through this, and I'm going to support you in any way that I can. You're one of the bravest people I know, and if there's a time when you feel weak, I'll carry you until your strength returns." I drop a kiss onto her upturned lips before resting my forehead against hers. "It's you and me, Rose. No one or nothing else matters." The weeks ahead would put those words to the test. But tonight, we would make love as if tomorrow would never come.

CHAPTER FIFTEEN

Rose

I wake to the now familiar feeling of a warm body at my back and a hard cock pressing into the crack of my ass. I have grown to love these early morning moments when I'm snuggled in my warm bubble and not yet hit with the worries of the day. I refuse to consider how I nearly failed him last night. *How I nearly failed me.* Max and I usually make love in the mornings—and at night. For a straight-laced lawyer, he continues to surprise me with his kinky side. The man does love his dirty talk, and I have to admit, I could almost come from his words alone.

He's still snoring softly, and it's so adorable. I ease away, careful not to wake him. He gives me so much of himself that this morning I want to return the favor. Since neither of us bothered with clothes last night, it makes this much easier than it would be if he were wearing his boxer briefs. Almost as if he knows my intention, he rolls onto his back and flings a well-muscled arm over his head. I'm temporarily derailed as I pause to admire his masculine beauty. Broad, muscular shoulders, strong, slightly hairy chest, tightly toned abs, a glorious happy trail ... and then his cock. My man is smoking hot and hung like a horse. I giggle to myself as I imagine torturing Lia with those very lines in a few hours at the office. The nice part is I don't even have to exaggerate. Max is all that I claim and more. I knew he had a banging body, his suits showed that much. But I hadn't been expecting the six—no eight pack—and that great big, gorgeous penis. Truthfully, I'd never enjoyed oral sex with Jake, but I'd been dreaming of having Max, from start to finish. He seemed to love going down on me, and I was more than ready to return the favor.

So with my plan of action in mind, I crawl between his thighs and put a hand on either side of his waist. A bead of pre-cum glistens at the top of his staff, and I watch it in fascination for a moment before lowering my head to lick it off. The musky, salty flavor explodes on my tongue and I am ready to go back for more. His hips shift just a fraction, but otherwise, he remains still. I lean over again and dip my tongue into the tiny hole that is quickly filling with liquid again, and this time, a moan escapes his mouth, but a quick glance shows his eyes are still closed. I grip his base and marvel at the fact that my fingers don't touch. I feel like woman of the year for being able to take this hefty bad boy. *Do they give awards for conquering Mt. Cock? Maybe a T-shirt saying I scaled Mt. Cockmore?* I begin laughing at that thought, before biting my tongue and attempting to stay quiet.

I pump my hand up and down his length before taking him in my mouth. There's still a lot of him left over, and he's already hitting the back of my throat. I read a lot of smutty romance, so I know there's supposedly an art to taking one all the way down without choking on it, but I've never tried it. And it wasn't a big issue with my one and only other sexual partner as his dick wasn't even in the same zip code as the one I'm currently enjoying.

I lick and suck with pure enjoyment and am surprised to find I'm so wet just from bringing Max pleasure. I'm not rushing through it as I did with Jake. I bob my head up and down on his shaft, then squeak when I feel hands thread through my hair and a voice groaning my name. He's such a dominant lover that I'm never in control for very long, which suits us both. But at this moment, I own his pleasure and the heady sense of power I feel from it is indescribable.

His hips begin pumping upward, but he never goes farther than I can handle. "Mmm," I moan around his width. The vibrations drive him wild, and his cock swells impossibly bigger. I drop one of my hands to rub my clit as we both race toward completion.

"I'm going to come, baby," he rasps, and then attempts to pull out. But I'm not having it. I want all of him and, this time, I'll have it. "Ah fuck," he hisses, just as jets of thick liquid hit the back of my throat. I swallow frantically until I've taken it all then I leisurely lick every last trace from his cock before releasing him with a popping sound. He looks down to where I'm still working myself and quirks a brow. "Looks like you need some help, sweetheart. Bring that dripping pussy over here and sit on my face. I want to eat you for breakfast."

I should be embarrassed at his words and at my eagerness as I all but leap up his body and lower my cunt onto him. I hold the headboard as he braces my thighs before taking one, long lick. "Oh, my God," I moan as my sex quivers in delight. The man has a magic tongue and he knows how to use it. He sucks my clit into his mouth, and I almost jump from the bed. Only his hand holding my thighs keeps me in place. He alternates licking, sucking, and penetrating me with his tongue and fingers. "I'm … coming!" I shout as my body convulses.

"That's right, baby, come all over my tongue. You taste so fucking sweet," Max continues with his dirty talk. Each word seems to extend my orgasm until I'm just a puddle of mush. He lets me collapse against the pillows and smirks as if he knows damn well how good he is. Amazingly, his cock is bobbing around and eager for more attention. I'm debating seating myself on it when Max looks over at the clock and winces. "You have no idea how much I'd love to fuck you, sweetheart, but I have a meeting in less than an hour."

I look at his cock then back to his face. He looks surprised when I leap from the bed and run toward the bathroom. I stop in the doorway and throw over my shoulder, "Get your ass in here. If we multitask, we can save water and time."

"I love you," he says reverently before sprinting toward me. His penis is thumping against his stomach, and my nipples harden in anticipation.

"I know." I giggle as he grabs my arm and pulls me into the shower with him. In the end, we both ended up being a few minutes late for work with slightly wrinkled skin. On the plus size, though, Max made sure I was thoroughly clean after he did his best to dirty me.

Had I ever known life to be fun? Carefree? It was all Max. He's given me that. I knew he worried about me having a relapse and cutting, but he never hovered. With him, I felt like a normal woman in love. I know I haven't heard the last from my father after our altercation the previous night, but what else can he do? I'm over the age of consent and have friends whom I can depend on. Despite my newfound confidence, I still feel uneasy when I think of the people who gave me life. It's obvious that I'm a burden to them, but why do they try so hard to keep me under their thumb? It makes no sense to me. I feel uneasy as if I'm missing a huge piece to the puzzle. One thing I know for certain, though: I won't let them ruin this new life I'm making for myself. I'm stronger now, and if my father wants to go head to head with me, then I will. I've always caved to his wishes, but that's over. He'll see that the old Rose is slowly fading away and the new one is ready to fight for what she needs.

CHAPTER SIXTEEN

Max

"Hey, sugar," our local bartender, Misty, yells out in greeting as I walk in the door of Lucian's neighborhood pub. I have no idea why we keep coming here. Misty is loud, perverted, and a little scary, but she always manages to find us a table in the busy establishment.

"Evening, Misty," I call out over the noise. "Have you seen Lucian yet? I'm supposed to meet him here."

"Yeah, he's at the table in the back corner that you guys like. He's having a cheeseburger and a beer. You want the same thing?"

I nod my head and begin walking through the crowd. "Sounds good. Thanks." I see Lucian a few tables ahead. His fingers are flying across the surface of his phone and the sappy grin on his face tells me he's texting his wife. I've got little room to talk, though. I was a few minutes late coming in because I was talking to Rose from the car. It's been a few weeks since her father's visit, and I hope the bastard never shows his face again. She is gaining confidence—strategies—each day, but I don't want it tested by ugliness any sooner than we have to. She's also seeing Joanna twice a week, and I think she actually looks forward to the sessions now. For all intents and purposes, Rose is blossoming like a child who'd been denied attention all her life. She takes such pleasure in the smallest compliments. I am almost positive that her parents never praised her for anything, which is just fucking sad.

Lucian spots me as I reach the table and waves me to a seat. "Don should be here any time. I've got Misty on the lookout for him."

I wince. "Poor man, you know how she gets around fresh meat. Especially since she and the boyfriend broke up. Although, I don't really understand that. If you're in an open relationship where you both screw other people, what is there to fight about?"

"Hell if I know." Lucian shrugs. "Maybe he didn't take out the trash or do the dishes. It's the little shit that'll get you every time."

I always hate asking him this next question because I know it hurts, but I'm too curious not to. "Heard any more from Aidan? Did he answer the email you sent about his mom?" Aidan's mother had been having some health concerns and had undergone a battery of tests. Lucian had used Aidan's emergency email address, but as of a few days ago, there had been no reply.

Lucian shreds a napkin in his hand as he admits, "He hasn't emailed me, but his father called me this afternoon and said that Aidan had been in contact with them. Apparently, he's not coming back as of right now, but he told his father that he would stay in touch and wanted to be updated after his mother received her test results."

"Fuck." I sigh as I run a hand through my hair. "I hate that Aidan has something else to worry about, especially since he's not here. That must be hard for him, being an only child and all."

"Well then, why the fuck doesn't he come home?" Lucian snaps, sounding furious. He raps his knuckles on the table before taking a deep breath and pinching the bridge of his nose. "I know I'm supposed to be okay with all of this, and maybe it's selfish, but I miss the hell out of him. I can't stand the thought of him out there somewhere by himself and hurting when he could be here with the people who love him."

I take the risk of being punched when I ask, "You're pissed because he contacted his parents instead of you?"

Lucian appears angry for a moment before a sheepish look crosses his face. "That makes me sound like a real asshole." He shakes his head. "I know it's some grade school shit, but yeah, it sucked that I was the one to email him yet he completely ignored me."

"He doesn't blame you, Luc," I say quietly, knowing what's going through my friend's head. "It was an impossible situation, and Aidan made the only choice he could. He did the right thing, and he knows that. But he wouldn't be the man he's always been if he wasn't devastated over losing Cassie. He built his entire life on someone who never really existed. Hell, even he knew that in the end, but old habits die hard. He wanted to believe that Cassie could change and be the woman he needed her to be. But that didn't happen and he's making a difficult adjustment. I'm sure he was afraid that if he talked to you, it would be too hard for him to handle. You'd ask him to come home and he would say no. Cutting contact has kept him insulated from those feelings. He loves you like a brother and you two haven't been apart for this long since the day you met. Trust me, I'm sure it's killing him. But he needs this time to plot a new direction."

Lucian takes a long drink of his beer before answering. "You should have been a shrink," he says dryly. "You'd have a load of business just off our circle of friends."

"No thanks." I laugh just as Misty walks up with my food.

"Here ya go, sugar." She pulls her T-shirt down until her tits are in danger of popping loose before perching on the edge of the table. "Where's Aidan been hiding? I thought we made a real connection, but I haven't seen him since."

"He's out of town," Lucian mutters while staring down into his drink.

Undeterred, Misty looks from me to him. "So what about you two?"

Lucian sticks his hand up so fast to show his wedding band, he almost knocks his half-eaten cheeseburger on the floor. "Sorry, I'm married and have a baby now." He picks up a French fry and points it in my direction. "But Max is single. Maybe you should give your number to him. He really needs a good woman like you, Misty."

Holy fuck. She looks at me as if she's just spotted a water fountain in the middle of a desert. I kick Lucian under the table and enjoy his pain-filled yelp as I connect with his shin. "I'm seeing someone—actually living with her," I quickly add. When she continues to stare at me, I find myself rambling on. "We're in love with each other. You know, we sleep together and have sex. Actually, we have a lot of that. And—"

A hand drops onto my shoulder and Lucian gives me an amused look. "Man, I think we get it, no need to draw a picture."

Misty gets to her feet and shrugs her shoulders. "Well, if anything changes or your women want to include a third party, then you know where to find me."

"Um, yeah, got it." Lucian nods. "Thanks for the er … offer."

Misty points a finger in Lucian's direction and cocks it like a gun. "Sure thing, sugar. I've always gotcha covered." She walks off with an exaggerated shake of her hips that I admire despite myself.

"You know," Lucian muses as he stares after Misty as well, "she's about ten kinds of crazy and wears way too much hairspray, but I bet she could suck rusted lug nuts off a passing car."

I strangle on my beer, gasping for breath. We're both still laughing when Don shows up. He looks over his shoulder a few times as if in a daze but finally takes a seat.

Apparently, he's trying to process Misty as well. "Just don't go there," I advise. A wry smile tells me I was right in my assumption.

"So you've got something for us," Lucian prompts.

He hadn't bothered to bring his briefcase this time, which strangely disappoints me. The likelihood of him knowing much seems slim now. Don props an elbow on the table and gives his best poker face. "I've located and spoken to Daisy Wheeten."

Well hell, apparently I was wrong. "And?" I question as he pauses. Why in the hell do investigators do that? Can't they just blurt their findings out instead of being prodded?

"There's definitely something," he says. "She looked like a ghost when I told her why I was there. Then she began questioning me about Rose, and at one point, she called her Poppy before quickly correcting herself. After that, though, she clamped down and asked me who I was working for." Don gives Lucian an uneasy look. "I finally had to tell her. That's not usually how I operate, but she was paranoid I'd been hired by the Maddens."

"I don't have a problem with her knowing as long as she doesn't tell them about it," Lucian interjects. "Like you, I'd really like for them to remain in the dark for as long as possible."

"I can almost assure you that she isn't going to be in contact with them," Don says. "But the hitch here is that she wants to talk to you."

"Me?" Lucian asks sounding surprised.

Don waves his hand between us, adding, "Actually to both of you. I wouldn't answer a lot of her questions, so she's requested a meeting with the people who hired me. And trust me, guys, I know a stubborn woman when I see one, and she's not going to budge."

Lucian gives me a questioning look, and I nod in response. He turns back to Don and says, "Set it up then. Wherever she feels the most comfortable."

"What do you know about her?" I ask, curious as to this woman who may have given birth to Rose.

Don laughs before taking a drink of the beer that thankfully someone other than Misty had dropped earlier. "Her name is Daisy Wheeten Myers now. She married Joel Myers almost fifteen years ago. She began working for him as a receptionist when she was twenty. He paid for her to attend dental school then hired her on as his partner. He was fifty when they married and died a couple of years ago of a heart attack. He left the practice and all of his assets to her. Neither of them have ever had any children—at least not officially.

Lucian begins laughing abruptly and both Don and I turn to stare at him. "Myers Dental Center. That's Lia's dentist. They're just a few blocks from our condo. I tried to get her to use my dentist who is near my office, but she saw the Myers office when we were walking around downtown one evening and liked that it was so close to home. Fucking small world," he muses as he rubs his chin.

"No kidding." Don smiles, seeming to appreciate the irony as well. "She wants to meet as soon as possible. Tomorrow work?"

"Absolutely," I say quickly and am relieved to hear Lucian agree.

"I'll call her now." Don gets to his feet and walks away, leaving Lucian and me to absorb the additional information he's given us.

"So we're not really that surprised by what he had to say, right?" Lucian asks as he pushes away his probably cold burger.

I lean back in my chair and cross my feet at the ankles. "The fact that Rose may be Daisy's daughter? Not really. I think we both guessed that was a possibility. What I'm most curious about though are the details surrounding it. Why did she give her daughter to the Maddens? And the even bigger question of why wasn't it handled as a legal adoption if both parties were in agreement? I mean obviously Daisy knows where her daughter has been all of these years, and she hasn't done anything about it, so I believe we can forget a stolen baby scenario."

"I'm baffled by that as well," Lucian admits. "As much as some things make sense about this, others do not. I'm looking forward to getting some insight from Daisy. I just hope she doesn't shoot us a load of shit."

"Maybe you should ask Lia what she thinks of her tonight?" I suggest, only half joking.

"Oh, don't worry, I intend to do just that." He laughs. "She's probably gonna find it a bit strange though that suddenly I'm obsessed with her dentist."

"You can't tell her anything," I blurt out. I know that people in love have a hard time not sharing everything, but I feel guilty enough about doing this behind Rose's back without including her best friend as well.

Lucian holds up a hand and shakes his head. "I won't. I don't like keeping secrets, but Rose needs to know what we find out first. Lia might not like it, but she'll understand. Well, after she kicks my ass a little. She hasn't quite gotten over that whole withholding the identity of her father from her."

Before I can comment, Don is back. "Her office is closed on Wednesday. She's asked that you meet her there around eleven in the morning. I accepted on your behalf."

Lucian gets to his feet and tosses some bills onto the table. "Works for me." He claps first me, and then Don on the shoulder. "Max, I'll see you tomorrow, and Don, good work. We'll be in touch after our meeting with Daisy to decide where we go next." He rushes toward the door, and I smile as I see him glance warily at the bar to make sure Misty is otherwise occupied.

I get to my feet to follow after him. "You leaving now?" I ask the other man.

He remains where he is and picks up his beer. "Nah, I think I'll hang here for a while."

Uh-oh. Like Lucian, he looks toward the bar. Misty may have gotten someone else on the line, after all. "Good luck," I say dryly and smile when he attempts to play dumb before finally giving up.

"Yeah, thanks." He sighs and motions me on.

I reach my car uninterrupted and sit there for a moment. I'm normally in a hurry to see Rose, but tonight, I'm bogged down by guilt. Lucian's right; we're doing almost the same thing we did to Lia. It seems as if finding long-lost parents has become our specialty. No matter how much I try to justify it, it still feels wrong. I decide then and there that no matter what comes of our meeting with Daisy tomorrow, I'll come clean with the woman I love. I'm concerned about what it'll do to her mental state, but she is so much stronger now. This is too important to keep from her. Her world is possibly about to irrevocably change.

Am I doing the right thing?

It's with a heavy heart that I start my car and make my way slowly to enjoy what could very well be the last night with the woman who has become *my* whole world. At that moment, I wonder if doing what I know is the right thing, could very well be the costliest decision I've ever made.

Rose

I'm bouncing on my toes in excitement when Max walks in the door. He gives me a questioning look before crossing the room and encircling me in his arms. "Hey, baby. How are you?"

I stretch until I reach his lips and press a lingering kiss there. He groans, then complains as I pull back too soon. "You're not going to believe what happened today," I rush out. "I was completely floored and know you will be as well."

He picks me up into his arms effortlessly and walks through to the living room, before sitting with me on the sofa. It's become a bit of a nightly ritual for me to rest in his lap while we talk about our day, so I don't question the gesture. Although, he seems more ... reticent. He was out with Lucian and normally time with Lucian is not a chore. Maybe something is happening at work with a merger. He nuzzles against my neck for a moment then asks huskily, "What's going on, sweetheart?"

"My mom called me today," I blurt out. "She asked me to go to lunch with her. Of course, I said no immediately, but then she actually begged. It's the first time I've ever heard the woman say please in a manner that wasn't sarcastic. So I agreed because I was too surprised not to."

Max gives me what looks like a strained smile. "How did it go when you saw her? You seem pleased, so I'm guessing well?"

I wiggle until I'm more comfortable and grin as a groan escapes his lips. "It was a bit strained at first. You have to understand that we've never really been like what I would assume a traditional mother/daughter relationship would be. She asked how I'd been doing and then there were some uncomfortable silences. Finally, I asked her why she wanted to see me since she didn't appear to have anything to say. She shocked me by tearing up. She said she was sorry for not being a better mother, and she's missed me since I've cut contact with her. She told me that she wanted us to spend more time together and really get to know each other. She said that my dad had also missed me but wasn't good at expressing his feelings in the right way. I said, 'No shit,' and she laughed. Can you believe it? I know that seems small, but she's never gotten my particular brand of humor. After that, I don't know. Things just seemed almost normal. We chatted as friends. Well ... friends who haven't seen each other in ten years, but she tried."

"Wow," Max says as he twirls a strand of my hair around his finger. "That was rather out-of-the-blue, right?

Maybe they're concerned that you've cut them out of your life. Did she pressure you to go back home?"

I wrinkle my nose as I think back over my earlier conversation with my mother. "No, other than saying they missed me, that was it. I've never been out from under their thumb before, so this is certainly new for them and for me. Maybe it's gotten their attention."

Max purses his lips before shrugging. "It does sound that way. What do you plan to do about it?"

I'm a little surprised that he doesn't seem more enthusiastic about the lunch with my mother. In fact, he looks rather apprehensive. He's probably worried about me getting hurt again. I turn until I'm straddling him and take his face in my hands. His beautiful eyes stare back into mine and my heart stutters. "I love you," I whisper quietly before kissing him. He lets me set the pace for a moment before taking control. Our breaths mingle as our tongues meld together. A simple kiss from him is enough to send my pulse into orbit and thoroughly drench my panties. He rocks me against the growing bulge in his pants, and we're both quickly on the edge.

"I want you—now," he growls, and I can only nod my agreement. He stands and sets me on my feet and I think he's going to lead me to the bedroom. But, instead, he leaves for a moment, then returns with a foil packet in his hand. He motions toward the arm of the sofa, and I almost swoon in delight. He gives me no time to verbalize my approval as he hastily drops his trousers. He grips my skirt in one hand and rips my panties away with the other. "Bend over." I hurry to do his bidding. I felt vulnerable and exposed in this position, *and* more turned-on than ever. He comes up behind me and lines his cock up with my sex. There is no time to brace myself as he bottoms out inside me, pushing me forward. He grips my waist to bring me right back and impales me again and again. He wraps a hand in my hair and angles my neck back to nip the sensitive skin there. "I fucking love you so much," he rumbles.

"I … sweet shit," I yell, unable to stop myself. I have no idea why that's become one of my favorite phrases during sex, but I almost always say it when I'm close to coming, and tonight is no exception. "Max, I'm almost there. Harder, baby, harder!"

He's pounding me now, moving me off my feet with every thrust. "Fuck, I love this greedy pussy. It sucks me dry, then begs for me," he roars. I begin to spasm. His dirty talk does it to me every time. I'd have never thought that the word "pussy" could be so erotic, but it never fails to make my clit twinge. He's lying fully on my back now, still embedded deep inside me as he finds his own release. He continues to rock his hips forward, taking us both down from the peak at a more leisurely pace. I feel his tongue moving against my neck as he licks what are probably beads of sweat. I should be grossed out, but I'm the exact opposite. He lets me know with and without words that he loves every part of me, even the stuff I consider not so pleasant. "Love you, baby," he whispers in my ear before pulling out of me. My body cries at the loss of him. He's so much a part of me now. I curse the months we spent stubbornly avoiding each other. But I've come to accept that it wasn't our time then. I was still reeling over my boyfriend's infidelity, and I don't know if Max would have taken a chance on us had I not been thrust into his house with no warning.

He holds on to my arm as I turn to face him on shaky legs. "I love you, too," I murmur dazedly before allowing him to lead me gently to the shower. We take turns lazily washing each other and then throw on comfortable clothing. We fix a casual meal of omelets for dinner. One day, I'll actually make us that pasta I've been attempting for weeks.

Max works for a while after dinner while I clean up the kitchen. He comes to find me as I'm flipping channels on the television and coaxes me to bed. We curl up together like missing halves of a puzzle, and I'm dozing against his chest moments later. As I drift off, I'm blessedly content. I'm with the man I love, and my mother actually wants to be a part of my life. I feel almost invincible at that moment, but happiness in my experience is both fleeting and short-lived. Even as I try to enjoy the moment, I can't help but brace for the aftermath when something takes it away from me. Pleasure and pain go hand in hand and have for so very long. *Jake was pleasure until that too became pain.* Will I ever truly be able to have one without the other?

CHAPTER SEVENTEEN

Max

Lucian has an appointment the next morning, so we arrange to meet at Myers Dental a few minutes before eleven. When I arrive, I see his Mercedes idling at the curb and his driver, Sam, behind the wheel. I tease Lucian about his chauffeur sometimes, but truthfully, for a man of his wealth, he lives a surprisingly low-key lifestyle. He has a nice home and vehicles, but his biggest splurge is probably Sam. And even that makes sense because it allows him to work during his commute instead of what he sees as wasting time driving. Plus, Sam is like a second father to him, and I think he enjoys those moments with him every day. Of course, now that he's married, he sends Sam back for Lia most mornings, even though she argues about it.

When Sam spots me, he gets out of the car and opens Lucian's door. My friend and boss step out onto the sidewalk, and we both spend a few moments joking around with Sam before he leaves. Leaving Rose this morning had been bittersweet. Part of me hadn't wanted go, knowing I could very well be unveiling an alternate history in this meeting today. I had made love to her fiercely last night, which, despite feeling all versions of wrong, had been fucking incredible. She leaves me breathless. Awed.

We're a few steps away from the door when it swings open, and I halt abruptly. Nothing quite prepared me for this. *Shit.* Unable to stop in time, Lucian plows into my back and curses under his breath. "Sorry," I mumble as I continue to stare at the woman who looks so much like Rose.

Lucian moves out from behind me, and I know that he sees it too when he hisses, "Holy shit."

Daisy Wheeten Myers smiles ruefully at both of us. "I guess I've answered one of your questions without even opening my mouth." She steps back and motions us in, and I approach her on wooden legs. She shuts the door after us and points at a couple of sofas in what I assume is the waiting room. "This seems a little more informal than my office," she explains after we're all seated. She inclines her head toward Luc and says, "You're Lucian Quinn. I did some research after speaking to your investigator." Then she turns to me. "And you're his lawyer, Max Decker." Both Lucian and I lean forward to shake her hand before settling back against the sofa cushions. "Now that we've gotten the introductions out of the way, I'd like to know why you gentlemen are digging into my past."

Lucian gives me a look as if asking if I'd like to answer her question. "I'm involved with Rose Madden. We live together." *Shit, maybe I should have left out the whole living in sin thing to her mother.* "She doesn't have a particularly good relationship with her parents and has had some issues because of it."

Daisy looks pained as I pause in my explanation. She clears her throat and asks, "Be that as it may, why would you have any inkling that I exist? I'm certain that the Maddens have never said a word about me."

Lucian interjects. "Actually, I became suspicious when Rose told me about a recurrent dream she's had since childhood. In it, a woman screams that she doesn't belong with them and yells the name Poppy. I thought that it might possibly be a memory she's been suppressing instead, which is how Max and I got to this point."

I glance over and am surprised to find tears rolling down Daisy's cheeks. "I can't believe she remembers that. She was so young." Her head drops into her hands as she visibly fights for control.

Lucian clasps his hands together between his knees and asks quietly, "Can we start at the beginning? I promise you that we're only here for Rose. Other than her, we have no association with the Maddens. We only want to help the woman who is your daughter."

Daisy gets to her feet and paces the length of the room for a few moments. The air is heavy with tension as we wait to see if she'll trust us. Finally, she begins. "My parents had originally been hired by Hoyt Madden's father. Then when Hoyt married Celia, they went to work for them since the father wasn't entertaining as much anymore and was overstaffed. I was five years old at the time. When I started school the next year, I would get off the bus and stay until my parents left work for the day." She stares off into space before continuing in a dreamy voice. "I thought it was the grandest place. We lived in a small, one-bedroom apartment in a run-down area, so I felt like a princess for those few hours every day. On the rare occasion when I saw Hoyt or Celia, it was as if I were invisible. They completely ignored my presence, which was confusing to me at the time. I realized a few years later that they thought I was beneath them."

"That pretty much fits with the Maddens we know," Lucian adds dryly. Daisy pauses for a moment to get a cup of water from a nearby fountain.

"That's not surprising," Daisy agrees. "Those types of people rarely change. Anyway, things were mostly the same throughout my childhood. During the summer months, I spent the entire day there and the year I turned fifteen I met Camden Marshall. His family had been visiting the Maddens." Daisy's eyes seem far away as she says, "The first time I saw him, he took me by surprise by actually speaking to me. He introduced himself then asked for my name. I was so awestruck that he had to prompt me several more times until I managed to answer his question. After that first meeting, he sought me out every day. We were the same age, but he was wise beyond his years. He'd traveled the world with his wealthy parents, and I loved hearing his stories. Plus, every day, he'd bring me a handful of daisies from what I feared was the neighbor's yard. On the night before he was to leave, though, he brought me the most breathtaking bouquet of Poppies." Daisy shrugs her shoulders and adds, "I guess you can guess what happened before he left."

"Did you ever see him again?" I ask gently, deeply moved by her story.

Instead of answering, she walks away, and I see a light go on down the hallway. I look uncertainly at Lucian, wondering what's going on. Soon, she's coming back with a stack of envelopes in her hand. She drops the bundle onto the coffee table a few inches from our knees. "To answer your question, no, I never heard from Camden—or so I thought. When my father passed away almost two years ago, I cleaned out my parents' house because my mother moved in with her sister after the funeral. I found those letters addressed to me from Camden buried at the top of their closet."

"There's quite a few of them," Lucian remarks, looking as if he'd like to read one as much as I would.

"There are eighty-seven," Daisy says sadly. "He wrote me that many letters and I never knew until recently. He never knew I was pregnant and that our daughter had been taken from me. I've had those letters for almost two years and still haven't had the nerve to read them. I don't feel worthy."

The urge to stand and take Rose's mother in my arms is strong. She's just barely keeping it together now. I feel like an insensitive ass when I ask, "How did Rose end up with the Maddens?" We've come this far, and I have a feeling that just maybe Daisy needs to tell someone.

She winces, then admits, "My father was a gambler and a drunk. My mother covered for him on the job and did his work too if needed. He borrowed money from one of those shady loan places, then lost it all. Of course, they had no way to pay it back."

"So your father borrowed money from the Maddens?" Lucian asks the question I'd already been thinking.

Daisy surprises us both by shaking her head. "Oh no, that would have been too easy. Plus, he always liked to pretend he was someone he wasn't. Begging for a handout from Hoyt would have been too embarrassing. So instead, he stole some paintings and antiques from the attic that they never ventured into. Unfortunately for all of us, Hoyt was a paranoid man who had hidden cameras throughout the house and the theft was caught almost immediately."

"Fuck," I hiss out, then apologize for my language.

Daisy waves me off, not seeming offended by my language. "Add an 'ed' to that, Mr. Decker, and that's exactly what we were. Hoyt and Celia called us into the library that afternoon and showed us the video. I was six months pregnant at the time, and it had become impossible to hide the fact. Hoyt didn't bother beating around the bush. He said we'd all be going to jail. The items my father had taken were worth a lot of money, so it wasn't just a charge of misdemeanor he'd be facing. And Hoyt said my mother and I would be arrested as accessories. He calmly laid the whole scenario out. I was in shock and my parents were panicked. My mother cried and my father begged. I knew that there was more. Hoyt would have had the police waiting for us otherwise. He seemed puzzled by my lack of reaction—then angry. Finally, he dropped the bomb. He and Celia would be willing to let the whole thing go as a *simple misunderstanding* and do us a favor in the process by raising my child. After all, he had pointed out, it was obvious that none of us were fit to do it."

I drop back against the sofa heavily, sick to my stomach at the story she is telling. Beside me, Lucian looks as pissed and disgusted as I feel. "You were forced to give them your baby," I state because, at this point, it's no longer a question.

She takes a tissue from a nearby table and attempts to halt the tears that are again tracking down her face. "I tried to fight them on it, but what could I do? I was sixteen with nowhere to go and no money to support myself, much less a baby. Plus, if what Hoyt said was true, we'd be separated anyway when I went to a youth detention facility. So I was forced to live there for the rest of my pregnancy because they didn't trust me. They found someone discreet to homeschool me so I had no reason to leave. A few hours after I gave birth, my baby was taken from me and I was dropped at home. My parents were given enough money to keep their mouths shut. Not that they would have dared to do anything else. They were terrified of the repercussions. I fell into a depression after that and was little more than a zombie. A few years later, I got my GED and a job at a local restaurant waiting tables. When I'd saved enough to buy a car, I began driving by the Madden's every day on the way home, hoping to see some sign of Poppy. Then one day when she would have been five, I saw her. She was standing against the fence with a red ball in her hands. Before I even knew what I was doing, I'd parked on the side of the road and had run over to her. She'd looked at me curiously through the bars but hadn't appeared afraid. I talked to her for a few moments; I don't even remember what I said. Then Hoyt came thundering across the lawn. He grabbed her up into his arms and started threatening me."

Daisy is openly sobbing now and Lucian walks over to her and puts a supporting hand on her back. "That's the memory Rose believes is a dream," I say, and she nods through her tears.

"That's the only time I ever saw her, and I was screaming her name as he took her away." After she composes herself, she adds, "I had next to nothing to do with my parents after I left home. You know that I went on to marry Joel, and as much as I loved him, I never told him about her. I was too ashamed. After all, I had sold my baby."

"You didn't sell your baby," I interject firmly. "They took her from you. And I plan to find out why. There's more to this story, and it's time we figure out what the ultimate agenda was all those years ago."

"Absolutely," Lucian agrees.

"One thing I'm curious about," I begin. "Do you have any idea why they didn't legally adopt Rose? Were they afraid you'd say something to the judge if they tried?"

She shakes her head, then shrugs. "I've wondered how they got away with that. They never mentioned anything to me about the possibility, and I never signed any papers. In the years since, I've often thought that they seemed almost desperate for Poppy, which I find strange seeing as both Celia and Hoyt appeared to loathe children. They never even asked me who the father was, so I don't think they had any reason to suspect it was Camden."

"Have you never thought of contacting him since finding the letters?" Lucian asks.

"And say what?" she states flatly. She then turns to study me before asking, "Are you going to tell Rose about me?" She looks equal parts hopeful and terrified.

"I am," I say. "I can't hide something like this from her. She deserves to know." I don't tell Daisy about my fear that this will push Rose to cut again. This woman may be her mother, but she's also essentially a stranger and I won't share something like that with her.

Daisy fidgets nervously before taking a breath. "I ... I'm here if you need me." She grabs a piece of paper from a nearby desk and writes something on it before handing it to me. "That's my cell phone number. I realize that she'll likely hate me, but if, for some reason, she wants to talk, please call me."

Lucian and I stay for a few more moments to make sure she's going to be okay before we leave. Lucian turns to me and says, "Drop me at the office and then head home. Take some time to think everything through before Rose gets there." I've just shifted the car into drive when Lucian's phone rings. He answers and then shoots me a glance. "Don, how are you?" I feel my chest tighten. "No, we just left Daisy's office. Tell me what you've got. If you have answers, we need them now."

By the end of what seems like an hour, but is only about five minutes, I'm grinding my teeth together and ready to choke my best friend. Whatever Don has found out, it's certainly taking a long time to relay. When Lucian finally ends the call and sits silently in the passenger seat, I prompt him impatiently. "Well?"

Lucian points toward a Target store in the distance and says, "Pull in there and we'll talk. I'd rather you not hit anyone while we're talking."

I bite my tongue and take the next right. After another few moments and some erratic maneuvering, I slide into a space at the top of the parking lot and cut the engine. "All right, let's hear it."

"When Don was digging into Hoyt's past, he came across a copy of his father's will. He had died the year before Rose was born. There was a surprise codicil made to the will. Hoyt had to produce a Madden heir within three years or the entire estate would be distributed among a list of charities. I have no idea if she couldn't have children or simply didn't want to, but Celia was never pregnant and I'm guessing Hoyt was desperate."

"Daisy was like an answer to his prayers," I muse. "He must have felt like he'd hit the fucking lottery. And her father stealing from him was the golden ticket."

"Yeah, I'm guessing it was almost exactly like that. But, as hard as it may be to believe, that's not the most interesting part of the will," Lucian adds cryptically.

Fuck, the man has been spending too much time speaking with Don. Pulling. Teeth. "Well?" I prompt, impatient to hear the rest.

"Old Wilton Madden, it seems, had a bit of a mean streak where his only son was concerned. If Hoyt produced an heir, he was allowed to keep the family fortune until the heir—Rose—turned twenty-one. At that time, she would gain controlling interest, and Hoyt would receive a set allowance. Anything else would be up to Rose."

"But Rose doesn't have any money," I state, confused.

Lucian shifts in his seat before leveling a stare at me. "That's the tricky part. According to the records, Rose signed everything over to Hoyt on her twenty-first birthday. The papers were drawn up by a downtown law firm and filed with the court. We need to find out if she was somehow coerced into that or if it was done of her own free will. I know she's been under her father's thumb, so it's quite possible she signed anything he put in front of her."

"She wouldn't have wanted to disappoint him," I agree, feeling nauseous. Shit, when does this mess end?

"You have to talk to her tonight," Lucian reminds me. "I was on the fence for a while about it, but there's way too much going on here for her not to know. Hell, I'd like nothing better than to call the police and have Don turn over everything we know to them. But ultimately, Rose needs the voice that has been denied her and so does Daisy."

I promise to call Lucian later and let him know where things stand with Rose. After I drop him at the office, I drive to the house that has become a home since she moved in. A pang hits me as I wonder if that will be over after tonight. How will she react to the news I have for her? Celia's timing in reaching out to Rose makes a lot of sense to me now. Hoyt was probably nervous about losing control of her and ordered his wife to bring her back into the fold. Since her father's *visit*, Rose has almost returned to the sassy, quick-witted, bold woman I first met. Watching her unguarded joy at her mother's apparent initiation for a relationship had been difficult, especially knowing that moment of contentment was going to be brief if what I suspected was true. Now that it's come to pass, will she be able to forgive what she might perceive as betrayal? Has she gained enough strength from seeing Joanna to be able to recover as everything she knows goes up in ashes? *Will she still love me?*

Rose

I'm surprised to see Max already home when I arrive. I generally make it first, unless I stop off along the way. I drop my purse on the kitchen counter and go in search of him. I've checked all the rooms and have my cell phone out to call him when I walk by a window that looks out into the backyard. And it's there I see him, sitting on the arbor swing that we so rarely use. I smile to myself and quickly go to join him. "Hey, handsome," I call as I get closer to him. I drop down next to him on the wooden seat and wait for him to embrace me. He hesitates before he drops a tense arm around my shoulder. He silently moves the swing with his foot, and I lay my head on his shoulder, curious about his unusual mood.

When he finally says, "I don't know how to tell you this," my heart nearly jumps through my throat.

"What is it?" I manage to squeak out. *Oh dear God, he's breaking up with me. That's what this is.* I stiffen, trying to pull away, but he tightens his grip.

"It's not what you think," he rushes out. "Hell, it couldn't possibly be whatever is running through your head, trust me."

I still as his words reach me. "You need to tell me before I freak out," I say, proud my voice doesn't betray the squeezing anxiety that I feel.

Oh, how I wish I could take those words back as minutes later, he takes what little certainty I've always had in my life and obliterates it. He's looking at me now in near panic as I attempt to process his last question.

"Did I sign over my inheritance to my parents?" I repeat as if testing the words. "No, I haven't inherited anything. I have nothing."

I have nothing. Breathe, Rose. Accept the anxiety. Don't fight it.

I have nothing. Dark spots. Watch the anxiety. Imagine it's outside of you.

I have nothing. Clammy. Act normal. Carry on as if nothing is happening.

"Rose, baby, are you okay?" he asks as he cradles me in his lap.

Then I feel it.

My protective mechanism is kicking in and the stoic Rose—that I've always shown to the world—is emerging. Instead of hating it, I find comfort in the total blankness that descends upon me. I give him a bright smile that has no substance behind it and push his arms away to stand. "I'm fine," I say. "It's getting late, so I'll go make dinner. You stay out here and enjoy the sunset; it looks beautiful." *Oh, how pretentious and rehearsed those words sound. Just like my mother.* He gapes at me as I turn to walk away, but I don't care. I'm in the place right now where nothing can hurt. God help me when I can feel again because I don't think any amount of cutting can relieve the feelings lurking just below the surface.

CHAPTER EIGHTEEN

Max

Lucian and I look over the information Don faxed earlier that morning. It's the name and address of the attorney who handled Wilton Madden's will, as well as the contract Rose supposedly signed bequeathing her inheritance. In the brief time before she turned into a Stepford wife, she claimed to have no knowledge of having ever signed anything like that.

"How's she doing?" Lucian asks, looking grave. I'd told him that evening about Rose's strange reaction to my revelation, and as the days have passed, we've all grown more concerned.

"It's bizarre and a little unsettling," I admit. "On the surface, it's almost as if nothing has happened. The difference is any affection between us is very impersonal. She hugs me when I get home and asks how my day was, but that's it as far as contact goes. She chatters on about her day and the fucking weather, then goes to bed early—in the spare room. I spend the night walking the floor, wondering if she's okay. Then tiptoeing into her room and checking on her a dozen times. It's been a week, and when I look at her, there's nothing there but blank space. Her walls are up, and they are taller than ever. What about at work? Has Lia gotten any reaction at all from her?"

Lucian shakes his head. "None. She says that she's cheerful and upbeat there, but also distant at the same time. Apparently, she's not even discussing our dick sizes, which Lia says is very alarming."

I rub a hand down my face and grin for the first time in what feels like months. Then, just as quickly, I'm overwhelmed again. "You know, I've gone back and forth as to how to deal with this. A part of me feels I'm being selfish to want to force some reaction out of her. I mean, if this is how she can handle it without cutting, shouldn't I leave it be? But then, I can't stand the thought of the beautiful woman I know her to be hiding away from the world. Especially when in a state of distress. I want her to have the mother she always needed and to know that the people who raised, but never appreciated her are not her biological parents."

"I don't know, Max," Lucian admits. "You've spoken to Joanna. What was her take on it?"

"She thinks I should gently confront her in a controlled environment like our home and see where it goes. She's afraid that otherwise, one day Rose will crack and there may be no one around to deal with the potential fallout."

"Then you talk to her tonight," Lucian says, looking as nervous about the prospect as I feel. "After you do, though, Max, you need to watch her carefully. She won't like it, and she may rage at you, but this is bigger than anything she's ever dealt with before and we have no idea how she will react."

"I know that," I snap, then give him an apologetic look. I get to my feet, and as I have for the last week, I drive home with a heavy heart and a feeling of hopelessness. I feel her slipping away from me, and I don't know how to stop it. Tonight, I fear I'll poke a hornet's nest that has been waiting for just such a moment to attack. I can only hope there'll be survivors when it's over.

Max

The creepy smiling version of Rose with the empty eyes is putting dinner on the table when I arrive home. I take a moment to get my game face on, then ask pleasantly, "How was your day, dear?" Shit, I want to cringe. *Dear? When have I ever called her that? It's always baby, sweetheart, honey, or something along those lines. I'm turning into a Stepford husband as well.*

"Very good," she answers as if on autopilot. "And yours?"

"It fucking sucked just as the entire last week has," I blurt out before I even know what's happened.

She blinks at me like an owl trying to process my words. "I ... what?" she stutters out.

I'm probably completely screwing this up, but she's actually showing some reaction other than that hollow façade. So I press on. Moving close enough to where I'm invading her personal space, I add, "Yeah, having to watch you check out and act like a bad imitation of Martha Stewart hasn't exactly been a picnic for me, cupcake. I know you're all fucked up inside and are trying to hide from it, but that shit's not gonna fly around here any longer. Starting tonight, we're going to air things out. I'll tell you exactly how I'm feeling, and I'd love nothing more than for you to return the favor." When she opens her mouth, I quickly add, "And the word fine better not be a part of your vocabulary." Her jaws snap shut so fast that I swear, I hear her teeth grinding together.

"But ... dinner's ready." She points toward the pans on the stove. When I see mashed potatoes in one of them, I begin laughing. Of course, she would fix the blandest dish she could think of. No taste or color allowed in her world right now.

Continuing to push the envelope, I walk over and take the handle of the first pot and toss it in the trash. She gasps audibly behind me as I follow suit with the pot roast. *Shit, that pan was hot,* I think, and try not to wince. I lean against the counter and cross my ankles as I await her reaction. When she moves to the cabinet and begins surveying the contents, I fear I'll have a stroke on the spot. Her walls are still holding, despite the shock value of the last few minutes. So I go with verbal communication next in hopes of jarring her a little more. "I'll tell you what I'd really like for dinner. How about some communication followed by a side of emotion? Now, that's something I could really sink my teeth into. Or do you plan to continue the Prozac Barbie imitation you're so good at because I gotta tell you—"

"FUCK YOU!" she yells so suddenly that I jump. And then she begins throwing stuff in my direction. I duck as cans, boxes, and everything in between sails past my head or bounces off my arms. "Is this what you wanted, asshole?" she shrieks. Profanity spills from her lips in a non-stop torrent, and I hate to admit it, but I'm equal parts impressed, relieved, and a bit turned on. I block her air attack as best I can but make no move to stop her. She's finally showing some emotion, and I'll gladly take the black eye or whatever I end up with if it'll help her process what's happened.

She continues on longer than I would have imagined her capable of before sliding down the cabinet and collapsing limply to the floor. Then heartbreaking, wrenching sobs shake her small frame as she cries like she'll never stop. It's then that I throw caution to the wind and approach her. She fights me weakly as I attempt to pull her into my arms, but finally relents and allows me to cradle her against my chest like a child. I go straight to our bed where we've had some of our most important talks and simply let her purge the anguish from her soul. She weeps until I fear she'll make herself sick. Then thankfully, the storm tapers into sniffles and then silence.

I have no idea what to expect now, so I continue to rub her back soothingly before finally asking, "What can I do to help you, baby?"

I'm afraid I'll feel a knee to my balls at any moment, so I'm pleasantly surprised when she turns her head to my ear and whimpers, "Don't let me go tonight, Max. I can't be strong right now."

Joanna had suggested non-confrontational and gentle. Well, we all know how that panned out. But it worked. Literally smashing into her walls broke them down. Despite what she says, she is strong *and* resilient. But together … together we're stronger. *We* can do this. I curl my body protectively around hers and begin rocking her. "I've got you, sweetheart—always." She doesn't say another word; she falls asleep, no doubt exhausted. I doze a few times, but jerk awake to make certain she's still with me. My eyes are burning and my throat is dry as the first light of early morning begins filling the bedroom. Against all odds, we've made it through the night and she's back in my arms. Today, I'll begin the challenging task of making sure she stays there, no matter what battles I have to undertake.

CHAPTER NINETEEN

Rose

Max gives me a look full of love and wariness as he hands me a cup of coffee. He's probably frightened after last night that I'll throw it in his face. And I'll admit that the urge is there, but I love the man, no matter how much I resent him for fucking up my life. *What life? You can't stand your fake parents, and they certainly have never had any love lost for you. You should give the man a medal for finding you a new mommy.*

"Good morning, sweetheart," he says softly as he sits beside me on the sofa. "I let Lucian and Lia both know we wouldn't be in today. I hope that's all right with you."

I can tell he expects me to be pissed off at his high-handedness, but I'm actually relieved. I need to work some stuff out in my head before I face my best friend. I love her dearly, but I know she'd handle me with kid gloves and I'm too weary to deal with more sympathy.

"Could you please go over everything that you told me about my parents and the ... other woman ... from beginning to end? I'd like to attempt to process it again." He seems surprised by my request, but like the outstanding lawyer he is, he covers each point clearly and concisely and pauses to answer any of my questions before continuing on.

By the end, my hand is tightly clutching the coffee mug I'm holding as if it alone can anchor me against the storm. "And you spoke to the woman who gave me away face-to-face?" I can't call her my mother. Hell, I didn't even know she existed until a week ago.

"Yes." He inclines his head. "Both Lucian and I met with her." He appears to hesitate before saying softly, "You may not want to hear it, but she's a nice lady. You were both victims of greed and have suffered in your own ways."

His words enrage me and I struggle to remain in control. "How has she suffered, Max? She's lived just miles away from me my whole life and didn't bother to take me back. I spent every day with people who hated me, and now, I know why. They resented the fact that I was the proverbial keeper of the keys. Without me, their money train would have slowed considerably. The same money that paid that woman to give me up!"

Max leans over and pries the mug from my hand before setting it on a nearby table. He then pulls me into his lap and holds me so tight, I have difficulty taking a full breath. "I'm so fucking sorry, baby. As much as the Maddens never deserved a gift like you, the last thing I wanted to do was take your family away from you. I know a part of you must hate me, but please know that I love you so much that the thought of losing you is tearing me to shreds. You need time to process, and I'll take anything you can give me at this point. Just stay and let me help you work through all of this. No decisions have to be made today. Take the time you need to think things through."

As much as I want to be angry with him, I am also calmed by his presence. When I think logically, he doesn't deserve my anger. Is he not just the messenger? Did he not love me enough to find out the cause of my disquiet? In some sense, he is like the white knight going after my parents for me. But he went behind my back and it feels as though he thinks of me as a child, and I'm incredibly sick of that. "You're afraid I'm going to cut if I'm not here for you to watch me, aren't you?" There's no judgment in my voice because I have the same fears. How could I not?

"It concerns me, yes," he answers truthfully. "But regardless, I want you with me. You're going through a trauma that most can't even imagine. You need me and I need you, sweetheart."

And so we spent the morning locked securely in each other's embrace. Neither of us mentions the situation with my parents during our long walk around the neighborhood before sleeping for a few hours. Max makes shrimp pasta for dinner, and I smile for the first time that day, thinking it's finally happened. A perfect pasta meal was created after months of trying. The sappy part of me wants to believe it's a sign that everything will be okay.

I return to his bed again that night without thought or discussion. There are no sexual overtures made. Simply put, it's about the giving and receiving of comfort. I'm close to drifting off when I say sleepily, "I want to confront my parents tomorrow. I can't go on with this hanging over my head. I won't know my next step until that's done."

He's still against me for a moment before sighing. "I told you, baby, whatever you need, I'm here."

That night I dream again of a girl named Poppy and a frantic woman yelling her name. This time, though, when I wake, I know that person to be my real mother and myself to be the child who has been lost to her for twenty-three years. That time can never be recovered, but can there be something more for the little girl inside me who's never felt wanted? I felt like a burden my whole life—to my parents, to Jake, and perhaps to Max too. Perhaps that is not a flaw but something that was imprinted on me at birth.

Max

Rose appears strangely peaceful as my car pulls into the circular driveway of the Madden estate. I'm tempted to frisk her for firearms as we step out onto the pavement but resist the urge. A part of me had hoped she'd back out of coming today, thinking it might be too soon for an encounter where tensions and emotions are bound to run high. We're effectively blindsiding her parents. But the other part of me has been in awe of her strength. Instead of being nervous this morning, she's been resolved.

Things between us are in no way back to normal. She has been courteous and allowed me to hold her when I thought she or I needed it. But there is also resentment there, and I can't blame her. Many a messenger had probably been shot through the years delivering far better news than what I'd heaped upon the woman I love. She's correct, though. The healing process cannot begin until she's faced Hoyt and Celia. I haven't asked her what she plans to say, and she hasn't volunteered it. Possibly, she doesn't even know.

She chose a simple black pencil skirt today but paired it with a bold magenta blouse. I fell in love with her a little more over that simple rebellion against the people who raised her. It's her silent way of saying she's not going to back down, no matter how unpleasant it may get.

I have a rare moment of uncertainty as my hand settles on her lower back to lead her up the walkway. Do I hold her hand when we reach the door or will she rebuff me? She takes the decision from me. After pressing the doorbell, she slips her hand into mine and our fingers intertwine. "I love you," I say in a strangely choked voice just as her father opens the door.

He looks confused for a moment then huffs impatiently. "Since when have you bothered to knock?" He leaves the door ajar and grumbles, "I was attempting to read the paper." I'd give anything to kick his pompous ass. He doesn't bother to acknowledge my presence, nor temper his disdain for his daughter in front of a guest.

"I need to speak with you and Mother," Rose says firmly. I wonder if Hoyt caught the pause in her words before she uttered the word "mother." I highly doubt it. He's far too smug to think that she might know something.

Without turning around, he tosses over his shoulder, "Then call back and arrange a time. We both have other obligations and can't drop them on your little whims."

He's almost through the doorway of what appears to be a study of some sort when her voice rises. "I know that I'm not your real daughter. A woman named Daisy gave birth to me and then you forced her to give me up."

I can almost hear his feet screech to a halt as he freezes in place. He remains facing away for long moments before slowing turning around. "What in the hell are you talking about?" he blusters, but there is little heat behind it. He knows by the confident tone of her voice that she has him.

"Go get your wife now and we'll meet you in there." She points at the room that he was in the process of entering before she knocked his world on its axis.

Without a word, he stalks off in another direction and there is nothing but the sound of our ragged breathing as we regroup. "You were magnificent," I say sincerely, in awe of the strength she's exhibited so far.

She chokes a laugh out of me as she admits, "I was scared shitless. I was afraid he would hear my knees knocking." She pulls on our clasped hands, and we walk into a decadently appointed room heavy with the smell of cigars. Wealth seeps from every wall. Rose and I have barely taken a seat on one side of the dark leather sofa when Hoyt returns with his wife in tow. Even this early in the morning, her eyes are glassy, and I'm fairly certain she's either hungover or has already started on the alcohol today—possibly both.

She pulls the concerned parent card almost immediately. "Rose darling, is everything okay? Your father said the craziest thing. Are you not sleeping again, darling? We can get you some more sleeping pills. You know how you imagine things when your insomnia is acting up."

I feel Rose draw into herself, and I fear she may lose her nerve. She's been manipulated for so long that it would be easy to fall back into the ingrained passive pattern of behavior the Maddens have created in her. But again, she surprises me by inhaling sharply and collecting herself. She holds up a hand and effectively cuts off Celia's sickening diatribe. "Please, just stop. I know everything, and if I should forget any of it, Max can easily fill me in. You're not my biological parents. You blackmailed the Wheetens and forced their daughter, Daisy, to give me up." She turns to stare at Hoyt before adding, "Otherwise, your father would have given the majority of the Madden money to charity. I was a means to a financial end, pure and simple."

It's Hoyt that then shocks the room. He shrugs indifferently and says, "That's exactly what you were, *daughter*." I gasp at the ease with which he confirms my accusation. *Does he have no shame at all?* "When Celia couldn't manage to get pregnant, we began looking at other options. The old man would have discounted adoption, so we were forced to get creative. I'll admit that I was close to giving up when I noticed how plump Daisy Wheeten had become. It was a happy day around here when some of my other staff confirmed that the little whore had gotten herself knocked up. Then when her drunk of a father stole some useless trash from our attic, it all fell into place beautifully."

"Hoyt, I think that's enough," Celia snaps. She gives Rose a look that *almost* appears apologetic. Hoyt's mouth drops open at the interruption by his wife, but surprisingly, he doesn't voice an objection. "I was never meant to be anyone's mother. There were times when I wanted to do right by you; truthfully, there were. But I could never forge the bond to make that happen. In the end, I had to believe that it was because you weren't of my blood. I talked Hoyt into letting you attend college and live on campus because I thought it was something small I could do for you." She shrugs as if to say, "that's all I've got," and then goes to a side table and splashes a liberal amount of amber liquid in a glass. *What the actual fuck? Is this some sick, twisted movie? They have no remorse whatsoever. I can only imagine the internal screaming going on inside Rose's head. Fuck.*

"So I guess that's it." Hoyt sneers and points toward the door. "You know the way out, Rose. Make sure you leave your key. Your pretend home here is no longer available to you."

Rose laughs as she gets to her feet. "I agree. We are finished today. But you'll hear from me again when I decide what I want to do about the papers you forged with my name." Celia gasps and Hoyt's face turns a sickly pale hue as he stares at the woman before him. "Thank you, Hoyt. Thank you for tossing me out on the street and denying me every financial privilege I had owned. You were so smug in your perceived cleverness thinking I'd come running back to you, but you couldn't have been more wrong. Without you tossing me away, I would have never found out the truth. How despicable and callous you really are, how vapid and fruitless your lives really are, and how thankful and appreciative I am that I am no longer a part of it or you in any way. Thank you." It's as if he's never seen her before. She pulls a key from her purse and tosses it onto the floor. "I'll be in touch," she says ominously. I rise and follow the splendid creature from the room and out of the cold house that couldn't possibly ever be a home.

We are a few miles away when she suddenly turns in her seat and asks, "Will you take me to the shooting range?" *Oh, fuck.*

"Pardon?" I choke out, thinking maybe I heard her wrong.

She gives me a grin full of mischief and says, "It's the one thing that bastard taught me that I enjoyed. I'd give anything to put a few clips in a target with his name written across it."

And just like that, I'm hard and a bit terrified. Who am I to judge what another person needs to move on? So I follow her directions, and soon, we arrive at the private club where she holds a membership. She's obviously well known here, and within moments, she's holding an impressive handgun. We both put on headphones and goggles. Then I nearly come in my fucking pants when she spreads her legs as far as her skirt will allow and takes up a stance that would make a professional weep. She shoots the first clip before ejecting it and smoothly loading the next one. She repeats the process six times before her arms are limp and her body is spent. I lead her back to the car, fighting the urge to fuck her against the shooting range sign. *So not the time for it, Decker.*

We arrive home thirty minutes later, and I help her from the car and into the house. I wasn't sure where we stood before we entered the Madden's house, and she has gone silent now. But I saw a mischievous smile on her face after the gun range. It's as if she is inwardly processing the events, and possibly following the advice of Joanna to see it from the outside in. She reeks of gunpowder, so I undress her and carry her to the shower. She stands quietly while I wash first her and then myself. Afterward, she shocks me by initiating lovemaking. Even though I want her so badly my teeth ache, I would have held off until she was ready for it both mentally and physically. But she seems to need the intimacy so I slowly worship every inch of her skin before joining our bodies together. I force myself to keep my thrusts slow and even as we build almost languidly toward the peak in the distance. When I feel her shudder around me, I increase my pumps slightly, bringing her to orgasm several more times before finally letting myself release into her.

As we are lying there afterward, she admits huskily, "I have no idea where I go from here, but I want you with me.

I have issues that won't be resolved next week or even next year, but I love you. I want to be the best version of myself for you, and I hope that you can accept that. I'm far from perfect—"

"*You* are the best version of *me.*" I interrupt her by putting my finger over her lips. "You brought me back to life and gave me a reason to live again, sweetheart. Without you, I'd still be sitting here night after night, too scared to take a chance on love again. We both have mountains to climb, but when you're tired, I'll carry you until you find your feet again."

"And I'll do the same for you," she promises.

There in the circle of her arms, the last of my fears fall away. We'll both struggle in the days ahead, but in the end, I have to believe we'll be stronger for it. I knew the first moment I saw the beautiful redhead in my arms that my life would change. I just never imagined we were put on this earth to save each other. Two damaged souls united in an imperfect circle of hope, love, and laughter. If she ever writes my name across a target while loading a clip, though, I will drop to my knees and beg for fucking forgiveness, even if I have no idea what I'm apologizing for.

The End

EPILOGUE

Max

"I think I'm going to puke," Rose warns for the tenth time in an hour. She fidgets with the tank top she's wearing. "This is too casual, isn't it? I should have dressed better."

"Honey, you're perfect," I assure her as I join my hand with hers. We walk into the small restaurant in the downtown area and I quickly scan the tables until I see Daisy's familiar hair in the distance. Next to her is a man of about the same age with dark hair, streaked through with a few silvery strands. "Just breathe, baby," I remind her as I steer her toward the table.

Mother and daughter stare at each other as if riveted. I wonder again why we chose such a public place for this first meeting but remember that Rose thought she'd feel more comfortable with others around. Now, I think she probably regrets that decision. "You're so beautiful," Daisy breathes out as she reaches a tentative hand to stroke Rose's arm. "Oh, Poppy," she begins before stopping abruptly. "I'm sorry. I know your name is Rose."

"It's okay," Rose says softly.

I clear my throat and extend my hand to the man whose gaze is darting between Daisy and Rose. "I'm Max Decker."

He jerks slightly before giving me a strained smile. "Camden Marshall. It's good to meet you." Daisy had finally read Camden's many letters and had found an email address to contact him. Amazingly enough, he'd never married, and he was living a few states away in Georgia. He had come to see Daisy the next day, and she'd told him the painful story of what had happened to her and to Rose. I can see the anguish of lost years in his eyes as he swallows hard before haltingly holding out a hand to his daughter. "Rose, I'm ..." he begins and then appears lost for words.

"You're my father," she says shyly.

I pull out a chair for Rose, and Camden does the same for Daisy. I can't help but notice the way the former lovers look at each other, and it seems as if twenty-plus years has done nothing to lessen the feelings there. Surprisingly enough, conversation flows easily. I'm enjoying seeing my love interact with her biological parents. Therefore, I'm taken completely off guard when Rose pulls an envelope from her purse and lays it in front of Daisy.

Rose

It's only been an hour, but I'm already half in love with Daisy and Camden. There's a comfortable ease between us that never existed between the Maddens and myself. They both look at me as if I hung the moon and stars—actually in the same way Max stares at me more often than not.

I'd had an idea last night and meeting them today has only reinforced it. Hoyt and Celia took so much from all of us that I can't possibly make a decision about their future without Daisy and Camden. Actually, I want to put them in charge of that area completely. I'll go along with whatever they decide.

"That's the legal document that my parents forged giving them control of my inheritance. They took away your choice when they forced you to give me up. They altered your future, and now, I'm giving you that control back. Take this information and think about it. I'll fully support whatever decision you make. This is the only gift I can give to you," I say with tears in my eyes.

Daisy gets to her feet shakily and leans down to embrace me. "Oh, Poppy, just knowing you were in the world, even if we weren't together, was always a gift to me. And I hope you'll let me get to know you and maybe someday be a mother to you." Camden echoes her sentiments and doesn't seem to care that he's crying openly in a restaurant full of people.

Six months later, the Maddens are left with their house and cars, but nothing else. In exchange for not alerting the authorities and bringing charges against them, they agreed to sign all other assets over to me, and I, in turn, donated them to charities for abused women in honor of my friend, Lia, and to organizations benefiting children.

Max asked me after that how I felt about Hoyt and Celia getting away with kidnapping with nothing but a slap on the wrist. And I told him that I agreed with Daisy. If we set out with vengeance in our hearts, how are we better than they were? Plus, considering the size of the fortune Hoyt lost, I had to believe he would suffer greatly knowing that eventually he'd be forced to get a job to maintain his lifestyle. Shit, as they say, runs downhill, and I had a feeling that Hoyt would be swimming against the current very soon. I know that my decision not to go to the police is a hard one for the lawyer in him to handle. He would have rather I gotten justice in the traditional manner, but I had no desire to put myself through the media circus that would have ensued.

As for me, I still struggle with the urge to cut myself when life becomes stressful. After confronting Hoyt and Celia, I'd even purchased a razor. But again, I'd been strong enough to hold back. I wasn't healed as such, because like with any addiction, it remains within your psyche. But I'm slowly working out why I first started. Yes, it had been about taking back control, but the constant berating, constant belittling, constant control had demeaned me so completely that the pain became my friend. I don't need it as my friend anymore. *One day at a time*, Joanna constantly drills into me, and that's exactly how I'm living my life. I'm grateful for each and every moment with my love.

ALSO BY SYDNEY LANDON

The Danvers Novels
Weekends Required
Not Planning on You
Fall For Me
Fighting For You
Betting on You (A Danvers Novella)
No Denying You
Always Loving You
Watch Over Me
The One For Me (Feb. 2016)

The Pierced Series
Pierced
Fractured
Mended
Aidan 2016

Coming May 2016

Pre-order available now at select outlets.

Made in the USA
Middletown, DE
07 May 2020